"So, Lauren Conway.
Do you know you have a twin?"

Lauren hugged the hospital bedsheet closer. "No. But I gather this Dana looks like me."

Alex cocked his head, then reached into his back pocket and withdrew his wallet. He leafed through several pictures before he stopped, pulled one out and handed it to her.

Lauren looked down. In the picture was a woman with long, luscious hair and curves to die for outlined in a wild-print bikini. She held a surfboard and leaned on the smiling, sun-burnished man whose arm was around her. The man was Alex.

The woman looked exactly like Lauren.

The similarity made her light-headed and caused her heartbeat to falter. What was going on here?

Dear Reader,

Welcome to my contribution to the CODE RED series. It's been a pleasure to participate in this project—three Superromance novels, an anthology, a twelve-book continuity, then four sequels—all about my favorite people, rescue personnel. It was a joy to work with the other authors involved in this series. I liked getting to know them and contributing to the story lines. But don't worry. *The Unknown Twin* can stand alone, too.

As many of you know, I wrote some firefighter books for Harlequin a few years back, and it was a pleasure to revisit America's Bravest. I did have to do some additional research, though. Fire fighting in California is different from that in New York State, where I did my original research of riding the trucks, eating at the firehouses and participating in classes and drills. I met with a wonderful former California firefighter, who helped plan out the staff and station house for us. I also called on my other friends in the Rochester Fire Department, particularly Joe Giorgione, who was always there to help out with technicalities and plot elements. All of the firefighters I worked with were wonderful and gave me very important information.

Lauren and Alex's story is a classic romance about opposites attracting—the macho, charge-right-in hero and the creative, sensitive heroine. I love to put people who are so different together and see what happens. I didn't expect all of what transpired in the book. It was fun to watch Lauren and Alex wrestle with their relationship. I hope you enjoy their trek to happily-ever-after.

I love to hear from readers. My e-mail is kshay@rochester.rr.com and my Web site is www.kathrynshay.com. Though few use it, I still have a snail-mail address: P.O. Box 24288, Rochester, New York 14624. Write and tell me what you think.

Kathryn Shay

The Unknown Twin
Kathryn Shay

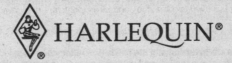

HARLEQUIN®

TORONTO • NEW YORK • LONDON
AMSTERDAM • PARIS • SYDNEY • HAMBURG
STOCKHOLM • ATHENS • TOKYO • MILAN • MADRID
PRAGUE • WARSAW • BUDAPEST • AUCKLAND

ISBN 0-373-71206-5

THE UNKNOWN TWIN

Mary Catherine Schaefer is acknowledged as the author of this work.

This edition published by arrangement with Harlequin Books S.A.

® and TM are trademarks of the publisher. Trademarks indicated with ® are registered in the United States Patent and Trademark Office, the Canadian Trade Marks Office and in other countries.

www.eHarlequin.com

Printed in U.S.A.

Books by Kathryn Shay

HARLEQUIN SUPERROMANCE

659—THE FATHER FACTOR
709—A SUITABLE BODYGUARD
727—MICHAEL'S FAMILY
760—JUST ONE NIGHT
774—COP OF THE YEAR
815—BECAUSE IT'S CHRISTMAS
871—FEEL THE HEAT
877—THE MAN WHO LOVED CHRISTMAS
882—CODE OF HONOR
908—FINALLY A FAMILY
948—A CHRISTMAS LEGACY
976—COUNT ON ME
1018—THE FIRE WITHIN
1066—PRACTICE MAKES PERFECT
1088—A PLACE TO BELONG
1123—AGAINST THE ODDS

Don't miss any of our special offers. Write to us at the following address for information on our newest releases.

Harlequin Reader Service
U.S.: 3010 Walden Ave., P.O. Box 1325, Buffalo, NY 14269
Canadian: P.O. Box 609, Fort Erie, Ont. L2A 5X3

CHAPTER ONE

IT WAS TOUGH having an imaginary friend at thirty-two. Lauren Conway stared down at hers, now captured in living color in a brand-new comic strip, *Dee and Me*, that she'd agreed to create for the Courage Bay *Courier*. She'd moved to the California-seaside town two weeks ago to begin drawing the cartoon, which was based on the imaginary friend she'd first made when she was a child.

Looking down, she reread the strip she'd just finished.

Frame One:

You got yourself a job, Lily! Twelve-year-old Deirdre's smile is pleasant. It always is, even when Lily does something stupid.

Lily looks nervous. *Yeah, for the summer.*

Frame Two:

Lily is first this time. *I hope I don't blow it. Like I do everything else.*

Don't be lily-livered. Dee laughs at her pun. *You're not gonna blow it.*

Frame Three:

Flexing her muscles, Deirdre picks up the free weights and raises them in an arm curl. Lily stares helplessly at her.

Deirdre asks, *You wanna try it?*

Frame Four:
Lily appears horrified. *Dee, please. I can't.*
If you think you can't, Lily, you're right.
Frame Five:
Lily stares helplessly out at the reader. *Easy for her to say.*

Lauren studied her drawings. "Is it any good?" she asked aloud. Leaning back in her chair, she stared up at the ceiling; the cheerful fresco of blue sky and sun she'd painted there made her smile. She'd worked in a cubicle on the other side of the building for a week while she fixed up this office on her own time. It was so small, so run-down, nobody else at the *Courier* had wanted it. And since she had just started as a part-timer, she hadn't been high priority for amenities. Rising, she crossed the room to two oversize beanbag chairs she'd stuffed in the corner, since there wasn't room for much else. Kicking off her canvas sneakers, she stretched out on one and put her feet on the other. She continued to stare up at her own personal sky, inhaling the spicy scent of potpourri she'd scattered throughout the office and pondering the direction of her cartoon.

Her new boss, Perry O'Connor, had studied the prototype when she'd presented the concept to him in an interview several weeks ago. "It's got a lot of potential, Conway." He nodded to the drawings. "I like the self-effacing nature of the klutz. Cute dynamic with her alter ego. Puberty adds a lot. But you need a focus. A tack." His expression was thoughtful. "We're looking for something to draw readers to the *Courier*'s Web site. Maybe we could do this cartoon on the fly."

"On the fly?"

"Yeah, have readers write in saying what they like

and what they don't like, and see if we can roll with it. It doesn't have to be in every day. Then you could tailor the cartoon to public opinion.'' He stared hard at her from beneath bushy gray brows. ''Think you can do it?''

Could she? ''Yes.''

''Okay, let's give it a shot. You're hired. Don't let me down.''

''I won't.''

So she'd moved from Benicia, in the northern part of California, to this small community of Courage Bay, close to L.A., hoping she'd be able to realize a dream she'd had for a long time. And realizing that dream was why she was at the office at midnight.

She shot a look at her battered oak desk. Tomorrow, Saturday, she would come in and strip and re-stain it.

Maybe you should come in and work on our cartoon. Ah, that voice. Her imaginary friend, Deirdre, aka Dee. Just as Deirdre advised Lily when she was at her wits' end, she was also there for Lauren in the worst of times. There had been a lot of those lately.

Placing her bare foot on the carpet remnant she'd put down—it was thick with a geometric print—Lauren sighed. ''I can do this,'' she said aloud. ''I *want* to do this.''

Then do it, Deirdre told her. *Make me come alive like I am in your imagination. Like you have since we were little.*

Lauren concentrated on visualizing the face of her imaginary friend—and sometimes alter ego. Lauren's face. Red hair—though Lauren's had turned auburn now—dark brown eyes, freckles and a bow-shaped mouth. ''Come on, Dee, help me out here.''

Okay, close your eyes. Picture me on the surfboard. Picture Lily on the dock, wishing she could surf.

"Lily would wish she could *swim*." Just like Lauren did.

Breathing in, Lauren lost herself in the scene. The rush of the ocean was loud. The air was hot, tempered by a delicious breeze. It kissed Lily's skin. Overhead, seagulls swooped and dived. Ah, it was so peaceful...

BING-BONG!

Alex Shields bolted upright from his cot when the alarm went off. Lights blinked on, and ten other firefighters bounded out of their bunks alongside him as the dispatcher's voice crackled over the PA. "Fire at the Courage Bay *Courier*. Engine One, Ladder One and Paramedic One go into service."

"Hell, that's right in our backyard," Louis Alvarez said as they threw on their uniform pants over the gym shorts that, along with T-shirts, all firefighters wore to bed. They raced to the bays, where the rigs were parked and ready to go.

As senior captain of Courage Bay Fire Department's Squad Two, the shift currently on duty, Alex ducked into his office and yanked the printout from the computer. He scanned it as he headed for the trucks. Fire in the newspaper office. Occupants unknown. Alex knew the presses worked until about two, but who would still be there at 3 in the morning?

At his locker, he shoved on his bunker pants and boots, grabbed his turnout coat and air-pack and snatched up his red captain's helmet. He was on the truck in seconds, along with the other four assigned to Ladder One. The bay doors went up almost simultaneously, with a teeth-grating iron screech. Sirens blared in unison as the three vehicles raced out of the house, onto Jefferson Avenue and around the corner to Fifth. They lurched to a stop in front of the *Courier*'s building.

Alex bounded off the truck and took a quick tour of the exterior. Thick smoke billowed out the Fifth Street side—from lower floors, as well as the roof—disappearing into the dark, warm early morning. No flames on the west side or the back of the building, but there was an open window at the front west corner. No light on inside, though. Back at the trucks, he set up a makeshift Incident Command from which he could direct the maneuver, called for generators to be put in place and calmly gave his orders into the radio. "Engine One. Attack from primary entrance on Fifth Street. Check to see if there's a guard." His engineer—the rig driver and second in command—would know where to position the units. "Ladder One, get the aerial up to the top of the west side and start a master stream." It looked like the fire was contained in one side of the building, but the flames could spread fast.

Minutes later, the hoses were laid for both an exterior and interior attack. Alex listened over the radio as his men worked.

"I got water," Robertson shouted when he reached the basement. He'd taken one hose and aimed it at what he perceived to be the seat of the fire.

The aerial dumped water on the roof.

Two of the truck's men had followed the hose in and were now dragging out the guard. Gonzales, a paramedic, rushed over to the unconscious man. The truck crew hurried back in to search and rescue. It didn't appear they were going to need roof ventilation.

Now that everything was in place, Alex strode to the rig. He dragged out a single ladder, meant to mount a one- or two-story wall, and hauled it to the corner of the building.

Kellison, another paramedic, jogged over. "What's going on?"

"I saw an open window at this end. Somebody might be in there working late."

"Any lights on?"

"Can't see any. Still, I'm gonna check it out."

Together they positioned the ladder. Donning his face mask and starting his air, Alex glanced at Kellison. "Stay here. I'll need somebody to heel the ladder if I come down with a victim." Grabbing the rails, Alex shinnied up the rungs, then climbed inside the open window.

The smoke wasn't opaque, but it was thick enough to do harm. And it was getting hot. He shone the flashlight he carried into the room and surveyed the area. The shapes were amorphous in the smoke, but he could make out a desk, a chair. A tiny beacon of light, invisible from outside and obscured by the smoke, lit the corner and something near it, which resembled a couch. Then he heard, "Ohhh…"

He raced over and found a sleeping woman, stretched out on something. He bent down and tried to rouse the victim. He couldn't see her clearly, and she was tough to wake. "Ma'am, can you hear me?"

"What?" She was too slow to respond, so he picked her up. She was slight and easy to carry.

Striding back to the window, he yelled out to Kellison, "I got one. Stay with the ladder. I can carry her easy." Setting the victim down, he shook her again. Finally, she awoke, but she was groggy. Kneeling her against the sill, he climbed outside and reached in. She went over his shoulder like a bag of feathers. Grasping the ladder, he descended. She stirred partway to the bottom. "Shh," he said gently. "You're all right, I got you."

When they hit the last rung of the ladder, Kellison, assisted by Gonzales, took her from him. They laid her on the ground and, in the light of the generator his men had set up, Alex got his first good look at her. Though her face was covered with a thin layer of grime, he recognized her instantly. "Dana?"

"What happened to her hair?" Kellison asked, popping the canister to activate the oxygen.

Standing over them, Alex shook his head. "I have no idea. What the hell is my EMT doing in the newspaper office at three in the morning?" She was supposed to be at an Emergency Medical Systems training seminar in San Diego.

She coughed and sputtered. Alex stared at her. Something wasn't right. Not just the hair; she'd felt lighter, too.

"Shields," a voice called out over Alex's radio. "We need you on the east side."

"She's all right, Alex," Kellison said. "Her vitals are good. Go."

Alex took one last look at the woman he'd once loved, and headed around the corner.

LAUREN COUGHED and breathed into the oxygen mask. Looking at her gown, she wondered if the pretty pink sweater she'd worn earlier was ruined. She'd smelled like the inside of a barn when she arrived at the hospital. Lauren smiled, remembering the sweet firefighter who had rescued her. That was the good news.

The bad news was that everybody had lost his senses.

First it had been the paramedic. "Come on, Dana, baby, take more oxygen."

Then the hunky, if deluded, firefighter. He'd picked up her hand as they were putting her in the ambulance and kissed it, for God's sake. Even though he was a stranger, she'd been moved by the tender gesture. But then she'd realized the guy must have inhaled too much smoke because he'd said, "I thought I was past these feelings for you, Dana."

Finally, the nurse at the hospital, Jackie Kellison, acted as if she and Lauren were best buddies.

Hell, maybe Lauren was still out cold and hallucinating.

A doctor poked his head in her cubicle. An older man, he had a full head of gray hair and a kind smile. He looked familiar. "Hello. They treating you okay here?"

"Yes."

"I'm George Yube, chief of surgery."

Ah, yes. Perry O'Connor's friend. Lauren had seen him at the office once.

"I'm Lauren Conway."

He gave her a fatherly smile. "I know. Perry told me who you were last time I was at his office. And then I recognized you when they brought you in. I just had to make sure you were all right."

She smiled back.

After asking a few questions about what had happened to her, he squeezed her arm. "Well, glad to see you're doing fine." Then he left.

She'd just closed her eyes and sunk into the pillows when the nurse entered. "Look who I found."

The firefighter who'd kissed Lauren's hand was behind her. He'd cleaned up and changed into tight-fitting blue jeans, a green Nike T-shirt and sandals. Lauren had often watched the Courage Bay firefighters from her office window in the week since she began work, though she hadn't met any of them. The whole rescue unit—fire department, police and hospital—was located in a small, two-block area, and was lauded as an exemplary prototype. Their comings and goings had fascinated her. Though macho, high-profile men scared the daylights out of Lauren—and Lily—they were exactly Deirdre's type.

The firefighter's hair was damp. He smelled like soap and citrus aftershave, despite the fact that there was still a growth of beard on his jaw. His smile was thousand watt as it broke through the shadow. "Hey, how's our girl?"

Swallowing hard, she closed her eyes. This was ridiculous. "I'm fine, but I think you have me confused with someone else."

The nurse and firefighter exchanged worried looks.

"Dana." He picked up her hand again with that same tenderness as before. "Are you playing another one of your practical jokes on us?"

She shook her head.

As if he had a right to, the guy brushed the long bangs out of her eyes. His fingertips were callused. "And when did you cut all your hair off?"

"About twenty-five years ago," she said dryly.

The nurse frowned. "Dana, does your head hurt?"

"Look, I'm not Dana." Discomfited, she picked at the hospital sheet. "But in any case, thanks for rescuing me."

"You know you were in a fire at the newspaper office. You remember that, don't you?" The man's tone was patronizing but concerned. "What were you doing there at three in the morning?"

"I work there."

After exchanging another look with the firefighter, the nurse said, "Alex, maybe she got hit on the head."

The man—Alex—raised his dark brows, and his eyes, the color of aged whiskey, narrowed. "Don't you know who I am?" he said.

"No, I'm sorry."

"Call Doc Murdock."

"Who's that?" she asked.

"A psychiatrist."

"Look, I don't need a psychiatrist. I know who I am. Lauren Conway. I just moved here from Benicia."

Alex ran a big hand through his hair. If she had the chance, she'd paint the color with different tones of brown and gold to achieve his natural color. She'd call the painting "Confused Hero."

He took her hand again. "Honey, no more jokes. We're worried about you."

"This isn't a joke. Look in my purse. At my driver's license."

"You don't carry a purse!"

"Of course I do. It's got all my stuff in it."

They just stared at her. She felt her heartbeat speed up. Whipping back the sheets, she made to get up but went into a fit of coughing.

Jackie stepped around Alex and stopped her. "Here, sweetie, get back in bed." She eased Lauren against the pillows and started to draw up the covers.

But Alex held up his hand. "Wait a minute." He grabbed hold of her left foot. "What's this?"

Lauren felt uncomfortable. Right above her ankle, she had a small brown spot which resembled a leaf. "It's a birthmark."

"Dana's birthmark is on her right foot," Alex said. "But it looks just like this."

"I told you, I am not Dana!"

Awareness dawned on Jackie's face. "Wow. Except for your hair, you're a dead ringer for Dana Ivie. She's a friend and a firefighter on Alex's squad."

Alex peered closely at her. "Not exactly." He reached out and tipped her chin. "Your features are more delicate. I can see that now that it's light out and you've cleaned up." He stared hard into her eyes. "And your eyes are a shade darker."

Jackie frowned. "How could this be?"

Alex shook his head. Whipping out his cell phone, he punched in numbers. "Give me the San Diego Days Inn." He looked at the nurse, then back to Lauren again. "Yeah, hi. Dana Ivie's room, please."

Lauren hugged the bedsheet closer to her chin.

After a moment, Alex's eyes widened. "Dana? Is that you?" He chuckled. "Nothing, I just wanted to make sure...okay, okay, I know it's seven. Sorry for waking you. Go back to sleep."

He clicked off.

"She's there?" Jackie asked.

"Uh-huh." He turned his interesting eyes on the patient. "So, Lauren Conway. Do you know you have a twin?"

"No. But I gather this Dana looks like me."

Alex cocked his head, then reached around into his back pocket and withdrew his wallet. He leafed through several pictures before he stopped, pulled one out and handed it to her.

Lauren looked down. In the picture was a woman with long luscious hair and curves to die for outlined in a wild-print bikini. She held a surfboard and leaned on the smiling, sun-burnished man whose arm was around her. The man was Alex.

The woman looked exactly like Lauren.

The similarity made her light-headed and caused her heart to trip. *What* was going on here?

"THIS REALLY WASN'T necessary." Lauren, dressed in baggy hospital scrubs, turned in the front seat of Alex's Blazer to face him. She'd showered before she was released and her hair curled softly around her face. He didn't know if she normally wore makeup, but without it, he could see the few freckles smattering her nose. Just like Dana's. It was hard to believe she wasn't related to his friend. "But I appreciate it."

"I don't mind. I was on my way home, anyway."

"Still, it was nice of you." She coughed. "I didn't feel like driving."

"Smoke inhalation can be bad. You should take it easy today." He reached for the door handle. "The landlord said he'd meet you here, right?"

"Yeah." She glanced down at her watch; her wrist so slender he'd be able to encircle it with his fingers. She touched the timepiece lovingly.

"A special possession?" he asked.

"My mother gave it to me."

"Does she live in Courage Bay?"

"She and my father were both killed in an accident." A shadow crossed her pretty eyes. "A little over a year ago."

"I'm sorry."

She gave Alex a half smile that did something to his insides. It was a smile similar to Dana's when she was being soft and feminine. "At least the watch was spared in the fire."

He smiled. "You'll probably get your purse back. The flames were contained to the east side of the building. Smoke damage is the worst your office got, and that can be cleaned up."

"Thank God I'd moved out of the side that burned. I'm lucky, I guess."

"Well, at least you weren't hurt badly."

"When do you think I'll be able to move back into my office?"

"As soon as the arson team finishes."

Her eyes widened. "Arson team?"

"Yeah, we couldn't determine the cause of the fire, so the arson investigator, Sam Prophet, was called in. It could have been an incendiary blaze."

"That means set intentionally, right?"

"Uh-huh."

She shivered.

"Come on, let's get you inside."

Rounding the car, he opened her door and helped her stand. She was trembling. It was about seventy degrees, warm enough at eight o'clock in the morning. "You cold?"

She rubbed her bare arms. "A little."

"Shell-shocked, I'd guess."

"It's sinking in." She peered up at him with doe eyes. "I could have died in that fire."

That was true. People slept through fires and never woke up.

Something made him slide his arm around her. Just a little human compassion, he guessed. Still, it felt good when she leaned into him. She *was* slight—a lot slighter than Dana. That had registered when he'd carried her down the ladder, but didn't make sense until now.

And she was a lot more fragile. Alex was accustomed to being around women who could beat him now and then at racquetball or who were at least worthy opponents in pickup beach volleyball.

The landlord pulled up, inquired after Lauren's well-being, unlocked the house, then left them alone. She turned in the doorway. Wrapping her arms around her waist, she smiled at Alex. "What do you say to a man who saved your life?" she asked softly. Her voice was different from Dana's, too—mellower, more feminine—but her speech patterns were the same.

"Thanks is enough." But the scared look on her face made him add, "Or maybe offer him a cup of coffee. Us smoke eaters really need our caffeine, ma'am."

Laughing, she stepped inside. "That's the least I can do."

She led him into her home. Studying the room, he let on a low whistle. It literally took his breath away. He'd never seen such a wide array of colors, textures and unusual furnishings. The living-room rug was raspberry and so thick that his sandals sank into it.

"Make yourself comfortable. I'll fix the coffee." Before she left, she opened two huge windows. The tinkle of wind chimes drifted in. Then, she disappeared into the kitchen.

He bypassed the off-white, nubby couch and sat on a long chaiselike thing that conformed to his body when he stretched out. Plump rose-colored cushions enveloped him. Picking up one of the several geometric-patterned pillows that accented the blues, grays and pinks in the room, he scanned the rest of the place.

Jeez, look at that. In the corner was a full-size hammock. He got up and crossed to it. He'd never seen one indoors. The wall behind it was decorated with an array of mesmerizing paintings. He circled around the hammock to examine them closely. The artist's signature read "LAC." Delicate, wispy strokes etched out the water, the mountains, the forest. They were abstract, but he knew for certain what each painting portrayed.

"What do you think?" He turned to see her holding a small tabby kitten. As he watched, she rubbed her cheek on the animal's furry little head. Another kitten scurried at her feet.

"Are you kidding?" He pointed to a small picture. "It feels like I'm wading in that lake. I can smell those flowers."

Her smile was broad. "I'm glad you like them." She set the kitten on the floor—it stayed at her feet like a toddler would its mother—and, crossing to the wall, reached up and took a painting down. "Here, as a thank-you for saving my life."

"You don't have to do that. Just tell me who the artist is and I'll look him up."

"The artist is a she."

He cocked his head. She seemed…proud. "You, Lauren?"

She nodded.

"They're wonderful. They should be in a gallery. For sale."

Her frown was instantaneous. "No. I wouldn't want to do that." She fingered the delicate teak frame. "It would be like selling a child." She handed him the canvas. "You can adopt it. It'll be safe with you."

Grinning, he took the painting. She was downright charming.

"Who's this little guy?" he asked, squatting to scratch one kitten's head. Both sidled against his legs, making him smile.

"Butterscotch. The other's Caramel."

He chuckled at the names.

When the coffee finished dripping, they sat together on the couch, sinking deep into the overstuffed cushions. Over the rim of his mug, also one of her works of art, he watched her drink. She'd made herself tea—Dana preferred it over coffee, too—and she inhaled the scent first, then sipped. She closed her eyes when she swallowed. Smiled. When she finally licked her lips, he felt his body respond. He had to look away.

"I hope you like hazelnut."

"Hazelnut?"

"The coffee's flavored."

"Um, sure. I do." He had no idea what he was drinking.

He searched the room for something to focus on instead of her mouth. A picture sat on the odd-shaped end table next to the couch. It was an eight-by-ten close-up of two older people and Lauren. He slid over so he could see it better. The couple was attractive;

both had vibrant blue eyes, thick gray hair and they were smiling. In the photo, Lauren was laughing, too, her brown eyes sparkling. He stared at it for a minute, then glanced at her.

"Your parents?"

"Uh-huh."

"You were adopted." It wasn't a question.

"What?" She grinned. "Oh, no. I wasn't. I know I don't look like them, but I wasn't adopted."

This was odd. "Lauren, you had to be adopted. Two blue-eyed parents can't have a brown-eyed child."

"That's what they say. I studied eye-color genes in biology class. When I asked Mom and Dad about it, they said I must be some kind of mutation because she saw me come out of her body and Dad cut the umbilical cord. Actually, *I* saw it on the home video they took."

Alex shook his head. "This goes against everything I know. I studied genetics—my mother's a geneticist—before I decided to follow in Dad's footsteps. From what I learned in my courses, this is a scientific impossibility."

She shrugged. "I guess I'm a rare breed."

He scanned her place again. He didn't doubt that. But something wasn't adding up. And it bothered him. What about her similarity to Dana? What were the chances of someone looking almost exactly like his friend? Slim. What were the chances of a genetic abnormality—impossibility, really—with that same person? Nonexistent, in his mind. But he said only, "Well, I'll ask Mom about it to be sure."

Her look was indulgent. "Don't bother. I know who I am."

Suddenly he hoped—for her sake—that was true.

CHAPTER TWO

THE FIREHOUSE WAS a kaleidoscope of sights, sounds and textures. As Lauren stepped through the open door into one of four bays and onto the cold concrete floor, she ran her free hand over the rough wall. And sniffed. Gasoline. Oil. The faint acrid smell. The bays were full. Huge red trucks towered over her; they were different sizes and shapes and, she assumed, performed different tasks, as one had ladders, the other hoses. Another was the medical truck she'd ridden in. Walking up to it, she ran her hand over the cold steel surface, sensing the strength emanating from it. Everything here was so big and *powerful*. Intimidating. Still, she had a delivery to make. She crossed to the station house and entered the building proper. She found the kitchen by scent. It was noontime, and somebody was making lunch. The aroma of cooking beef, French fries and coffee made her stomach growl.

The kitchen area was mammoth. A hulk of a guy bent over the stove against the far wall; he was humming off-key as he mixed food in a huge frying pan. Another man prepared salad at the counter. He was also big. Two more men and a woman were seated by the window at the long oak table, which Lauren knew would be smooth and cool to the touch. It overlooked the rec area, where, from her own office window, she'd watched the firefighters play basketball and sometimes grill outside. Today, they were dressed in the dark blue uniform of Courage Bay firefighters, complete with badges on their chest pockets, a Maltese cross patch on their short sleeves, and name tags.

"Hello," she said softly.

They peered over at her. "Dana?" the woman asked. She was more diminutive than the rest, but well-defined muscles stood out beneath her short sleeves. Briefly Lauren wondered what it would be like to be brave enough, strong enough to do what this woman did.

A woman like Dee.

"No. I'm Lauren Conway. I was at the newspaper's offices when they caught fire last week."

"Hey." The man at the table stood. "I'm Mick Ramirez. Now I recognize you."

"They said you were a carbon copy of Dana, but wow." This from the woman again. "It's hard to believe you could look so much alike and not be related. You sure you're not?"

Lauren shook her head. "I'm sure." She held up a huge shopping bag. "I brought you all something by way of thank you."

"Something to eat?" the chef asked. "I'm Nick LaSpino, by the way."

Everybody else gave names Lauren knew she'd never remember.

"Cookies. I made them myself." She glanced around. "I particularly wanted to thank Alex Shields. He, um, carried me out."

The men exchanged knowing looks.

"Alex is out back playing a pickup basketball game."

"Oh." It was just as well. She'd thought entirely too much about the sexy captain in the few days since the fire. Since she'd last seen him. "I won't disturb him. I'll be on my way to the *Courier.*"

"You aren't back in the offices yet, are you?" LaSpino asked.

"No, we're still in the temporary space set up in the vacant building next door."

Ramirez pointed outside. "Go out through the back. You can get to the newspaper that way and catch Alex before you leave."

"Showing off, as usual," the woman noted in a patronizing tone.

Lauren hesitated. "All right." She said her good-byes and made her way to the door. One of the guys got up and opened it for her. He towered over her. Jeez, were they all giants?

Just because you're a shrinking violet around manly men.

Damn, she thought. Go away, Dee. She didn't need her imaginary friend nagging at her any more than she had all week. *Call him, stop by the fire house,* act, *you sissy.*

She smiled at the man who's name tag read Begay as he opened the door for her. "Alex'd kill us if we let you go without talking to him." His voice sounded teasing. "They're playing over there."

"Thanks." Once outside, she walked the few feet to the blacktop court, which sparkled in the May noonday sun. She stood behind a barbecue pit so she could observe.

And was mesmerized by the sights and sounds.

Grunts.

Heavy breathing.

A word of direction.

Several curses.

At one point, Alex grabbed the ball, leaped up and seemed to freeze in the air—she'd title the scene "Poetry in Motion" if she had a chance to paint it. He released the ball. It arced, then swished into the net.

"Hot damn, I'm good." He executed a high five with another guy; two others swore.

One man grabbed the ball, jogged to the top of the court and cracked his hand on it. That must signal game in play because the four men began running all over the place.

"I'm open," somebody yelled. The ball handler hurled the ball at him, just as Alex stepped in front. He intercepted it and turned, but somebody rammed into him, landing him right on his fanny.

"Oh!" she said with a gasp.

As a group, they turned. Alex, from the blacktop, smiled up at her. It was a male smile, one that said *I'm glad to see you.* "Hey, Lauren, hi."

"Are you all right?" she asked, edging up to the court.

"Yeah, sure."

"His butt's as hard as his head," one guy put in.

From the firehouse, somebody called out, "Lunch in ten, guys."

"We're done, anyway," another player said. They bade goodbye, leaving Lauren alone with Alex.

Lithe as a cat, he rolled to his feet and crossed to her. She fought the urge to back up. She hadn't remembered him being quite so big, but today, out here, he looked…overwhelming. Tall, at least six-two. Really broad shoulders under a sweat-soaked gray T-shirt. His hair was damp, his face ruddy and dripping. He wiped his forehead with his sleeve. It didn't help. "Good to see you."

"You, too." Her voice sounded raw, even to her own ears.

He gave her a studied look. "Still not feeling well?"

"Why would you ask that?"

"Your voice is hoarse."

She shook her head. "No, I'm fine. I, um, came by on my way to work to bring you some cookies I baked as thank-you."

He propped a foot up on a nearby bench and leaned over, resting his elbow on his knee. His legs were corded with muscles and covered with a sparse growth of dark hair. He wore heavy high-tops on his feet. "I got a beautiful little painting for my bedroom wall as thanks from you."

"You put it in your bedroom?"

His light brown eyes darkened. "I will as soon as my house is painted." He nodded to the fire station. "Hey, you wanna stay for lunch? We're having sloppy joes and French fries."

Oh, God, and eat with this one hundred eighty pounds of pure male flesh? "I don't think so."

"Why?"

She bit her lip and his eyes focused on the action. She felt his gaze in her stomach—and lower. "I'm going to the office."

"You're up and running again in the place next door, right?"

"Yeah. Lucky thing it was vacant. Our press is still operating in the old building's basement, though. It wasn't damaged."

"How long will you be working out of the temporary offices?"

"Another couple of weeks, I guess. The west side will have to be rebuilt, but they'll wall it off and we can work in the rest of the space."

"I've been wondering how you were."

Then why didn't you call me? she wanted to ask. But didn't, of course.

"As I said, I'm fine."

His eyes flashed with male appreciation. "I've been thinking about you, Lauren."

"Oh?"

"I saw your first cartoon. I recognized Deirdre—she looks like you."

"Did you like it?"

"Sure. Is it autobiographical?"

Yes. "Of course not. It's just a cartoon."

"By the way, I talked to Dana. She was fascinated to have a look-alike right in town. She's dying to meet you when she gets back."

"That would be nice."

He scowled. "I still can't get over the resemblance. My mother's away at a conference and I couldn't reach her."

"Oh, well, that's not necessary." She stepped to the side. "I'll let you get to your lunch."

He laid a gentle hand on her arm. "Want to have dinner some night with me, Lauren?"

"Dinner?"

"Yeah, you know, like on a date."

"A date?"

"Uh-huh, where two people agree to go somewhere together."

"Um, I'm busy." She raised the purse she carried to her chest, effectively shrugging off his touch.

"I didn't give you a day or time."

She sighed.

"Look, if you don't want to go out with me, just say so."

"It's not that." She studied his sturdy, rugged form. His handsome face. "I just don't think we're very well matched."

"Never know until you try."

She shook her head. "I don't think so. Thanks anyway." She had to get out of there. "I hope you enjoy the cookies." And coward that she was, she scurried through the backyard of the firehouse, crossed the street and ducked into the new offices.

She didn't look back. If she did, she might change her mind. And that was not a good idea. She didn't date men like Alex. She liked the poetic, sensitive, *smaller* kind of guy. Felt more comfortable with them.

Oh, yeah, sure. Deirdre was back. *Dating men like James Tildan is a great idea.*

Well, her ex-fiancé *had* been her type.

Until he stole from you.

God, that stung. Lauren had buried the hurt and didn't let it surface too often. Just because James had turned out to be a creep didn't mean all men like him were.

Except for James, you haven't kept one of those sensitive types around yet.

No, and she didn't miss them all that much. Though she did miss sex. A lot. As she stepped into her makeshift office, she let herself think for a minute what sex would be like with Alex.

Dazzling. Exciting. Adventurous.

She remembered how strong he was, carrying her down the ladder. How safe she'd felt when he put his arm around her in front of her house. But damn, she couldn't handle a big, strong, tough firefighter. His physical presence intimidated her.

Nope, she'd made the right decision.

Yeah, sure you did, you lily-livered wimp.

THEY WERE GATHERED around the window when Alex strode into the firehouse. Which was *all* he needed. He was good and pissed.

"So, she say she'd go out with you?" Robertson asked.

Ramirez snorted. "She get swept away by your charm like all the ladies, gringo?"

When he remained silent, Robertson winked at the others. "Don't tell us you didn't ask her out. We know you did."

"Like hell." They'd never let him hear the end of it if they knew she'd blown him off.

LaSpino called out, "Hey, come look at these."

Saved by the chef, who had a legendary sweet tooth. Alex crossed to the table and looked down at the cookies Lauren had brought. "Holy hell."

There had to be twenty dozen of them. He picked one up. "A Maltese cross." The insignia of firefighting. "It's beautiful." Frosted in red and yellow, Lauren had even put a badge number on it. 527. His.

"There's some boots and helmets, too," LaSpino murmured. They were also frosted with details—a black line for the sole, yellow reflectors.

"They had to take her forever," Janey Lopez said.

Another asked, "Why'd she wrap each one in plastic?"

"So they'd stay fresh, moron," LaSpino told him. "Didn't she know we'd chow 'em down right away?"

Still, nobody moved to take one.

"Well, lookee here." This from Alvarez. "A helmet, frosted in red."

"It's probably for me," joked Will Begay, the captain on the engine. Captains wore colored helmets so they could be found easily in an operation. Everybody knew, just like the badge number, this cookie was for Alex.

Then why the hell had she said no to a freakin' date? "Women!" he quipped, and stalked out of the kitchen to the bathroom. The guys' razzing followed him.

Under the shower's spray, he thought about her. She wasn't exactly Miss America. Still, she *was* pretty. As pretty as Dana? Hmm. He hadn't thought about Dana in those terms for years. But Lauren was definitely as pretty, only in a different way. He could still remember how she'd drunk the tea, how she steeped herself in it. Cherished it. Hell! Just thinking of that had an effect on his body.

And she was softer than Dana. Delicate. But delicate women were probably a lot of trouble. They'd need coddling. You'd have to do things for them. They had never been his type. Out of the shower, he pulled on sweatpants in deference to the woman subbing on their shift and grumbled, "I don't need any wilting flowers in my life."

"She looks more like a vibrant little rose to me."

Damn, he didn't know anybody else was in here.

Will Begay had come out of one of the stalls and was washing his hands at a sink. Rubbing his head with a towel—it was too late for backpedaling—Alex mumbled something unintelligible.

At least Will was trustworthy. The only Native American on Alex's squad, he seemed more self-possessed than the rest of the guys. He and Alex had been friends for years.

Will leaned against the wall as Alex dried off. "She said no, didn't she?"

"Yep."

"You haven't been shot down in a long time."

"Nope."

"Giving up?"

"Uh-huh. Before I invest. I got a feeling she's high maintenance."

"She seemed pretty interested in you. I looked out the window, and she was watching you on the court. Acted like she was studying a foreign species, but she was fascinated."

"Yeah?"

"And the red frosted helmets weren't for me."

He snorted.

Begay hesitated, then spoke. "She's a dead ringer for Dana."

There was something about his tone....

"So?"

"That's not why you're interested, is it?"

"Nope."

Will pushed away from the wall. "Good."

Alex asked, "Will? Your wife, Mareeta?"

"Yeah?"

"Is she high maintenance?"

"In my experience, Shields, all women are. You

just gotta find one who's worth it." He nodded to the bay. "We saved you some food. What time are we training?"

"This afternoon. About four, if there are no calls."

"On what?"

"Orientation for that new warehouse they just finished over on Twelfth Street."

The PA blared. "Car accident at Ronstat Street. Truck One and Paramedic One go into service."

Alex grabbed his stuff. "That's me," he said, and raced out of the john.

When he got back, he did some paperwork until four, then called the group together. There were nineteen of them, including the HazMat guys, who were also housed in the Jefferson Avenue firehouse. They'd need this training, too, because the warehouse would contain hazardous material.

When the crowd settled down, Alex explained the purpose of the session and told them they'd be going to the site on their next shift to check out the place before it opened. He gave them stats with questions to go with them. "I'd like you to look at the information I've got here. First, the warehouse is three thousand square feet. How long will it take to search it out for victims?"

"Not usually a lot of people in a warehouse." This from LaSpino.

"No, but a thorough search still needs to be done."

Somebody suggested a time frame.

"So how long does one SCBA last?"

They got the picture and discussed ways to search effectively and divvy the warehouse into manageable parts to accommodate their air supply.

"Second point—which hoses do we lay?"

Janey tackled this one. "Our usual? The one and three-quarters."

Alex said, "It's only forty-five feet long. Can it make it to all the walls?" When everybody shrugged, he said, "Let's figure it out." They did the math on a blackboard Alex had set up behind him. That length of hose would stretch to some walls and not others. They discussed alternatives.

In the next hour, Alex covered other points: he talked about what would be housed in the warehouse from the list provided by the owners. They studied it.

"Now let's analyze the conditions here that you wouldn't encounter in a bedroom fire. Any suggestions?"

The guys speculated there would be additional oxygen from all the doors that would be open when they attacked with water. They also mentioned decreased visibility.

Alex ended the session with some recommendations of his own: "We need to use the closest access doors. We need to back up with larger lines. And accountability is an absolute." He waited for this to sink in. "Last thing to talk about is the trusses…"

When they finished training, it was after five. Restless, Alex wanted some fresh air and privacy. He grabbed the paper and headed outside before dinner. Telling himself he was just curious, he sat at the picnic table and flipped to the comics. Lauren's cartoon, *Dee and Me*, wasn't in every day, so it probably wasn't even here.

It was.

Frame One:

The ocean. Deirdre and Lily stand on the dock.

Deirdre wears a chic suit, holds a surfboard. *Come on, Lily, let me show you.*

Lily is dressed in a dowdy bathing suit, horn-rimmed sunglasses and has zinc oxide on her nose. *I can't swim. You know that.*

Frame Two:

Dee is in the water. *You said you were taking lessons.*

The bubbles indicate Lily's thoughts. *I wish I was more like her.*

Frame Three:

Lily stands on the dock looking dejected. She's at the very end, where waves crash, watching Dee, mumbling *Some people have all the fun.*

Frame Four:

Other swimmers jostle Lily as they jump into the water.

Lily teeters on the edge of the dock after one particular shove.

Frame Five:

A big, muscle-bound boy skids into view, grabs her from behind before she falls.

A little *eek* comes from Lily.

Alex reread the cartoon. Hmm. A shy retiring female being rescued. Did this have something to do with her? With him? He glanced up at the building temporarily housing the newspaper. He'd never been a no-means-yes kind of guy, but the comic, coupled with the cookies, made him think trying again for a date was a good idea. He'd just whipped out his cell phone to call her, when she emerged from the building.

With news reporter Toby Hanson. Toby covered the fire-department beat and often showed up at their calls. The guy was her height, slender, nicely dressed. He wore wire-rimmed glasses. Alex remembered thinking before he was kind of nerdy, not really a man's man. Right now, he had his hand at Lauren's back. They walked toward a small Toyota, and Hanson opened the passenger door for her. She was just about to get in when she looked up. She must have seen Alex staring, phone in hand, because she gave a slight wave and slid into the car.

I'm busy.

For some reason, he had never thought about her having a boyfriend. So that's why she'd blown Alex off.

It made him feel better to know that.

Sort of.

LAUREN STARED at Toby Hanson and realized that she'd never been more bored. Immediately, she chided herself for the unkind thought. Toby had been sweet and sincere with her since she arrived in Courage Bay. "I'm sorry about not sitting on the rooftop," he said. "My allergies are bothering me."

"That's all right." She'd have preferred to be in the outdoor restaurant. Would Alex have wanted to sit up there? "This is a great place inside, too." It was. The Courage Bay Bar and Grill was an off-duty hangout for the rescue personnel in the community and bore signs of its main customers.

"Isn't it? The father of the owners, the Goodmans, bought this building when it was an old movie theater, then converted it to a restaurant. His son Larry and daughter-in-law run it now. They're all descendants of the sailors of the *Ranger* who settled here."

Lauren had researched the history of Courage Bay

before coming here. The ten-mile strip of coastal area, near Los Angeles, had been inhabited solely by Native Americans until a ship called the *Ranger* came upon the coast during a horrific storm. The ship was ready to capsize when twelve very brave natives had risked their lives to save the sailors, who ended up staying and intermarrying with their rescuers. Lauren loved reading the stories, especially the somewhat mystical connection of the town's current rescue personnel and those brave natives who'd put themselves in danger for others.

"Lauren?"

"Sorry, I was just thinking about the *Ranger*." She glanced around. "I love the interior of this place." The dining room was softly lit, with buttery-cream walls and smooth, rich oak trim. It smelled like seafood and the freshly baked bread they'd served before dinner. She broke off a piece and brought it to her mouth. It was flaky. Light. "I hope all the food's as good as this."

His eyes were riveted on her mouth. "Did anybody ever tell you you have a really sensuous way of eating?"

"Yes, people have said that. I enjoy food."

"You savor it."

"Observations from an ace reporter."

He shook his head.

"What? Your coverage of the goings-on with the police and firefighters is very insightful."

"I wish Perry would give me more challenging stuff. Or that I'd have the gumption to leave the *Courier*."

The waiter arrived and took their orders for Veal Marsala. She and Toby were well matched in tastes.

Alex would no doubt have picked the prime rib. A man's meal. Toby was more her type.

Deirdre's voice broke into her thoughts. *Then why are you thinking about the hunky firefighter so much?*

I'm not.

"Lauren, you look like you're someplace else again."

"Oh, sorry. You were talking about your job."

"I like it well enough. I just think I'm underappreciated."

"Then you should do something else."

"Is that why you moved here?"

"No, I came to Courage Bay because my roommate from college teaches school here. After my mother and father died a year ago, I was at loose ends in Benicia. I'd been trying to get the cartoon off the ground, so this seemed like a good opportunity." And since her parents, who were both lawyers, had left her a lot of money, she was free to pursue her interests and work only part-time.

She didn't tell him about her broken engagement. Or James's deception.

"Do you mind doing the layout Perry assigned you until you get the cartoon going?" he asked her.

"No, it's fine. I like helping with the artwork."

He nodded to her clothes. "That jacket's a work of art itself." It was several shades of pink and wine, like a patchwork quilt. Gold threads outlined each small square.

"I made it."

"A woman of many talents."

They managed small talk while they ate their salads, then their meals arrived. She sipped the white wine he'd ordered for them both and cut the veal. "This is so tender, it melts in my mouth."

Again he watched her. Smiling. Hmm. Seemed as if he was interested. She wondered what he'd kiss like. Then she wondered what Alex would kiss like.

The dinner finished pleasantly. "I'd like to see the rest of this place," she told Toby. "I've only been in town two weeks and I've never been here. Would you mind if we looked around before we left?"

"No, of course not. It's cool. You'll love the Wall."

"What's that?"

"I'll show you."

He led her to the far side of the room to the Remembrance Wall. It was filled with names and pictures of rescue personnel who'd died in the line of duty. "This is remarkable." Lauren ran her finger along the frames, studying the faces of the men and women who'd lost their lives saving others.

"The Goodmans' son is here." Toby pointed to a picture.

A young, redheaded boy stood, looking proud in his fire department blues. She saw so much life there, so much missed. It made her sad.

"He was a paramedic. After he died, Larry and Louise put up this wall."

"A lovely tribute."

They headed to the back, to what was called the Function Room. She laughed when she saw it. It was a man's paradise: three huge TVs, pool tables, darts and framed photos and articles around the perimeter. It even smelled male—with a faint hint of aftershave. "Did you write any of these articles?"

"I've written some they've hung in the bar, though

I don't think there are any of mine in this room. I don't hang out much in here. I'm not good at these games.''

Lauren perused the pictures. One was captioned "Captain Saves Little Girl." The captain was Alex. He was smiling broadly, holding a small child. His face was grimy, and he was dressed in turnout gear, which was dirt smeared. For a moment, she couldn't take her eyes off him.

She followed Toby, looking at other articles, photos and various memorabilia in the back room, then they went to the bar. More accolades were out there.

More Alex. A casual shot of him with his crew. Lauren's eyes zeroed in on a woman. Dana. Damn. She looked even more like Lauren in this picture.

Toby gave voice to her thoughts. "She could be your twin."

Lauren peered over at him. "You must know her, Toby. Why didn't you ever say anything about how much I resemble her?''

He shrugged. ''You've only been here two weeks. Truthfully, I thought maybe you were related, and since you didn't say anything, you must not want to talk about it.''

"That was thoughtful. But we're not sisters, or anything else.''

"Okay. Just fate, I guess.'' He nodded to the wall. "Here's an article I wrote.''

She moved closer. *Please don't let it be about Alex.*

It was an off-the-job rescue. Alex had been out of town on vacation and drove past a house on fire. He'd spotted a kid in the window two stories up. He'd called 911 and then shinnied up a tree to rescue the child. On the way down, a limb had cracked and they'd fallen. The girl was fine, but Alex had broken his arm. He'd received a medal from the mayor for his actions.

By the time they left the grill, Lauren felt she'd been to dinner with Alex Shields—he'd been in her thoughts so much and his pictures had been all around. Damn. She got her car from the newspaper office parking lot and drove home, wondering about her preoccupation with the man. She was distracted as she parked in the driveway, got out and hurried up to her house. When she had moved here, she'd wanted her own space. Since she had the money, she'd rented, with an option to buy, this small stucco one-story home on a quiet street. The landlord had even agreed to go half on any redecorating. She liked the place, she thought, as she reached the porch and unlocked the door.

But once inside, she stopped in her tracks.

It could be nothing, but...the room smelled different, almost like cologne. The scent was male.

And the desk drawers were slightly ajar.

And her throw pillows were on the floor.

Lauren was neat, and knew she hadn't neglected to close the drawers. She hadn't scattered pillows on the floor before she'd left, either.

With a sinking feeling, she realized somebody had been in her home.

CHAPTER THREE

ALEX STARED out at the second-graders and thought about the fact that by now he could have had a seven-year-old child. He was thirty-four. Sometimes he regretted that he hadn't already married and started a family. Sometimes, he was glad as hell. Still, he wanted a woman to share his life with, to eventually have kids with. It just hadn't happened yet.

"Alex?" The teacher, Hannah Nielson, smiled up at him. She was engaged to his friend, Vince Wojo-howitz, a cop, and Alex liked her. "You with us?"

"Yeah, sorry I'm a little vague. I was on last night and we had calls." Then, when he finally did get to sack out, he'd dreamed of...damn, he wasn't going to do this.

"Well, we're ready to start if you are."

"Sure."

"Hannah?"

Both of them turned to the door. Lauren. Jeez, what was fate up to here?

"Hey, Lauren." Hannah smiled. "Have you met Alex Shields, one of our bravest?"

Lauren bit her lip. Some lipstick—the color of rum—came off on her teeth. "Yes, I have." She smiled. "He's the one who pulled me out of the fire."

Hannah's brows arched. "Oh, Lord, I didn't know that."

Lauren's eyes filled with emotion. "I'm very grateful to our *bravest*."

"Just part of the job, ma'am. And those cookies you made—we feasted, I'll tell you."

"I'm glad you liked them."

"What are you doing here?" he asked her.

"I volunteer in Hannah's classroom."

Hannah squeezed Lauren's arm. "We were roommates at UCLA."

As with Toby Hanson, Lauren had thought it curious that Hannah hadn't ever mentioned her likeness to Dana. She had asked about it earlier, and Hannah said she'd never met Dana personally in the year she'd been in Courage Bay. She associated more with Vince's cop buddies. When Lauren had found a picture of her on the Net and showed Hannah, her friend had gasped at the similarity. She, too, found it hard to believe they weren't related. Lauren wished people would stop saying that.

"How about you?" Lauren asked. "Why are you here?"

"Alex does most of the fire instruction in this school. I think he's a frustrated teacher."

"Please, I could never handle them on a day-to-day basis." He nodded to the class.

"Speaking of which, I think the natives are restless."

Flushing, Lauren stepped away. "I'll just go to the back of the room."

Alex watched her walk away. She wore a gauzy sage-green skirt, which swirled around her calves, and a matching top. It was a peasant kind of style with the tie around the neckline. Her dangly earrings accented the outfit. They were made of tiny green stones.

Damn! What was wrong with him, noticing every little thing about the woman. He turned to the students. "Hi, guys. Remember me?"

"Captain Shields." They all spoke at once.

One kid asked, "We gonna get to do the fire extinguisher again?"

"Not today. We're going to talk about what a person should do if he or she catches on fire."

From the back of the room, Lauren gasped.

He threw her a knowing grin. "Some people think we shouldn't scare you with all the possibilities of what could happen, but we've already talked about how to prevent fires and precautions to take. It's important to know what happens in the event of a fire."

Lauren blushed. He gave her a smile that was meant to ease her embarrassment. She blushed deeper.

"So, look up here." He turned and wrote on the board. "Everybody repeat this for me."

The kids yelled, "Stop, drop and roll!"

"I don't suppose there are any volunteers who want to help me illustrate the technique?"

Sixteen hands shot up. God, he loved this. Maybe he *was* a frustrated teacher.

THE MAN UNNERVED HER. Lauren was right to have said no to a date with him. So what if she couldn't get him out of her mind? She *would,* if she could stop having contact with him. Who would have guessed that he'd be at school today? She'd agreed to help out Hannah with some end-of-the-year art projects, and never imagined she'd run into the one guy she'd been thinking about way too much.

Concentrating on the stars she was drawing, she listened to his strong baritone and the rumbles of laughter from him and the kids. She stole a sideways glance at them. He didn't seem to mind being on the floor with the kids, even though he wore a nice outfit: a red silk T-shirt that outlined his broad shoulders and washboard abs, and pressed khakis, which highlighted his trim hips and long legs. "Man At Ease With Children," she'd title the scene at the front of the room. He had the kids circled around him. A little girl was demonstrating the technique of Stop, drop and roll. Alex spoke softly to her. Gently he eased her down to the mat he'd spread out. The tender gesture made Lauren think of husbands and fathers. Her own father had been a wonderful man, even if both her parents had been as different from her as desert to ocean. They'd loved her dearly and were stymied by the fact she'd always felt a sense of not belonging. Thoughts of the loving man and woman who had raised her made her eyes mist.

Damn. She was feeling too much today. Probably because she hadn't slept enough last night. When she'd gotten home, she'd been sure someone had been in the house.

First, there was the scent of the man's aftershave in the air. The policeman who'd come had thought she was crazy....

"Let me get this right," Officer Carlos Jerado asked after he'd checked out the house and taken her statement. "You *smelled* somebody?"

"I know it sounds silly, but I have a heightened sensory awareness. Besides, there were the other things."

Like the pillows that weren't where she'd put them.

"You know where every pillow is?" Jerado had asked, indicating the ten or twelve in the living room. "As for the desk drawers, you sure you closed them?"

By the time the cop left, Lauren had felt like a fool.

Still, she knew she wasn't imagining things.

Would Alex have believed her?

Ah, back to the sexy captain, who right now was laughing so hard with the kids he was holding his stomach. It made her own stomach do a funny little two-step.

"GOODBYE, CAPTAIN SHIELDS." Interesting how a group like this could speak in unison.

"Bye, guys. I hope I see you next year."

Hannah came up to him. "Thanks, Alex. I'm going to take the kids to an assembly now." She looked to Lauren, who sat facing the back of the room. "Lauren, I'll see you in a bit."

Lauren glanced over her shoulder. "Okay, Hannah. Goodbye, Alex." She returned to her task.

After Hannah left, Alex stared at Lauren. Drawn to her like fire to air, he ambled back, not exactly sure what he was going to say. Over her shoulder, he saw she'd cut out stars and was sketching faces on them. The faces were those of the kids who'd just left.

"Those are beautiful."

She jumped. "Oh."

He put his hand on her shoulder. Her hair gleamed in the overhead lights. He could smell the lemony scent of her shampoo. "Sorry."

She pivoted in the chair, dislodging his hand. "No, that's okay, I'm just spooked today." She smiled up at him. Mauve smudges shadowed her eyes. "Sounds like you had a good time there."

"I love working with kids."

"They obviously love you. I'm sorry if you thought I was critical before."

"No, it's okay. A lot of people are afraid to talk to kids candidly."

"Yes, I know. I always felt that protesters of sex education in schools were nuts."

Sex, huh? "Me, too." He studied the lines on her face. "What did you mean you were spooked today?"

"It's nothing."

"Tell me."

She stood then, so she was more on eye level with him. "Last night when I got home, I thought somebody had been in my house."

"What?"

"No, let me clarify that. I know somebody had been there." She told him about the clues. "The policeman thought I was crazy. He said there were no signs of anyone breaking in." She shrugged. "He finally suggested the landlord had come in without telling me."

"Did you ask the landlord?"

"No, he wasn't answering his phone last night or today."

"Does anybody else have a key?" Alex asked.

"Hannah. She told me she wasn't at my house last night."

Arching his brows, he couldn't help flirting with her. "No guy has a key?"

Her brown eyes twinkled. "No, no guy."

"I'm sorry."

"What, that there's no man or about the break-in?"

"Definitely about the break-in."

She shook her head, then turned, as if uncomfortable with the exchange. "Well, I've got to get back to this." She nodded to the artwork. "I wanted to finish before the kids return from the assembly."

Her dismissal stung. "Sure." He straightened. "Take care."

Feeling like a second-grader himself, he headed out to his car. This was dumb. The lady was definitely not interested. He tried to shrug off his pique as he strode to his Blazer and slid inside. He was tired, so he'd go home, sack out, then find something interesting to do tonight. For a minute, he stared at the school. Lauren was an enigma. And it looked as if she was going to stay that way.

He caught sight of the morning's paper that he'd tossed on the front seat. Hell. He picked it up and leafed through the pages. Sure enough, another *Dee and Me.*

Frame One:

The muscle-bound boy, still holding on to her arms, smiles at Lily. *You okay?*

Lily is being shy. *Oh, sure.*

Frame Two:

They're off the dock now. Lily peers up at the boy. Bubbles indicate her thoughts: *Jeez, he's so big. So handsome. Eyes the color of amber.*

Amber? Alex's eyes were light brown. That was amber, wasn't it? He read on.

The boy has a goofy expression on his face. *Wanna go get a soda with me?* he asks.

Frame Three:

Um, no thanks.

Oh, okay. Looking dejected, the boy walks away.

Frame Four:

Lily appears despondent.

Deirdre is on the scene. *You wanted to go out with him. Why didn't you?*

He makes me uncomfortable.

Frame Five:

Deirdre shakes her head in disgust. *Boys are supposed to do that to girls. It's their job.*

Alex stared at the cartoon. If this wasn't a message, he didn't know what would be. Right then, he saw her exit the building. He got out of his truck as she walked toward her car, which, apparently, happened to be near his. Must be fate, he decided.

She came up to him. "Something wrong?"

His grin was cocky. He held up the newspaper. "Not that I can see. I read today's *Dee and Me.*"

Talk about being uncomfortable. She shifted on her feet. "Oh, did you, um, like it?"

"Lauren, you really do want to go out with me, don't you?"

"I said I didn't think it was a good idea."

He tapped the newspaper on his leg. "Then why did you write this?"

"It's a cartoon, Alex." But he could see her blush. "And from the input on the Web site, readers like the hook of the muscle-bound boy."

"I think your unconscious mind knows you want to go out with me."

Her smile was dazzling. It gave the sun competition. "Are you always this persistent?"

"I don't usually have to be." Never in his life had he pursued a woman so aggressively. Like jealousy, it just wasn't in his dating repertoire.

The arrogant comment drew a smile from her. "I don't doubt that." His phone rang. "Well," she said, like a prisoner given a late pardon. "You'd better get that."

"I will." He grasped her wrist, his fingers easily encircling it. "*You* are staying, however." He dug out his phone and flipped it open. "Shields."

"Alex, this is Sam Prophet." The arson investigator. "The cause of the fire at the newspaper office has been officially declared arson."

He saw Lauren's quizzical look.

"I see."

"We've already done interviews with everybody, but we're going to talk to your men again, as well as the occupants of the building that night."

That would include Lauren. "Sam, hold on a second." He covered the mouthpiece. "The fire was arson."

"Oh, dear."

"The investigator wants to talk to you again."

"Of course."

Sliding his fingers from her wrist to her hand, he spoke into the phone. "Sam, I'm with Lauren Conway. You should talk to her right away."

"I'm swamped this afternoon."

"I think you'll want to do it soon. Her house was broken into last night."

The investigator muttered an expletive. "Do you think the incidents are connected?"

"I wouldn't rule it out."

"Can she come over right now?"

Her face had paled when Alex told her about the arson. Now that he'd made a connection with the break-in, she was ashen. He felt an urge to protect her.

"Lauren, can you talk to the investigator now?"

She nodded.

"I'll bring her," he told Prophet, and clicked off.

She squared her slim shoulders and withdrew her hand from his. So she had some grit. That trait reminded him of Dana. Thoughts of his friend made him wonder if Lauren's resemblance to Dana had any bearing here. He'd been…disconcerted by that right from the start. Was the fire somehow linked to her similarity to Dana? Was there something sinister in that connection?

She said, "You think the fire and the break-in at my house are connected?"

"Let's just say it's a big coincidence."

"So you think…" Her voice broke off. Fear flashed in those dark brown eyes. "You think somebody wants to harm *me?*"

"It's a possibility. Come on, let's go see Prophet." He took her elbow and began to usher her around to the other side of his Blazer.

"My car…"

"We'll come back and get it."

She looked away. "All right. Thanks, I appreciate you going with me."

He grinned, trying to lighten the moment. "Well, I'm sure Dee would approve."

She smiled and he opened the car door for her.

SAM PROPHET WAS a big man—they seemed to grow them that way here in Courage Bay. He was over six feet tall with dark blond hair and smoky gray eyes.

Though he smiled, he was all business. "Ms. Conway, nice to see you again."

Lauren stared at the arson investigator. This whole thing was turning into a surreal dream. "Nice to see you again, too."

He shook his head, watching her. "I can't get over how much you look like Dana Ivie. I thought that when I first met you."

"Everyone's been saying so."

"It's somewhat uncanny."

She shrugged.

"I take it you've recovered from the fire."

Nodding, she said, "The smoke inhalation wasn't that bad."

"So, it's arson." Alex sat beside her facing the captain. She glanced at him when he spoke. His long, rangy body was stuffed into a small chair, and his legs were stretched out to accommodate his size.

"Yeah, and we know the source of the fire. I wanted to talk to you again, Lauren, to see if you've remembered anything more that might have looked or felt suspicious."

Concentrating hard, Lauren sighed. "I don't think so, Captain. I fell asleep in my office about midnight, which means I'd been out three hours before Alex rescued me."

"Hear or see anything when you came into the office?"

"I'd been there all day. The only people I saw that night were Perry O'Connor and Toby Hanson."

"Yeah, they were working late, too, you said."

"Truthfully, I just assumed they were working late. But Toby told me the other night he'd left at the end of the day and come back."

The investigator knit his brow. "Then he wasn't there the whole time…"

"Is it important?"

"It may be. We're trying to get a bead on the comings and goings of everyone who works in the building."

"What was the cause of the fire, Sam?" Alex asked.

"It was set in a storage room where back issues are kept. The torch ignited them. We found evidence of gasoline. Definitely amateur. It doesn't fit the arson-for-profit profile."

Lauren didn't understand. "Excuse me?"

"There are several types of arsonists." He held up a folder. "We've got profiles on each one. They're broken down by kinds of fires set, accelerants used, personality types for each one." He pointed to the computer. "With new software, we can draw some of our own conclusions."

"That's good," Lauren said. "Then you know what you're looking for?"

"Except in this case, the guy doesn't really fit any of the profiles."

"You know it was a man?" she asked.

"Most arsonists are male, Caucasian, young, below-average intelligence, have some kind of criminal history and have difficulty establishing normal social relationships." He sounded as if he was reading from a report.

"Wow."

He leaned forward in his seat and out of the corner of her eye she saw Alex scowl. Sam Prophet seemed to be showing off a bit. Was it for her? "Some studies say forty percent of all fires are set for profit. Half are set for revenge, the remaining ten percent are for fun—pyromaniacs, juveniles.''

Alex asked, ''What about vanity fires?'' Jeez, was he showing off, too? He addressed Lauren. ''Those are started by the guy who sets the fire sticks around to help out firefighters, to get credit for assisting.''

''They're often ex-firefighters or wanna-bes.'' Prophet again.

''I had no idea arson was so…predictable. It's fascinating.''

''If this case doesn't fit the arson-for-profit profile who are you looking for?'' Alex asked.

''Well, three areas come up as possibilities. Concealment of a crime leads me to suspect a juvenile fire starter, although those kids usually set fires in vacant buildings or at home in garages or basements. It could be a thrill seeker, since the devices they use tend to be simple, like this one. Or it could be hate/revenge arson.'' He focused intently on Lauren. ''That's what I want to talk to you about, especially since Shields said you had a break-in.''

''Well, *I* think I had a break-in, but the police don't.''

His gaze was razor sharp. Lauren realized she wouldn't want to be a suspect questioned by him. ''In any case, is there anybody you know of that would want to harm you? Or scare you? I think if this guy was really after you, the fire would have gotten to your office sooner. The fire department had plenty of time to put it out before it reached your side of the building.''

''That's good to hear.''

''Can you think of anybody?''

"Seriously, no. I don't have any enemies, as far as I know."

Alex grinned. "Now why doesn't that surprise me?"

She smiled at him.

"How about disgruntled boyfriends?"

She looked taken aback.

"I'm sorry to pry, Ms. Conway, but this is a criminal investigation. I'm a police officer, too."

"Oh, sure." She moved restlessly in her seat and glanced at Alex.

"Would you like Captain Shields to leave?"

"No, of course not." She lifted her chin. "I was engaged before I left Benicia."

She saw Alex stiffen.

"Who broke the engagement?"

"I did."

"May I ask why?"

"He stole from me."

"*What?*" Alex blurted out.

"James and I were engaged. He's an investment broker. I inherited some money when my parents died and he offered to invest it for me."

"Did he get a lot?" Alex asked.

"No, I caught on quickly."

Prophet had written down what she was saying. "Has he contacted you since you moved here?"

"Yes."

"Has he come down to Courage Bay?"

"Once, to try to talk me into coming back to Benicia."

She sighed, thinking of James's sensitive face and lying tongue.

"Tell me about the theft."

"He has a gambling problem. He contends it's an addiction and he meant me no harm."

"As I said, torches often have prior criminal records."

"I didn't prosecute."

"Why not?" Alex sounded outraged.

"Several reasons. One was because I got most of the money back. The others I'd prefer not to discuss, if you don't mind."

Prophet seemed okay with that, but Alex's look said *he* minded.

"We'll need to talk to him," Prophet told her.

Her heartbeat sped up. "I don't really want to see him again." It was too painful to confront the man she thought she loved. And to confront her own feelings of inadequacy regarding James.

"No reason you have to," Alex told her. "Right, Prophet?"

"Not that I can see." He glanced at his watch. "Could you give me the particulars on him now, Ms. Conway?"

The litany Lauren gave of James's vital stats—forty, divorced, no history of violence or uncontrolled rage—drained what little energy she had. Finally she finished, stood and bade goodbye to Prophet. As she and Alex left headquarters and drove to get her car, she could feel the strain in her sagging shoulders.

In the school parking lot, Alex pulled to a stop by her Accord and turned in his seat. He was really good-looking, with his sculpted features and strong jaw. "I'm sorry, Lauren. This stuff about James must be hard on you."

"On my pride, maybe." Now that he knew about

James, she wondered how a man like Alex could still be interested in her.

Tenderly Alex reached over and smoothed his knuckles down her cheek. "The guy must have been nuts to blow it with you."

"Thanks for saying that."

"It's the truth."

Glancing out his windshield, she stared at the setting sun. At the clear blue of the sky. She loved this time of day in California, just before supper. "Alex?"

"Yeah?"

"How would you like a home-cooked meal tonight?"

His smile was so sexy it made her heart trip in her chest. "I'd love one. Especially if you're gonna cook it for me, pretty lady."

"I've already cooked it. I was restless this morning and made quiche, an ambrosia salad and fudge brownies."

Again, the smile.

She gave him a sideways glance. "Unless you don't eat quiche."

"Is this some kind of test, Lauren?"

"Of course not. Guys don't actually believe in the adage, 'Real men don't eat quiche' anymore, do they?"

"No, 'course not, ma'am." His eyes were twinkling. The red of his shirt highlighted their amber color.

"Have you ever had quiche, Alex?"

"Sure. Lots of times."

"Did anybody ever tell you you're a very bad liar?"

"Me, lying?" He nodded to her car. "I'll follow you."

Lauren hummed on the drive home. She and Alex laughed all the way up the steps to her house. The mirth stopped, however, when she opened her front door. And felt the breeze.

"Did you leave your windows open, Lauren?"

Fear paralyzed her.

"Lauren?"

"No, I didn't leave any windows open."

CHAPTER FOUR

VINCE WOJOHOWITZ LOOKED like a younger version of Arnold Schwarzenegger. Alex had called his friend, a police detective, when he and Lauren discovered the open window in her living room. Not wanting a repeat of last night, where the cop, who turned out to be Vince's partner, had doubted Lauren, Alex had decided to call in his buddy.

"Okay, Lauren, let me get this down on paper." Perched on the edge of her lounger, Vince whipped out a pad and grabbed the pencil from behind his ear. "Shoot."

Lauren ran a shaky hand over her kitten Caramel's back. The movement of her fingers was slow and languid, and Alex's eyes were glued to it. Hannah, sitting next to Lauren on the couch, touched her friend's shoulder. She and Vince had been about to go to dinner when Alex called.

Alex listened to Lauren's melodic voice retell the simple facts: they'd come home, she was certain she hadn't left the window open or unlocked, especially after thinking someone had broken in the night before, yet the window was ajar. Alex bent down and picked up Butterscotch, Lauren's other cat. The appropriately titled feline burrowed into him, much like Lauren had when she'd discovered the window. He'd been moved by her vulnerability. "Be sure to tell Vince about last night."

"I already did."

"You need to again, so I get it right." Vince glanced at his fiancée and smiled.

After they finished, Vince rose. "Well, I'll be going."

From where he stood by the window, Alex saw Lauren frown. "What do you mean, I?"

"Honey, I'm going to stay with you." Hannah gave her a sympathetic look. She was dressed to the nines in a slinky black dress and killer heels.

"No way. I've already interrupted your evening. I'm fine."

The couple looked torn.

Hannah said, "You shouldn't be alone."

"I'll stay." Alex grinned. "Lauren promised me dinner anyway."

Hannah shot her a quizzical glance. "Oh, well then." She rose and leaned into Vince. "I'll come back after dinner to spend the night."

Watching Vince's face, Alex had to bite back a smile. Police officers and firefighters routinely sacrificed personal time for the job. But Alex could tell his buddy had romance in mind, and the guy was struggling to conceal his disappointment.

"Absolutely not." Dislodging the cat, Lauren stood. "Under no circumstances will you do that." When her friend started to object, Lauren insisted. "I won't let you in if you come back, Hannah. I mean it."

Alex liked her spunk, well hidden under her demure manner. Not to mention her unselfishness. She'd been mighty scared when she thought someone had broken in a second time.

"All right. But if you get frightened after Alex leaves, promise you'll call my cell."

"I promise. Now scoot so I don't completely ruin your evening out."

Dropping the cat on the floor, Alex walked them to the foyer with Lauren. "Thanks, buddy," he said, punching Vince in the arm. "I owe you one."

"Call Sam Prophet about this."

"We will."

When they left, Lauren turned and faced him. "You're a nice guy, Alex Shields."

He couldn't help it. Reaching out, he pushed a stray tendril of silky hair behind her ear. He brushed the knuckles of his other hand over her equally silky cheek. The *texture* of Lauren entranced him. "You okay?"

She wrinkled her nose. "I hate inconveniencing anybody."

"People care about you, Lauren. They want to help."

"I know." She smiled. "Thanks for staying."

"Hey, it's a tough job, but somebody's got to do it." He watched her. "I want to be with you, Lauren."

She smiled and leaned into him. Man, he liked that. He held her close, though he'd never seen himself as a cuddler. Lauren brought out unexpected reactions in him.

"I want to be with you, too." She drew back. "Now, come to the kitchen with me and I'll start dinner while you get us a drink."

He cocked his head. "What does one drink with quiche?"

"Something sweet and syrupy."

He grimaced.

"Just kidding. I've got Scotch, I think. Maybe a beer or two."

"A woman after my own heart."

As he followed her to the kitchen, Alex wondered if Lauren Conway was going to be the one to capture his heart permanently. The thought wasn't at all unpleasant.

THE QUICHE, CHEESY AND HOT, tasted as good as she had hoped it would. The bread was as light and airy as froth. The wine was tart. But Alex kept distracting Lauren from the food. "Didn't your mother feel bad when you switched majors in college?" she asked after he told her about his jump from genetics to fire fighting.

"She didn't seem to. My mom's a special person." His smile was warm and loving. It made Lauren's heart clutch, thinking about her own mother. It had only been a year, and she still missed her parents so much she found it hard to talk about them.

Alex, on the other hand, seemed to love to talk about his mother. "She and Dad are so different. She met him when he was treated at the hospital for burns and she was in med school."

"Did she worry about the danger of fire fighting?"

"A smoke-eater's wife can't afford to worry."

"What about a smoke-eater's mother?"

He knit his brows. "Probably. Though she never showed it."

"I'd worry. I can't imagine the man I love risking his life every day. Or my son. I'd be a wreck."

"It's funny. Before nine-eleven, I never heard spouses of firefighters talk about that. But now that time has passed, the worrying seems to have leveled off." He sipped his Scotch. Leaning back in his chair, he draped his arm over the back. She'd title this picture "Man After Dinner." He said, "Tell me about *your* parents."

Emotion constricted her throat. She fiddled with the napkin in her lap. "They were a lot alike. Both lawyers. Both right brained. Serious people. I was a surprise to them."

"Having you, you mean?"

"No, my creative streak. Most of the time, they didn't know quite what to make of me."

"I'm sorry. Were you unhappy as a kid?"

"Not in the way you mean. They loved me to pieces. I fascinated them, though, in how different I was." She frowned. "They did everything they could to make me feel accepted and loved. I was, I know that. It's just that I've always had this feeling of not…belonging, I guess."

Alex looked concerned but didn't respond.

"What?"

"Nothing."

She studied him. "Tell me."

"It's just the eye-color thing. And if you were that different from them…" He let the suggestion trail off, but she got the implication.

Shaking her head, she toyed with her fork. "That doesn't mean I'm adopted, Alex. My mother *saw* me being born. I have the tape."

"Lauren, I think you should meet the Ivies."

Her heart rate sped up. "Why?"

"Because of your likeness to Dana."

"That would be giving this whole thing credence, don't you think?"

"Not necessarily. What I do know is they shouldn't just run into you on the street. It would upset them."

She wouldn't want to do that.

"If it was my mother, or yours, wouldn't you want to prepare her?"

"Of course. This is just...disconcerting."

He leaned over and took her hand. His was calloused and big. "I'm sorry. I didn't mean to upset you."

She squeezed his fingers, enjoying the rough feel of his fingertips and palm. "No, it's all right. You're just looking out for the Ivies. I'll meet them."

"Good."

Studying him, she fit together a few more pieces of the puzzle that was Alex Shields. He was a man who cared deeply for his parents, and others in his life. "I guess we have one thing in common—a nice childhood. Acccptancc."

"This feeling of not belonging that you told me about? Is that where Dee comes in?"

"Dee?"

"Your cartoon. She's everything Lily's not."

She's my imaginary childhood friend, and current alter ego. But Lauren wouldn't admit that to Alex.

Embarrassed, Lauren shook her head. "I told you, Alex, it's only a cartoon. It has nothing to do with me."

"Well, damn. I kinda liked the idea of being the muscle-bound boy."

Oh, God, what had possessed her to let the story go down that road? She'd been fooling around with several plotlines and Perry had favored that one, so she went ahead with it. Then there'd been a ground-swell of approval from the Web site. *I love Dee... poor Lily, can't you give her a boyfriend...yummy for the muscle-bound boy.*

The doorbell rang, making her jump.

"Easy," Alex said, but she noticed how his big shoulders tensed under the red T-shirt. A wave of tenderness calmed her unease. She was so glad he was here.

"You expecting anybody?" he asked.

"No. I hope it isn't Hannah. I think they have better things to do than baby-sit me."

Despite the intrusion, his eyes sparkled. "I think they do, too."

Whoever was at the door was getting impatient, first pounding on it, then yelling. What the hell? Alex threw back his chair, said, "Stay here." He strode to the foyer.

Ignoring his instructions she got up and followed him. The kittens, who'd been sleeping by the window, awoke and Caramel scampered after her.

Alex peered through the peephole. "Some guy's out there."

From the other side of the door, she heard, "Open up, Lauren."

"Damn."

Alex pivoted. "You know who it is?"

Sidling in front of him, she took a quick peek. "It's James."

"Lauren, I hear you inside. Let me in." He paused, then added, "Please."

She sighed in frustration. Despite what he'd done, Lauren felt sympathy for him. He was simply a weak man. "It's all right. He's harmless. Physically at least."

"Sam Prophet wasn't so sure."

"Well, you're here. And I can't let him disturb the whole neighborhood."

She pulled open the door, coming face-to-face with the man who had made her feel like a failure. She was swamped by the insecurity a woman inherits when a man she loves uses her.

James was a few inches taller than she, about five-eight, and had a runner's body, the type Lauren had *thought* she liked. His light brown hair was cut short, and his hazel eyes were troubled. Uncharacteristically, his gray pin striped suit was wrinkled. "I want to talk to you."

"I'm busy, James."

He looked past her. The belligerence drained from his face. "Who is he? Don't tell me you're dating somebody else." He swallowed hard. "Lauren, you're my fiancée."

"Not anymore. I'd like you to go away."

When James shook his head and said no, she felt Alex come up behind her and place his hands possessively on her shoulders. Instead of feeling overwhelmed by his presence, like she often did, this gesture made her feel safe.

"The lady asked you to leave."

"Yeah, well, I'm not going until I get some answers." With that he tried to step into the foyer.

Nimbly Alex blocked James's path, towering over him. "I wouldn't try it, pal."

At her feet, Caramel scurried away. Lauren said, "It's all right. I'll answer his questions." The air crackled with tension. She put her hand on Alex's arm. "Please, Alex."

He moved aside and James crossed into the living room, which connected to the dining area. He stopped short when he saw the table. Lauren tried to view the setting through his eyes—lit with softly flickering candles, pretty mauve tablecloth, blue napkins, the remains of their food. The soft crooning of Harry Connick Jr. filtered in from the background. She'd title the scene "Seduction."

He turned on them. "Lauren, I—" There was hurt etched in his face.

Ignoring it, she folded her arms over her chest. After what he'd done, she couldn't afford to feel sorry for him. "What do you want, James?"

He glared at Alex. "I want to talk to you alone."

"Ain't gonna happen," Alex said.

She faced James. "Whatever you have to say, it will have to be said in front of Alex. Tell me what this is about."

"A man came to see me today." James scowled. She remembered trying to figure out that scowl on so many occasions. Had she caused it? Why was he unhappy? She'd spent hours on end deciphering the puzzle that was James Tildan. "A Sam Prophet. He wanted to know where I was last night. If I'd come here to see you."

"Oh."

"Did you tell him you thought I'd broken into your place?"

"No, of course not. He asked me a lot of questions. Your name came up."

"And what you did to her." This from Alex, who was standing stiff and uncompromising.

James swore, crudely.

Alex grabbed his arm. "Watch your mouth around Lauren, or I'll personally throw you outta here."

Shrugging Alex off, James gave him a sizzling look before turning back his gaze to Lauren. "This isn't over, Lauren. I made a mistake in what I did to you, but now I'll do anything I have to to rectify it." Without giving her a chance to respond, he stalked to the foyer and out the front door.

"Well, that was fun," she said, just as Alex's cell phone rang.

He fished it out of his pocket. "Shields." He watched Lauren. "Yeah. Uh-huh. We already know, Sam. I'm at Lauren's. He showed up here. Pissed as hell." A worried look. "Okay, I'll tell her." He clicked off. "Ready for this one?"

She sank onto the couch and picked up Butterscotch, who'd settled there. "No, but tell me."

"Your friend James lied about his alibi for last night."

Before she could react to that news, the phone rang again. This time it was hers. "Hell," she said, and looked up at him.

He shrugged. "Want me to get it?"

"No." She picked up the phone. "Hello."

"Ms. Conway?"

"Yes?"

"This is Hank Holmes." Her brain spinning, she drew a blank on the name. "I own the house you're renting."

"Yes, Mr. Holmes."

"You been tryin' to reach me?"

"Uh-huh. I was wondering if, for some reason, you were in my house last night when I was out."

"I was at the dog track last night. Lost my shirt." He hesitated. "Something happen?"

"No, it's okay. Thanks for returning my call." She hung up and faced Alex.

"I take it the landlord wasn't here."

"No."

"That settles it."

"Settles what?"

"I'm staying the night."

"Excuse me?"

"I'm staying the night." Alex nodded to the corner of the room. "In that man-size hammock over there." He gave her a lopsided grin. "Unless you have a spare bed."

"The other two rooms aren't furnished yet."

"Then it's me and the hammock." He arched a brow. "Is it comfortable?"

"Yes, but it's not necessary for you to stay tonight."

He crossed to the couch and squatted in front of her. He grasped her free hand and cradled it in his. "Humor me, then. I won't sleep a wink knowing you're here alone." He shrugged. "It's in a firefighter's genes to protect women, ma'am."

Her heart was beating fast. She didn't know if that was from the news she'd just gotten about James, from the landlord's call or Alex's suggestion that he sleep here. "That's ridiculous. I've got a dead bolt, I'll put it on."

"Does the regular key fit the dead bolt?"

"Yes."

"If someone's been in here, he'd have the key to that lock."

"I suppose."

"Look, I'll stay tonight, then call one of my crew who's a locksmith on the side. He can come out tomorrow and change your locks."

She had to smile. "Do you know everybody in town?"

"Comes from growing up here. Anybody I don't know, Mom and Dad do."

Trying to conceal her concern, she glanced at the door. "I could call Hannah."

"Oh, yeah, they'd appreciate that. Imagine what they're doing right about now."

She could. And it caused heat to flush her face. Because she could imagine doing the same thing with the sexy, smart man before her. Who wanted to stay the night.

As if he read her thoughts, he brushed her hair back, letting his hand rest at her nape in a possessive gesture that made her shiver. "Lauren, you know I'm attracted to you. I want to see you. To date. But the offer to stay tonight doesn't come with strings."

A branch batted against the window, and she jumped.

His arched eyebrow taunted her. *See, you are afraid.* "Do you think that I'd take advantage of you? Pressure you in some way?"

Like he'd have to do that to women. "No, of course not. I just hate to inconvenience you."

"You can cook me breakfast in the morning."

Smiling, she reached out and squeezed his shoulder. His eyes lit with her touch, and she couldn't stop herself from caressing the soft silk of his shirt, feeling his muscles flex under her hand. "What do you like for breakfast, Alex?"

Way to go, girl. Flirt your heart out.

Lauren smiled.

Alex smiled.

"Anything you're serving."

They watched a movie—*Backdraft*—and Alex explained what was portrayed realistically and picked on some of the *Hollywoodisms*.

At one o'clock, she yawned.

"Time for beddy-bye," he joked.

"I'll get you a pillow and a light blanket." She pointed toward the back of the house. "Bathroom's through there."

He rose. "I've got a gym bag in my car. I'll go get it."

"Keep it on hand for unexpected overnighters?"

He didn't take offense. Instead, he drew her up from the couch. Once again she felt dwarfed by him. He rested his hands lightly on her arms, and the weight of them felt good. "Lauren, I like women. I go out. I've had some serious involvements—I was almost engaged once—but I'm not promiscuous. Or indiscriminate. Basically, I'm just a normal guy."

"I didn't mean to insult you."

He looked over at the hammock. "However, if you get the urge to join me there during the night, feel free."

Chuckling, she said, "Go get your stuff."

He crossed to the door. Before he opened it, he turned. "I meant it, Lauren—you're safe with me."

After he left, she whispered, "I really doubt that, Alex."

Still she felt good that he was staying.

Surprisingly she slept well, though she dreamed about Alex. And the dreams that sketched themselves out in her unconscious mind were graphic. Delicious.

At eight the next morning—she was working in the afternoon today—she climbed out of bed. From the living room, she could hear birds chirping outside and a light tinkle of wind chimes. The shades were drawn and the hammock was in the shadows, but she could see Alex's form stretched out. Drawn to him like paint to canvas, she crept across the room, careful not to wake him.

She'd call the scene "Masculinity at Rest." He filled the hammock to capacity. She grinned. His right arm was thrown up over his head, his face turned to the side on the pillow. His navy fleece shorts and fire department T-shirt fit him…very nicely. His legs were corded with muscle—she'd noticed that when he was playing basketball.

But what tugged at her heart was his left hand, clutching the two kittens nestled into his side. She wanted, badly, to climb right into that hammock with him, let him cuddle her. And more.

You're dead meat, Deirdre told her, in the soft, sultry morning.

Smiling, Lauren thought, *Looks like!*

ALEX TRIED to roll over but he couldn't get any traction. Instead, he *swayed.* Jeez. He became aware of something soft and furry in his face. He went to swat it away and connected with a tiny body. He pulled his punch just in time. Awake now, he came face-to-face with green cat eyes. "What the…"

Then he remembered. He'd stayed at Lauren's, in her hammock. He hadn't slept well, thinking about the woman down the hall. Was thinking about her still. Glancing down he quickly realized that with all those thoughts about Lauren, his body had hardened.

"Damn." One kitten jumped off; the other stayed, nuzzling his neck. He set her on the floor.

But before he could get up, he heard Lauren coming out of the kitchen. Quickly he grabbed the blanket and threw it over his middle.

"You're awake." She carried a steaming mug. And she looked like pure sin. Tousled hair. A baggy T-shirt with Picasso on it that read, I Sleep With The Masters. She wore boxers. Had bare feet.

Damn, the light blanket was never going to do it! He shifted a bit. "Hi. What's that?"

"Try it."

All right. Swinging his feet over the side, keeping the blanket in place, he took the mug. It smelled minty and tasted not too sweet. Herbal. "Tea?"

"Yep."

"It's good."

She watched him. "But you'd rather have coffee."

"Would you mind?"

She shook her head, and her bangs fell into her eyes. He thought about kissing them away. Kissing her, period. He wanted badly to touch her. She smiled. "No, I don't mind. This is mine anyway. I already made you coffee."

Interesting. Dana didn't drink coffee, either. Actually, it made her ill. Had he read somewhere—in his genetics courses, maybe—that identical twins often favored or disliked the same things?

Lauren trotted back to the kitchen and he thought about dashing to the bathroom, but she was back before he could move. She handed him a mug of coffee. "Sleep well?"

"Great." He sipped. God, this was heaven. Rich. Flavored with vanilla.

"The cats good company?" she teased, perching on the arm of the chair.

"I managed not to be too lonely." He sniffed. "What do I smell?"

"Cinnamon, a bit of nutmeg. Thick crusty bread."

"Oh, God, French toast?"

"Uh-huh. Payback, for staying here with me."

He could think of better payback—which involved her tangled up in bedsheets—but his stomach growled.

She nodded to the bathroom. "Want to clean up first?"

"Yeah. Mind if I shower?"

"There are clean towels laid out for you. Take your time."

"You don't have to work?"

"Not till noon."

His group was off for a twenty-four-hour shift. *They could spend the whole morning in bed.* With that image, his lower body began to throb.

As if she sensed it, she slid off the chair and headed back to the kitchen.

The shower calmed his rampant reaction to Lauren, so when he came out, dressed in khaki shorts and a loose brown-and-white-checked sports shirt, he felt more in control. Until he reached the kitchen and saw her up on her toes, trying to reach something in the cupboard. Her long legs were bare, her butt tight and cute. Her shirt rode up, and he could see a patch of pale skin at the base of her spine. Hell, his body snapped right back to attention. At least he was dressed.

She glanced over her shoulder. "Can you help me?"

"Sure." He crossed the room. She smelled like flowers and sunshine. Her hair glowed in the beams sneaking in the window, a thousand shades of red. And he was only human. He got the dish down, set it on the counter, but didn't move away.

Placing his hands on her waist—she was slender but taut—he turned her around. Her eyes shone and she was smiling. He lifted her and set her on the counter. Her eyes widened. They seemed to say, *You can kiss me.*

Which was good, because he fully intended to. "You are so lovely." He cupped her cheeks in his hands, then lowered them to her shoulders.

"Mmm." She raised her palm to his face. Brushed his jaw, which was bristly. He'd forgotten a razor. "So male," she said, running supple fingers back and forth.

He swallowed hard.

Her hand slid up to his hair, which was still damp. She sifted her fingers through it. "It's coarser than it looks."

He smiled, which seemed to lure her fingers to his mouth. She outlined his lips, like a blind person studying braille. "Soft."

Automatically he moved in closer, so he was standing between her legs. Her hands settled on his chest. Rubbed. Kneaded.

Never in his life had he had such a strong sensation of being…explored. Leaning in, she inhaled the scent of him. "Mmm."

Somehow, gently, he raised her chin. He wanted to explore her, too, but his hands were shaky with the need to kiss her. Lowering his head, he covered her mouth with his. Hungrily. More forcefully than he wanted. She met his passion, edging her body to the end of the counter. Linking her arms at his neck so that her unbound breasts crushed against his chest. His breath hitched and he wrapped his arms around her.

His mouth opened, his tongue teasing hers to do the same. She tasted like the tea, and something else, something that was just her. It sparked his passion. As did the knowledge that she was letting him take her like this.

The buzzer on the oven began to ping.

"Coffee cake," she whispered against his jaw, then nipped him with her teeth.

"Huh?"

"Breakfast is ready, Alex."

I'm ready, he thought but didn't say it. Instead, he clasped her neck and held her close for a moment. "Lousy timing."

She made to slide off the counter.

He gripped her hips. "Wait a sec."

She looked up at him. Her pupils were big. Her face was flushed, and her nipples were tight against her shirt. She was clearly a woman aroused, thank God, because he could easily combust at any second.

"This cinches it, sweetheart."

"Cinches what?"

"We're going to start seeing each other."

Her smile was broad and sensual. "Yes, I guess we are."

He gave her a quick kiss. "Good, that's settled."

She shimmied into him, bumping his middle with her crotch. "It's anything but settled, Alex," she said against his mouth.

He chuckled. Oh, *this* was going to be fun.

CHAPTER FIVE

"GET THAT SHOT, Hanson." Perry O'Connor, Lauren's editor, yelled at his news reporter/cameraman, then continued to stare ahead at the dramatic scene unfolding before them.

Lauren stared, too. She'd entitle the scene "Man vs the Elements." Though her heart galloped at the sight, she couldn't take her eyes off Alex as he waded into the gasoline. It burned hotter than the sun. She'd been having lunch with Toby and Perry when the news had come over Perry's pager about a rescue call to a nearby gas station. A tanker had overturned and caught fire. The three of them had raced from the restaurant—Toby and Perry to get the story, Lauren to observe.

As she watched Alex, she tried hard to tamp down the fear she felt for him.

He's just doing his job.

Of course, Deirdre would relish this kind of thing. It'd scare Lily to death.

Cool as summer rain, in full turnout gear, Alex gripped the huge hose. "I got foam," he shouted, as white stuff that looked ridiculously like bubble bath spurted from the nozzle. The force bucked him backward, but he was braced by the firefighter behind him.

Slowly they moved farther into the lake of fire, smothering the red and yellow flames in a white blanket. She wondered how he could stand the heat. From a safe distance away, she was sweltering. He had the fire half-out and had just reached the middle of the pool when somebody yelled, "Shields, behind you!"

"Oh, my God!" Lauren clutched at the handle of her purse. The gasoline in back of them had reignited and now the two firefighters were surrounded by hungry flames feasting on the accelerant. Her knees went weak as the fire moved toward its prey—Alex.

He turned and, without breaking stride, retracked his steps, dousing the fire with the foam as he went along. Then he pivoted as easily as he had on the basketball court and finished the job.

By the time he was done, Lauren was light-headed from holding her breath. It was one of the bravest, most terrifying things she'd ever watched.

"Got it." Toby had been clicking pictures rapidly.

"See if we can talk to Shields right now." Perry glanced at Lauren. "You okay, Conway? You look a little pale." Then he added, "Not used to the news beat, are you?"

"Um, no." And not used to seeing a man who'd kissed her senseless a little more than twenty-four hours ago swimming in fire.

Ain't it grand, Deirdre commented.

"Come with me, Conway," Perry told her. "We'll show you how we interview our bravest." He grabbed her arm and pulled her closer to the scene.

Toby was already talking to Alex by the truck. He'd taken his helmet off and his hair was soaking wet, his face ruddy. He scowled when he saw Lauren. That was odd.

Toby joined Lauren and Perry. "He'll be right here. He wanted to give some orders for the cleanup."

Leaning against a post, Lauren studied Alex. He removed his turnout coat; his suspenders and T-shirt dripped with sweat. Finally he headed toward them. Up close, she noticed red welts on his neck. "Hi, O'Connor," he said, his voice gruff. "Lauren. What are you doing here?"

"We were having lunch when the call came through."

"Oh." His voice was as cool as mountain snow. "I see."

"So, hero of the day again, huh, Shields?" This from Perry.

Annoyed, Alex turned to Toby, who was scribbling madly. "Don't print that, Hanson. It takes a team to put out a fire."

Lauren listened as he answered some questions. Finally Alex said, "Go talk to Ramirez. He was inside as much as I was."

Perry nodded. "Go on, Hanson. I want to see the chief." Perry had told her that Fire Chief Dan Egan was directing the maneuver at Incident Command.

When both men were gone, Alex peered down at her. He smelled like gasoline. She reached out toward the marks on his neck. "You're burned."

"Heat gets around the Nomex Hood. Doesn't hurt much." Still his voice was gruff.

"What's it like to wade into a fire like that?"

"It wasn't so bad. I've laid a foam blanket before."

He glanced pointedly at Toby then back to her. "You dating him, or what?"

"We were having lunch."

"Yeah, so you said. You went out with him Tuesday night, too."

She just watched him, entranced by the color in his cheeks, the adrenaline-induced gleam in his eye. Even his hair seemed richer, more vibrant.

"Forget it. I shouldn't have asked." He gave her a weak smile. "We still on for tomorrow?"

"I'm looking forward to it." She shifted from one foot to the other. "I'm a little nervous about meeting the Ivies, though." Alex had set up the meeting for her and Dana's parents for tomorrow, then she and Alex were going out on a real date.

"They're great people. I've known them all my life."

"And Dana, too."

"Sure. It'll be fine. After, we can get something to eat on the pier before the shindig you wanna go to."

She cocked her head. "You sure you're up for an art show on the beach?"

"Yeah, why not? We'll stop by the party the gang's having out there afterward."

"I'd like that."

"Fine." Like a little boy checking out a rival, he glanced back at Toby, scowling again. "I gotta go."

"All right." As he started to walk away, she called out to him. "Alex?"

He pivoted. He made a striking picture—dressed in the light tan turnout gear, the yellow reflectors on his pants picking up the noonday sun—against a backdrop of the remnants of a very dangerous incident. She couldn't have composed the scene any better herself. "Yeah?"

"I was really impressed. Terrified for you, but impressed."

He shrugged again.

"And I'm not dating Toby."

A grin spread across his face. "I like hearing that, pretty lady." He winked. "See you tomorrow night."

FROM THE DRIVER'S SEAT in his Blazer, Alex glanced over at Lauren and resisted the urge to rest a hand on her lightly tanned knee. It peeked out from a green, yellow and white skirt that looked like a garden of daffodils. The yellow knit button-up top she wore with it hugged her like a lover. For some reason this woman triggered all kinds of physical reactions from him faster than matches lit kindling. Thinking of her with Hanson, he admitted that she also elicited a possessiveness—a jealousy, for God's sake—that he had never felt before. "Nervous?" he asked.

"A little. It's eerie being the double of somebody. Even if it is coincidence."

"Hmm."

"What?"

"I talked to my mother. She contends it's impossible that your natural parents had blue eyes."

"I know. I researched it on the Net. There aren't any documented cases. But Alex, like I keep telling you, I've seen the video of my birth."

"So you said." He passed a large Tudor house. "That's where my parents live. I'm staying with them for a few days till my living and dining rooms are painted and the floors refinished." He swerved the car into the driveway of a sprawling white stucco ranch two hundred yards down. "We're here."

Lauren stared at the house, fingering a tiger's-eye stone she wore at the end of a small ropelike cord. She frowned.

"What is it?"

"Oh, nothing. I just had a...feeling or something." She indicated the stone. "This is for strength. Wisdom."

Extending his hand, he fisted the stone. And was surprised as hell to feel an immediate jolt of well-being.

They got out of the car and headed up the driveway to the Ivies' small home. "I never thought to ask, is Dana an only child?"

"Yes."

She halted. "Are you, Alex?"

"Nope. Got two older sisters."

"I always wanted a sister," she said idly.

"Be careful what you wish for," he joked. At her look, he added, "Mine moved East with their husbands and families. Since they'd tormented the living daylights out of me growing up, I was shocked how much I missed them." He reached the door and started to open it.

"Alex, aren't you even going to knock?"

"I practically grew up here. Dana and I lived in each other's back pockets."

"You speak so affectionately of her."

He shifted uneasily. Things were cool between him

and Dana, after their foray into romance. But would Lauren understand that? And would her uncanny resemblance to Dana make her suspicious of his motives? "I think of her like another sister." He pushed open the door. "Hello," he called out, then they stepped inside.

It was so familiar here. Same carpet the Ivies put down when their daughter graduated from high school. Same couch he and Dana used to sit on and watch TV. The house even smelled the same, like flowers and furniture polish.

"We're back here," Tim Ivie called out. Alex led the way through the kitchen into a screened-in porch he'd helped them add on a few years ago.

"Hi—" He halted when he saw his parents sitting on a white wicker couch. "Hey, you two." He started to cross to them when he saw the four staring at Lauren. Openmouthed. Even his mother was silenced, which happened about as often as snow in California.

Moving in close to Lauren, he put a hand on her shoulder. This had to be hard for her. Though her face was composed, he felt the tension under his fingers. "This is Lauren Conway. Lauren, Helen and Tim Ivie, gawking from the right side. My mom and dad, Wes and Vera Shields, staring—*rudely, guys*—from the left."

"Oh my!" His mother recovered first. She stood and came forward. Dressed casually in white slacks and a purple top, she wasn't much taller than Lauren. Even with her graying hair, she seemed young. "Hello, Lauren. I'll apologize for us all. It's just that, except for your hair, you could be Dana."

"Well, look a little harder. She's not quite as big as Dana, or as...hardy." He squeezed her shoulder. "But do it later, okay? I think we're embarrassing her."

As if waking from a trance, Helen Ivie rose from the love seat and came forward. Plump and hardy herself, she had the warmest smile Alex had ever seen. "Lauren, hello. I'm so sorry. It's just startling to see someone who looks so much like my daughter."

They all sat and made small talk until the tension eased. Alex noticed, though, that Lauren kept fiddling with the tiger's-eye. And she seemed preoccupied. Finally she said, "I wonder, Mrs. Ivie. Do you have a photo album of Dana growing up?"

"Yes, of course. Several."

"I'd like to see them, if I could."

In minutes, Helen produced four photo albums.

Lauren opened the first one. Alex watched her. She frowned at page one. She touched something on page five. "May I take these out?" Her voice was shaky and when she glanced up, she looked pale. She reminded Alex of a patient who was sick but trying to hide it.

"Of course," Helen told her. Her tone was concerned, as if something ominous was going on.

Lauren gasped when she opened the second album. Swallowing hard, she removed the first picture.

Alex went to crouch by her, touching her knee. "Lauren, what is it?"

Slowly she raised her head. Then she mirrored his actions that day at the hospital and reached for her wallet. From inside she took out three pictures and handed them to him. They were of Lauren and her parents. In the first, she was an infant. The second was an elementary-school photo. In the last, she was about thirteen. Her parents, also in the pictures, aged accordingly and seemed happy as clams. Then Alex picked up the photos of Dana she'd removed from the albums.

Holy hell!

The pictures of Dana with the Ivies—in pose, in a child's crooked smile and facial expressions—were almost identical to those of Lauren and her parents.

"FEELING BETTER?" Alex asked Lauren as they made their way to the outdoor art exhibit, which had come down from Benicia and the surrounding areas. It was about the last thing he'd have chosen to do, she guessed.

The early evening glimmered around them, the dying sun bouncing off the water, accompanied by a warm breeze. Lauren inhaled deeply. Felt the air surround her. Drench her skin. Soothe her. "How can you not feel good in weather like this?"

He took her hand in his; it dwarfed hers. She felt safe. "Those pictures were a jolt."

"They were." Lauren had been absolutely confounded by the similarities in the photos. "But the Ivies were so upbeat about it, so sane." She stared out at a seagull as it swooped down, skimmed the water and flew back up. "Just like my parents would have been."

"My mother wasn't so cool. It's like a puzzle to her. She won't stop until she figures it out."

"They're very nice. You seem close to them."

"I am. Me and my dad are best buddies. My mom's my confidante." He grinned down at her. "I—"

Suddenly she was drawn away from him, spun around and encompassed in a bear hug. "*Ma chère.* You came."

Laughing, Lauren hugged her old friend. "François. *Comment allez-vous?*"

"*Très bien. Vous?*"

"The same."

Always a toucher, François smoothed a hand down her hair. "We *miss* you." He indicated the stalls of artists gathered on the wooden decking. "You should be exhibiting here with us."

"I think so, too." Alex. Oh, dear, she'd forgotten about him.

Lauren drew back, but François didn't let go of her arm. She turned. "Alex, this is my friend François Trudeau." She smiled affectionately. "We call him Dali."

"Dali?"

"After the painter. He was—"

"Yeah, the guy with the clocks." Alex held out a hand. "Nice to meet you."

Tall and very thin, François studied Alex. She knew he was seeing the differences in Alex from the guys she usually dated, beginning with his I'm-too-sexy jean shorts and the black T-shirt that showed off his pecs. "You know Lauren's work?"

"I have one of her paintings on my wall."

François smiled, and he turned back to Lauren and hugged her again. "So you are selling. *Très bien. Très bien.*"

"No, I'm not. I gave it to Alex."

François frowned. "Come, see Jacques. He will convince you." He grabbed her hand and dragged her ahead.

She glanced over her shoulder. "Alex, come with us."

For a while, Alex trailed behind her as she went from stall to stall, then he excused himself to get a beer. That had been an hour ago. In the meantime, he'd checked out some pottery that he liked and some Native American bowls his mother would appreciate. Now, he stood by a drink vendor, sipping his Molson's.

Lauren seemed to know everybody here. And they loved her. And they didn't stop touching her, male and female alike. For some reason, their open display of affection irritated him. Again, this jealousy stuff was so not like him, he couldn't fathom why her friends' intimacy bothered him. Maybe because he'd looked forward to being with her, and she was more interested in them. Clearly this was her element.

God knows it wasn't his.

He glanced over at the nearest stall—François's. The artist's brightly colored ceramics looked like jellyfish. That had been squished by somebody's foot. Several times.

Her friend Ariel's booth was down a ways. It appeared as if the painter had simply tossed paint at canvas. She was selling the paint that stuck.

And the female couple's sculpture just past that— he shuddered thinking about what they'd done to the male anatomy.

"You don't like it, do you?" Lauren approached him from behind. She was sipping champagne— which everybody but Alex seemed to know she favored—and smiled. She looked so pretty, her face lit with delight, her skin glowing. Seeing her old friends was good for her, and he felt bad for being annoyed by it.

"Should I lie?"

Her eyes narrowed. "Don't ever lie to me, Alex. Even by not telling me something."

Squeezing her hand, he said, "Nope, I don't like this stuff. Sorry, I know they're your friends." He brushed back a strand of her hair. "I like your work, though."

"Well, you obviously have *some* taste."

"They care about you, Lauren. Why did you leave Benicia?"

"When Mom and Dad died, and then after what happened with James...I needed a change of scene. I wanted to paint my horizon with different colors, I guess. Hannah was here...I got the chance at the cartoon..." She sighed. "The rest, as they say, is history."

"Speaking of the cartoon, how's Lily these days?"

"As nerdy as ever. Deirdre's trying to help, but Lily's a tough nut to crack."

"She making any progress with the muscle-bound boy?"

Lauren gave him a sideways glance—it was a flirty gesture. "Some." He watched her enjoy the sights—the colors, the people. Finally she said, "I'm ready to go when you are."

"My crowd's rowdy compared to this."

"Hey, if you can handle modern art, I can handle…what will it be?"

"Beer and crab. Dancing in the sand. And volleyball."

"Oh."

He chuckled. "Deirdre would be up for all that, Lauren."

"She would, huh?"

Staring down at her, he said, "So am I. I'd like you to give it a shot."

She smiled. "Okay, for you. And Deirdre, of course."

"BORED?"

Lauren turned to find one of the firefighters from Alex's squad behind her. He was tall with ink-black hair and dark eyes. She'd paint him in Native American garb, if she got the chance. "Excuse me?"

"You look bored." He held out his hand. "Will Begay. We met the other day when we drowned you in names and faces."

"Hi, Will. And no, I'm not bored." She was, but she wouldn't want that to be obvious to one of Alex's friends. She nodded to the group assembled on the sand; they were playing like they were in the Olympic trials. "I'm afraid I don't know the rules of volley-ball, though."

He chuckled, softening the harsh planes of his face. "Sometimes, neither do they."

"How come you're not playing?"

Holding up his other hand, she saw it was ban-daged.

"What happened?"

"I got burned at a kitchen fire. I'm off for a few days."

"Sorry. Does it hurt?"

He shrugged as if he hadn't thought about it. "I guess."

"Heads up."

Lauren stepped back just in time to avoid getting hit with a renegade ball. The abrupt motion jarred her arm, though, and the beer she was holding. The liquid splashed over her blouse. Some went down the open vee at her neck.

A tall, striking woman with black hair, dark eyes and a body to kill for jogged over. "Sorry." As she bent to scoop up the ball, Will swatted her on the fanny. "Go get 'em, slugger."

Straightening, the woman gave him a haughty look. "Don't get fresh."

"Oh, sure, I'll save that for later." When she hurried away, he said, "My wife."

"She's gorgeous."

"My Mexican beauty."

Lauren scanned the men and women on the make-shift court. They were a mix of ethnicity, creating a swirl of color and sound. That, at least, interested her.

In awe she watched them leap and slide, yell and cheer, while Will made small talk. Of course she enjoyed watching Alex stretch his lithe body, punch the ball. He joked with his friends; they liked him, it was obvious. Once in a while, they looked pointedly at her.

It didn't take her long to realize she was an oddity here. When she'd gone to use the rest room, she'd overheard two women who didn't know she was in the next stall.

"Who's the wallflower with Alex? She's not quite his type...maybe because she looks so much like Dana..."

Lauren had hurried out to avoid the sting of their comments.

And what implication about Dana were they making? Because that puzzled her—maybe even frightened her—she suppressed it and tried to have a good time.

When the game was over, Alex was engulfed in a group hug that could crack ribs. Then he swaggered over to Lauren and Will. "Am I good, or what?" Sweaty, he leaned over, kissed Lauren's cheek and took a sip of her beer. "You movin' in on my woman, Begay?"

"Fat chance. Mareeta would slice me in half and hang me out to dry. Just trying to entertain each other."

Alex seemed shocked. "You bored?"

"No, of course not."

Lauren handed him the beer. He chugged, then offered it back. She shook her head. "This place is great.'' Tucked away in a cove of rocks, the volley-ball court was down from a pavilion where the group had gathered before the games began. The night was bright with stars and the moon, but they'd set up torches, too, so they could play in the dark.

"I'm gonna go see my bride.'' Will squeezed Lauren's shoulder. "Nice to meet you.'' He took a bead on Alex. "Don't bully her. She's china, Shields.''

"China?'' Lauren asked after he left.

Alex drew her away from the crowd to stand under a tree. Bracing his arm against it, he cradled her cheek in his hand. Still sweaty, he was the consummate male, in sight, smell and intimidation. "Fragile. Precious.''

"I'm not fragile.''

"Sure you are.''

"I'm not.''

"Prove it.''

"How?''

"Play the next game.''

"You're not done?''

"No, this will go on for hours. Then we dance.''

"Oh.'' She glanced down at her clothes. "I'm not dressed to play.''

"Kick off those pretty little sandals and you'll be fine. Maybe ditch the jewelry.''

She grasped the tiger's-eye like a talisman. "I don't know the rules.''

"I'll explain them to you.''

"No, Alex, really, I can't.'' Not to mention that she didn't want to. Gym class had been torture for her, and she'd always steered away from any kind of athletic competition.

Oh, go on, you wimp. It's just a little game.

Listening to Deirdre was usually a mistake. But Alex's continued wheedling finally wore Lauren down. "Okay, I'll try."

Twenty minutes later, from the back of the court, Alex watched Lauren, who was up front, suffer through another play. It had been a mistake to coax her to participate. She was clearly *not* enjoying herself. When she missed yet another shot, he cringed.

"Your girlfriend isn't much of a jock," said Julia Cummings, who was on the line next to him. He'd dated her a couple of times.

"Guess not." For some reason, he felt compelled to add, "She's got other talents."

"I'll bet."

The line moved, and it was his turn to serve. He took his place, called out, "Seven to fourteen," and punched the ball over the net. Will's wife spiked it back, and one of Alex's teammates at the net fell to his knees and rocked it up. It went high and came down fast. Reflexively, Lauren stepped away when the ball headed straight for her. It thunked at her feet. Alex saw a couple of his teammates roll their eyes.

Lauren shook her head. The ball went back to the other side, and Mareeta served it. Though Julia dived for it and slid through the sand, it was an ace. The bad guys won. Alex tried to make his way to Lauren, but he was crushed in the throng of his teammates' banter and razzing. A couple of people joked about

Lauren's ineptitude. By the time he got away, she was nowhere to be found.

Begay came up to him. "That was a mistake, buddy."

"A mistake?"

Will stared at him. "You don't take a fish out of water and expect it to line dance with you." He nodded to the shore, partly hidden by some rocks. "She walked down that way, nursing her embarrassment I'd guess."

"Alone?"

"I offered to go with her, but she said she'd like to be by herself." He hesitated. "Maybe I was wrong the other day, Alex. Maybe you were right about not being well suited."

All indications tonight pointed that way. Still he was drawn to her, and now he was worried. She shouldn't be walking the beach by herself. If it was Julia or Dana, he wouldn't have worried. But Lauren didn't know the shore's nooks and crannies. He went after her. When he got a distance from his friends, he called out. It was too dark to see where she was.

There was no answer. Then he remembered something Lily had said to Deirdre. *I can't swim.* If the comic was indeed autobiographical, did that mean Lauren…holy hell. Alex started to jog. "Lauren!"

He found her about a half mile down the shoreline. She'd stopped at an old, abandoned lifeguard hut. Closer now, he could see the breeze play tug-of-war with her hair and the moonlight on her skin. She stared out at the water like some mermaid newly emerged from the sea, trying to decide how to function in this new two-legged world.

His heart beat fast as he reached her. "You shouldn't have gone off by yourself. You don't know the area."

"I'm fine."

"You can't swim." Jeez, how could somebody not know how to swim?

"How would you know that?"

"The cartoon."

"I'm okay, Alex." She nodded to the ocean. "I was thinking about the *Ranger*, and how Courage Bay came to be. Where exactly the ship was when it had to be rescued."

He didn't feel like talking about history. "I was worried."

"I'm sorry." She nodded down the beach to his friends. "I wanted to get away from that." Her tone was sober, and sad, as if she knew something she didn't want to admit.

Sighing, he ran his hand down her hair. "I shouldn't have forced you to play."

"I shouldn't have taken you to the art show."

He stepped back, bent over and picked up a stone. He tossed it out into the water. It was calm tonight, but waves still lapped at his feet. "Your friends thought I was a Neanderthal."

"Your friends wondered what you were doing with a klutz like me."

Neither denied the other's comment.

When he faced her again, she was staring out at the ocean again, her arms wrapped around her waist.

"Maybe I was right, Alex. Maybe this wasn't a very good idea."

"The date?"

She didn't look at him. "Us."

He moved closer. "We took a few missteps tonight is all."

"Clumsy leaps, is more like it." She stared up at him with fathomless eyes the color of the night sky. "You were confused and bored with the art show. And I hated every minute of that game. Everybody saw it." She added meaningfully, "Even us."

"I don't give a shit what everybody saw." That wasn't quite true. "I liked seeing you enjoy the art show. Didn't you like watching me play?"

"I did."

"So, that's enough."

"You're kidding yourself." Sighing, she grasped the tiger's-eye. "There's more, anyway. It's what I came out here to think through. This has been a hard year for me. My parents' death. All that stuff with James. I'm not in the best place emotionally. I'm feeling pretty raw. And—" she grasped his arm, her touch firm but tender "—I like you."

His heart did a little flip. He reached out and rubbed her arms, up and down. "I like you, too. Isn't that good?"

"Maybe not. I don't want either of us to get hurt. I'm afraid I'm setting myself up for more heartache."

"Lauren, we're adults. We enjoy each other's company." He watched the moonlight play along her skin. "And right now, I want to kiss you so bad I ache."

She made no move to stop him, so he went ahead. He drew her close, more forcefully than he intended. If she was going to dump him, he was going to show her what she was tossing away. Besides, he felt a need to connect with her, after the *disconnection* of the whole night. The water whispered around them as he lowered his mouth and took hers. Devoured it. His hands went around her back, slid to her waist, then to her fanny.

She leaned into him. Maybe she wanted the connection, too. He deepened the kiss; she clutched him hard. He couldn't get enough of her; she practically climbed up his body. The next thing he knew, he was moaning, stumbling the few feet to the hut, backing her against the outside wall. He yanked up her skirt. His hands found the creamy skin of her thighs and his body jerked into hers. She hung on to him, ate at his mouth, dragged fingers through his hair. He drew back and fitted his hands between them. He cupped her full, firm breasts through her sweater. "Oh, man." She was breathing convulsively. He thrust his lower body into hers. She thrust back. He cursed the clothes between them.

And then Alex lost the capacity to think.

THE BUTTONS on her knit top popped and rolled onto the dirt floor of the hut. "You're gorgeous," he said, as he released the front closure of her bra and filled his hands with her.

She ripped at his belt. When his zipper stuck, she said, "Damn it," and dug her hands inside the waistband of his shorts instead.

He groaned as she grasped him. He was big and full and she molded him in her palms. His flesh pulsed beneath her fingers.

When he snugged her skirt all the way up and grabbed for her panties, she felt the cool air filter into the little hut. He tore the scrap of lace off her.

He reached around to his back, where he fumbled for something. He swore, graphically. She was dimly aware when he found the condom, batted her hands away from her exploration and rolled the latex on.

She groaned when he bent his head and suck-led her.

His moan was loud and long as she found him again and gripped him hard. "Honey, I'm gonna…"

"I know. Now."

He braced her against the inside wall of the hut; she spread her legs and he yanked her up so they encircled his waist.

Near mindlessness now, she felt his first thrust in every nerve ending. Only two more and she climaxed. He captured her screams with his mouth. Then, one last thrust, and he groaned his own release into her.

ALEX COULDN'T REMEMBER a time when he'd felt more chagrined. As he pulled into Lauren's driveway, he didn't have a clue what to say. Apparently, neither did she. One minute they were talking about not see-ing each other again, the next, they were making it in an abandoned lifeguard hut. Neither had uttered a word all the way back from the beach.

Now, in lamplight from the house, he looked over at her. He couldn't see her clearly, but he guessed her lips would be swollen, and there were probably bruises here and there on her body. He winced, thinking about her softness, her tender skin. He should have been more careful with her.

"You don't have to see me in."

That was the last thing he expected.

"I got the locks changed, remember? I'll be fine." She reached for the door handle.

He stayed her arm. "You're kidding me, right?"

"I never felt less like joking in my life."

"Me, either. We have to talk."

"I don't think so."

"What do you mean?"

"I mean, I think this is best left undissected right now." She faced him then. "I don't want to see you again for a while, Alex. I need some time away from you to think about all this."

"What?"

"You heard me."

"There's nothing to think about. You can't honestly believe I'm going to waltz out of your life after..."

"After what? A quick pop in a hut on the beach?" She buried her face in her hands. "Oh, God. That is *so* not me. I've never done anything like that in my life."

He gentled his tone. "Are you sorry?"

She drew in a breath and raised her head. "Not sorry exactly. Just...confused. I hardly know you. And, when I'm with you, things are off-kilter for me. I don't like it. Doing that on the beach..."

"Lauren, we're both adults. Both unattached. It was a little crazy, a lot rushed, but we're—"

"Different as day and night."

"Well, obviously we have something in common." She just stared at him.

"Maybe it's enough," he said.

"Maybe it's too much. Maybe that's the problem."

"Listen, Lauren—"

"No! You listen to me. I like to process things. Analyze them. Make calculated decisions. I let you roadblock that, and look where it got us."

He didn't exactly mind where it had gotten them.

"I'm not sure I can handle you, Alex. Handle a relationship that makes me feel like this."

"You handled me pretty well in that hut. I lost my mind when you touched me. When I was inside you."

"Oh, Lord."

"Lauren—"

"I've got to go." When he started to object she snapped, "Alex, back off! I said I needed time and I'm going to take it. If you can't deal with that, then we're going nowhere." She flung open the door and slammed it shut behind her.

Well, hell! Confused, he let the anger surge inside him. Maybe she *was* too high maintenance for him. Maybe she hadn't been the only one who was right from the beginning.

CHAPTER SIX

Frame One:

You're pathetic. Deirdre holds up a volleyball, ready to put it in the air.

Lily sits on the sidelines, elbows on knees, chin on hands. *I know.*

Frame Two:

Deirdre punches the ball. *It's your fault.*

Lily looks even more dejected. *I know.*

Frame Three:

Deirdre joins her on the curb. *Why're you like this, Lil?*

Tears cloud Lily's eyes. *I'm afraid, Dee.*

Frame Four:

A coward dies a thousand deaths, a hero dies but one.

I know.

Frame Five:

Lily sits alone. She puts her head down. *All those deaths to look forward to.*

Lauren put her head down, too. After she balled up the sketched draft of the cartoon and tossed it in the trash. She wasn't going to get a message to Alex that way. If she wanted to keep seeing him, she'd tell him face-to-face.

Rising from the desk, she crossed to the hammock, where she'd spent a good part of the weekend, just lying where Alex had slept. Thinking about where else Alex's body had been. That night. And on the beach.

Lauren was surprised she wasn't embarrassed by the memories of those explosive few minutes in the hut. Instead, she was excited by them. She saw their encounter as a brightly colored eruption of fireworks in eighty different hues. In comparison, her weekend had been a blank canvas. If she closed her eyes, she could almost feel his muscles strain and bunch as he lifted her. She could almost smell his sweaty scent mingled with aftershave. It had seduced her even before they stumbled into that hut. She could almost hear him mumble "Oh, baby," her name, incoherent groans of pleasure.

Out of frustration, she'd called Toby and asked him out for Sunday. She wasn't looking forward to it. *You dating that guy?* Alex had asked.

"Arrgh...." The doorbell rang. "I wish it would be him," she whispered, bounding out of the hammock. The kittens had been playing in a corner but, at the noise, scampered after her.

It wasn't Alex. Instead, his mother stood on her porch. "Hello, Lauren."

"Mrs. Shields."

"Call me Vera. I hope it's all right I dropped by like this."

"Of course it is." She stepped back. "Please, come in."

Vera entered the house.

"I'm sorry I'm such a mess. I wasn't expecting company." Lauren had showered that morning but done nothing with her hair. It probably looked like a bird's nest. Smoothing down her most comfortable one-piece lounge outfit—she'd made it herself from some deep blue faux satin—she cast a studied glance at his mother.

Vera Shields had style. She wore her graying hair in a breezy cut around her face, and her eyes—the color of Alex's—were lightly made up. The two-piece designer skirt and matching blouse in burgundy made her eyes glow, just like that color did for Alex's eyes. Cool and classy came to mind.

"You look fine. Comfortable." She studied Lauren's face as Lauren had often studied subjects for a painting, only Vera's was a scientist's scrutiny. "Though tired." She arched a knowing brow—a gesture Alex had inherited. "Just like my son these last few days."

Lauren felt her heart speed up. "Did you come to talk about Alex?"

"No, but I will if you want to." She sat on Lauren's sofa. "This is a lovely place. Alex said it was unique, it was *you*. I can see what he meant."

"Alex talked about me with you?"

"Before this weekend. All he does now is sulk. He's staying with us while he's having some work done at his house." A mother's grin spread across her face. "He was always good at sulking."

"Vera, I—"

The older woman held up her hand. "No, we don't need to talk about him. I came for another reason."

Sinking into a chair, Lauren picked a cat up off the floor. "What?"

"Helen Ivie is my best friend, Lauren. Though she didn't show it, the similarities of the photos and the fact that you're a double for Dana upset her. I'd like to try to ease her mind and I was wondering if you might help me.''

"Of course. If I can."

"Do you have a birth certificate here?"

"Yes."

"I'd like to see it."

Something made Lauren shiver. She'd had the feeling before, when she went to art school, when she decided to market her cartoon, when she got engaged to James. Her likeness to Dana was surfacing all the time now, and had a lot of people questioning whether it was pure coincidence or not. "Yes, all right." She rose and went to her desk. Copies of her important papers were in a locked drawer at the bottom. One that hadn't been ajar that night of the break-in. Retrieving the document, she handed it to Vera.

Alex's mother donned reading glasses and scanned the certificate. She shook her head. "It's too much of a coincidence."

"What is?"

"You were born one day before Dana, in a hospital thirty minutes away from here, in L.A. Helen delivered Dana a month early, in Courage Bay."

"I was premature. My parents were traveling when my mother went into labor, so she had me at Los Angeles Hospital." Lauren swallowed hard. "Vera, I was early, too. A month."

Vera stood and crossed to Lauren. Reaching out, she squeezed her shoulder. "This is too similar to let go, dear. I was wondering if I might have your permission to look into this whole thing."

"Look into it?"

"Yes, I'm on staff at Courage Bay Hospital, but I

have connections in Los Angeles. I'd like to investigate.''

There was that shiver again. Lauren folded her arms over her chest. "What would you be looking for?''

"I'm not sure. Babies born during that time. In both hospitals.''

"This frightens me, Vera.''

"Yes, I can see that. It would me, too.''

"But if there's anything to find, or a way to put Helen's mind to rest, I'd like you to do it.''

Vera cocked her head. "I can see why Alex is so taken with you. Underneath that fragile appearance is grit.''

Lauren smiled. Together they walked to the door. When Vera opened it, she turned to face Lauren. "Since you've so graciously let me butt in thus far, I'm going to say something else. My son is miserable. He snapped at me tonight at dinner.'' She said it as if Alex had committed a felony. "And he was grumpy to his father, whom he adores.''

"I'm sorry I've made Alex unhappy.''

"Have you, dear? He wouldn't talk about what was bothering him.''

"Yes, I think it's me.''

"And is he responsible for your unhappiness?''

"No, I'm responsible for that, too.''

"I see.'' She smiled at Lauren. "Alex is a handful, Lauren. He can be pushy, and arrogant, and intent on getting his way. But he's also a compassionate, caring man with an inner core of true decency.''

"I know.'' She thought of James, whose decency was nonexistent. "I like Alex, Vera.''

"Well, I hope you work this out. I think I could like *you.*"

With that, Alex's mother left. Lauren closed the door and leaned against it. She felt sad, thinking about what she was giving up. Because she was a coward. Slowly she walked back to the hammock.

SCOWLING HAD BECOME Alex's favorite expression since Friday night. This time, he directed it at his father. "She went *where?*"

"Alex, what is *with* you? I can't remember the last time you raised your voice to me."

Alex was taking a pool cue from the rack in their rec room but halted before he chalked it to face his father. "Oh, Dad, I'm sorry."

"Don't apologize, tell me what's wrong."

Crossing to the table, Alex gave his dad a cue. "You wanna break?"

"Sure." As tall but leaner than Alex, Wes Shields was still an imposing man. He'd been a top-notch firefighter and an even better father. And as the only other male in the house, he understood his son well. Wes broke the stack, then called out a ball and pocket. "So talk, kid."

Watching his father sink the four ball, Alex sighed. "It's a woman."

"Now there's a surprise."

Alex raised his brows. "Am I usually this moody over women?"

"Never. Far as I can remember, you never pouted over or got jealous of any of them. But when a guy mopes like you've been doing, there's a female in the picture."

"Well, she's erasing herself from this canvas."

"Why?" Wes sank the seven ball, but missed the nine before Alex answered.

"Five ball in left corner." Alex took his shot and missed. And swore. He straightened and leaned against the table. "My concentration's shot."

His father just stared at him.

"She says we're too different. We are. But I'd be willing to risk it. She isn't. No, correction, she wanted time to think about it. Jeez, I hate when women keep you on hold."

"I doubt many women have done that to you."

Alex shrugged. Truth be told, he couldn't think of any. That didn't make him hate it any less. "She's got me going in circles. She writes this comic strip in the *Courier*. I've checked it three days running for clues as to where her head's at." He raked a hand through his hair. "I've driven by her house several times."

"Sounds serious." His father's tone was dry.

"It sounds like high school." Just like that night in the hut.

"You haven't known her long, buddy."

No, but he knew her well. In the Biblical sense. Jeez, he wished he could stop thinking about how she'd closed around him so tight he thought the top of his head might come off. "Doesn't change how I feel, though."

His father shook his head. "Didn't for me, either."

"What do you mean?"

A fond look of remembrance came over Wes's face, making him seem younger. He continued to play pool, as did Alex. It was easier to talk if they were doing something. "Your mother and I hadn't known each other very long before we…" He gave his son a very knowing look. "Got close. It was all over but the shoutin', then."

"Dad, you and Mom are so different. How'd you make it work?"

His father frowned. "It wasn't easy. Especially early on. We fought because of those differences. And trying to do things together was tough. I wanted to see a baseball game, she wanted to go to the opera. We tried at first to go with each other to those activities, but eventually, she went to the opera and I went to a baseball game. It worked, though it wasn't ideal."

"No?"

"Nah. She wanted to share more." He shrugged. "I guess I did, too."

"But you've been married thirty-eight years."

"Good years, too." His father was thoughtful. "There was one rough spot, a time when…" Wes trailed off. "Never mind. They were mostly good years." He stared at Alex. "You thinkin' about June weddings, Alex?"

"No. My guess is Lauren won't see me again."

"You gonna settle for that?"

"Yeah, Dad, I am. I made all the moves so far, and pressured her to go along. That was probably a mistake." He sighed. "I got a date tomorrow with somebody else." Julia the jock. Man, he wasn't looking forward to that.

"You don't sound too happy about it." His dad sank the last ball and put down his cue. "Life's short, so I wouldn't give up easily. If *I* had, you wouldn't be here."

Chuckling, Alex crossed to his father and hugged him. "Think Mom will say anything to her about me?"

"You can count on that, son."

TOBY HANSON PUSHED UP his glasses in an endearing gesture. "Do you mind being here, Lauren?"

"No, of course not." She did though. She had no interest in boats.

"I'm sorry. The guy assigned to this show got sick, so Perry asked me to cover."

Lauren squeezed his arm. "I'm afraid I don't know much about boats."

He smiled at her. "I did a series on them for the Benicia *Gazette*, which is the only reason I got this assignment."

"Benicia? You worked there?"

"Yeah, a few years ago. Why?"

"That's where I'm from."

"Really?"

That was odd. She was sure she'd mentioned it to him.

Toby's head snapped around. "Oh, look, there's the organizer of the show. Johnson. I've got to interview him."

"I think I'll just wander around." It was beautiful outside, this time of day. It had been just like this on the pier, the night she'd had the date with Alex. Turning abruptly, she walked right into someone. "Oh, sorry, I—"

"Easy," the familiar voice said. An equally familiar touch steadied her. It was Alex, looking as if he'd stepped out of a Gap ad, in a brownish black T-shirt tucked into tight black jeans. Sleek sunglasses shaded his beautiful eyes. She'd title him "Sexy Boy at Play."

"Alex."

He dropped his hands. "Lauren. What are you doing here? I wouldn't have pegged you for the boat type."

"I'm not."

He lifted his sunglasses. He did look tired, and unhappy, as Vera had said. It twisted her heart, because she knew she was responsible. "Who are you here with?"

"Toby."

His hands jammed into his back pockets. "You said you weren't dating him."

"I—"

"He doesn't scare you, I guess." Alex's tone was biting, tinged with hurt.

She didn't say anything.

"He doesn't change you into a different person."

She swallowed hard.

"Having fun?"

"No." Damn him. "Who are you with?"

He nodded. She tracked his gaze. It was one of the women in the volleyball game that night on the beach. The one who could play sports. Who chugged beer with him. Who even right now looked fit and athletic in tight jeans and sandals—and a T-shirt that screamed *Ready, set, go*.

Would she be playing with Alex tonight?

Surprised by the dread that thought instilled in her, Lauren averted her gaze.

"Don't do that to me!" he snapped.

"What?"

"Act hurt. You did this, Lauren."

"I know I did."

"Are you—" He cut off abruptly. "I'm not gonna do this again. Goodbye, Lauren. Have fun on your *date*." He stalked away, and she watched him go. He was all masculine grace and energy. Handsome in a macho way, yet sensitive, too.

Go after him, Deirdre urged.

No.

Then you deserve to feel bad.

Yeah, I do.

ALEX HAD TO FORCE himself not to scan the crowds for Lauren as he and Julia checked out the boats. She was looking to buy a used one, and they'd spent most of their time at the smaller crafts. "Let's check out a thirty-footer just for fun," he suggested, bored. His parents had a boat he often used and they were thinking about getting a bigger one, so the cruiser would interest him at least.

"Sure. I can dream." Julia leaned into him and her breast grazed his biceps. She entwined her arm with his, continuing the intimate contact. He didn't draw away. Since Lauren didn't want him, maybe he'd— funny, he couldn't even finish the thought. They headed for the cabin cruiser and he was proud of himself for not scouring the crowd for Lauren. Maybe she and her date had left. Where would they go? What would she do with Hanson tonight? His fists clenched at the thought of the guy touching her. And Alex was disgusted that he felt so strongly about a woman he'd only known a few weeks.

Well, he *did* know her pretty well.

He and Julia were down in the galley kitchen of the boat when she put the moves on him. Sidling up, she wrapped her arms around his neck. He remembered being in Lauren's kitchen and hefting her onto the countertop. And he remembered what happened then. Damn, he wasn't going to *do* this. The boat rocked as he tried to push Julia away. She wouldn't budge. The boat rocked again and they swayed to one side. He clasped her hips for anchor. She plastered her body against him.

Just as Lauren walked into the galley.

"Oh!" She stood before him in that damn soft yellow sundress, an expression on her face that cut to the quick.

Julia turned, and when she saw Lauren, she moved in even closer to Alex. "Hello."

"I'm sorry, I was just checking out...I..." Abruptly Lauren turned and raced away.

"Something's wrong." Alex stared after her. "She was green."

"Green-eyed monster, maybe." Julia turned back to him.

Firmly he set her away from him. "Not here, Julia."

"All right. Let's go somewhere."

"Yeah, sure. We'll go to the restaurant up the walk, then to the party at Pete's."

She shook her head but followed him out of the galley. Alex glanced at the head when they passed it. The door there was shut and someone was inside. Lauren. Damn, what did he care? He got all the way up top, before he said, "I'm going back down, Julia."

"Alex."

"I'm an EMT. Lauren was clearly ill. Why don't you go over to the restaurant and I'll meet you there."

"Would you even care if I just left?"

No. "Yeah, sure I would. Get us a table and order me a beer."

She walked away and he trundled back down into the cabin. At the head, he knocked. "Lauren, it's Alex. Are you all right?"

"Go away." It was mumbled.

"Lauren, I've got medical training. Let me in."

No answer.

"I'm not leaving."

Finally the lock snicked and she opened the door. Standing in the small space, she seemed even more fragile than usual—like a wilted flower now.

"Are you sick?"

She placed her hand on her middle. "My stomach." She drew in a deep breath. "I guess I still can't be on boats. But I was trying to prove I…" She stopped and raised her chin. "I didn't know you were down here."

"What did you mean, you can't be on boats?"

"I'm afraid of water. I fell off a boat when I was little. It's why I never learned to swim. To top it off, I get seasick like that." She snapped her fingers. The boat shifted. "I have to get out of here."

He stepped back as she brushed past him, resisting the urge to touch her. He wet some paper towels, then followed her up. Once they were on land, he led her to a bench in the shade. "Sit."

Weakly she sat.

He dropped down next to her. Lifting the towels, he blotted her forehead, her cheeks. She closed her eyes and sighed. As she did with everything, she relished the sensations. "Do you always get ill this easily?"

"Just on boats, which I normally steer clear of."

"Can you take medicine for it?"

"Yeah, sometimes it works. Sometimes not." She shook her head. "My mother always said I feel all physical things intensely. Pain and pleasure. I enjoy things more than most people, but when I get sick, I'm a basket case."

He stopped wiping her face. He trailed his hand down to her mouth, brushed his thumb over her full bottom lip. "I know firsthand how intensely you enjoy...things."

She peered up at him, her eyes full of feeling.

He whispered, "It was the same for me, sweetheart."

She leaned into him for a minute, then drew back, as if resigned to something. "You like to surf and water-ski, don't you?"

"Um, yeah."

"Do you have a boat?"

"My parents do." He could see where this was going. "And to address your unspoken point, yeah, I like to spend time on the water."

"I rest my case."

"You're giving up on a relationship because of a little motion sickness?" His voice was tight. "That tells me you don't want this all that much."

"I don't know what I want."

Swiveling, he faced forward, dangled clasped hands between his knees. "Yeah, so you said."

Reaching out, she touched his arm. "I've been miserable, if it's any consolation."

Again he sighed. "I don't want you to be miserable." He thought for a minute. "You know what, though? It really pisses me off that you are and you still won't let this happen between us."

The air between them crackled, like the atmosphere before a storm. "Alex, I—"

"There you are." Son of a bitch. Toby had arrived before he and Lauren could finish. Right behind him was Julia.

"Hi, Alex." Toby pushed up his glasses. "Where have you been?" he asked Lauren.

"I was checking out the boats."

Alex stood and Julia sidled in close to him. "We're eating, then going to a beach party," she announced.

Alex looked at Toby. "Where you guys going?"

"To a foreign-film festival at the Little Theater."

Julia shuddered. "I hate those flicks. No car chases. No action."

"Well, to each his own," Toby said, reaching for Lauren.

Alex watched the other man take hold of Lauren's hand. He gave her a piercing stare. "Yeah, I guess. To each his own. Bye, all."

Turning, he started to walk away. He didn't take Julia's hand, though, because he knew it would hurt Lauren, and no matter how angry he was, he meant what he said about not wanting her to be miserable. But Julia moved in close and slid her arm around his waist. Poor Lauren. He had no desire to make her jealous. He knew, for the first time in his life, how painful that emotion was.

All he wanted to do was make her laugh, to see her eyes light up with some new sensory experience. And bathe her in that pleasure she felt so intensely. But he was beginning to accept that she wasn't going to give him a chance.

IT WAS THAT ONE small thing that pushed Lauren to make a decision. Almost from outside of herself, she watched Toby take her hand and the hurt etch itself on Alex's face. Still, he didn't retaliate, didn't try to hurt her back, to make her jealous. When he turned away, *he* didn't cozy up to Julia. He didn't put *his* arm around her.

His mother was right. *He's a compassionate, caring man with an inner core of true decency.*

And as Lauren watched him walk away, she was hit with a realization. She was letting this wonderful guy go—no, pushing him away—because she was afraid of…what? Of giving their relationship a shot, of trying to work through their differences? No, it was more than that.

The truth was simple: she was afraid of falling in love with him and finding out they couldn't deal with their differences. That he'd come to see she wasn't woman enough for him, or at the least, the right kind of woman. After all, she hadn't been right for James.

Wimp. Coward. Deirdre hurled all kinds of epithets at her during the film she saw with Toby, on the drive home and as Lauren tossed and turned in her bed.

By morning, she knew what she was going to do. She got up early, worked until noon and made three stops before driving to the street where the Ivies lived, where Alex had pointed out his parents' house.

ALEX STARED at the computer, frustrated. It was just a bunch of squares, different colors, outlined in black. Still, he read the explanation. *Mondrian is clearly trying to show the racial inequity in society. Most people are white, hence the white squares. The Asian population…*

Alex sank back into the chair in his family's rec

room and rubbed his eyes. He couldn't buy all this. But he didn't have to. All he had to do was understand it.

I love modern art, she'd said. *It speaks to me.*

So, he'd make it speak to him. Even if it did seem to be in Greek right now. He glanced at the books he'd bought. *Art for Dummies. Who Was Vincent van Gogh? Cubism and the Philosophical Implications of the Movement.*

Taking the last one, he got up and wandered over to the couch. He dropped down on the old leather cushions and began to read. Hell, if he could understand genetics…

"Alex?" It was his mother's voice. He'd been engrossed and hadn't heard her come in.

"Hi, M—" He looked past Vera's shoulder. Behind her stood Lauren.

She wore a pretty green velour top and shorts, with gold sparkly sandals on her feet. "Hi, Alex."

"Well, I'll leave you two. Your dad and I will be back for dinner."

He couldn't tear his gaze away from Lauren.

Vaguely he realized his mother had crossed to him and felt her kiss his cheek. "Don't blow it, honey," she whispered. Aloud, she said, "Remember, it's your turn to cook."

Then she was gone. And they were alone.

The rec room had always seemed huge to Alex with its high ceiling, pool-table area, entertainment center, couches and a fireplace. But the entire room shrank to the six feet between him and Lauren. "What are you doing here?" he asked.

She stepped back as if he'd told her to leave.

"Not that I mind. I'm just shocked."

A smile spread slowly across her face. Her eyes lit up. "I'm a little shocked myself."

"That you're here?"

"Uh-huh." She held up a shopping bag he hadn't noticed she carried. "I brought you a present."

"More cookies?"

"No, you'll like this better, I think." She smiled again, then fiddled with the dangling earrings she wore. "Actually, there are three presents in here."

Closing the distance between them, she handed him the gift. Their fingers brushed. He took the package, sat back down on the couch and opened the bag. She stood over him.

He pulled out a shoe box with the Nike logo on the outside. Lifting the lid, he found pink cross-trainers. Six and a half. "Not my size."

She shook her head. "No, they're my size."

His eyes locked with hers. Then he looked back down and drew out a small pharmacy bag. Inside was a pill bottle for some new medicine on the market. "I don't get motion sickness."

"No, I do."

He was grinning when he pulled out the third gift. It was a folder from the Y in Courage Bay. He opened it and saw the forms inside. He glanced up at her. "I'm a certified water instructor, Lauren. I don't need swimming lessons."

"No, but I can't swim."

He dropped the bag and reached for her. She crouched in front of him, and he took both her hands in his. Kissed them with exquisite gentleness. "You'd do all this for me?"

"I would. If we're going to be spending our time together, we can't avoid what you love."

"I'm..." He kissed her hand again. "I'm touched."

"I was afraid, Alex. Actually, I still am."

"Of me?"

"No, that my feelings for you will grow, and we won't work out."

He ran a hand through her hair. "But you're willing to risk it?"

"Yes."

He stared into the brown depths of her eyes. And realized he already felt so much for her. And he wanted her to know that. He pointed to the other side of the room. "Go check out the desk, Lauren."

She frowned, expecting more, he guessed. But she did what he asked. "Oh, my," she said, picking up the yellow *Dummies* book. She bent over the screen. "God, I always hated that interpretation of Mondrian. I think he was just painting..." She stopped and turned to Alex. "You did this for me?"

"Yeah. Though, man, I didn't make much headway."

"Alex."

"Come here, sweetheart."

She crossed back to him. He tugged her down into his lap. Immediately her hand went to his neck, caressed it. Then she leaned over and inhaled him. "I love the way you smell."

He struggled for balance. She scrambled his brains when she did that kind of thing to him. And suddenly, he wanted what was best for this woman, more than he wanted to satisfy himself. As gently as he could, he raised his hand to stroke her hair. "Maybe we should backtrack a bit, here. We jumped headlong into something that night at the beach."

She smiled. "Yeah, we did. What do you suggest?"

"A kiss first. Then let's spend some time getting to know each other, doing things together before we go further, physically, again."

Shaking her head, she smiled. "Not your standard line from a man."

"I'm not your standard man, Lauren."

"No, I can see that." She whispered the words against his mouth. "All right. Let's start with that kiss."

CHAPTER SEVEN

FROM HER WINDOW, Lauren watched him as he washed the truck. Alex had taken his shirt off. The rays of the morning sun kissed his back, making it shimmer, making her hands itch to touch him. Though they'd made love, she'd never seen him without his clothes. His torso seemed bigger, his shoulders wider. Like a football player's. She'd title the scene below "Outdoor Beauty."

He glanced up, saw her in the window, and waved. Earlier, he'd conducted a drill with his group and then played some one-on-one basketball. He'd caught her watching him then—and she'd stepped back out of sight, embarrassed. Now she gave him a warm grin. Jeez, she was acting like a besotted schoolgirl mooning over her boyfriend. She'd felt the same way last night.

She and Alex had sat on his parents' couch for a long time, listening to music, talking quietly—and passionately necking. Her fingers tingled, thinking about how his body had pulsed under her hands. All hard muscle. Taut skin. Leashed strength. She also remembered how wonderful it had felt when he'd touched her. He made her head spin as he stroked her throat, her heart catapult in her chest when he caressed her breasts. They didn't take the physical contact to its natural conclusion, as they'd agreed. But their time together was…hot. Not Lauren's style at all, but she sure liked it.

Then, he'd asked her to stay for dinner—he was cooking for his parents—and she'd accepted. She felt no demureness now, since their encounter in the hut and their declarations that day. She'd enjoyed the time with him in a different setting, seeing him in yet another role.

He'd made stuffed zucchini, adding rosemary to the cheese, sausage and egg mixture at her suggestion. Everyone thought it was delicious, especially his mother. Enjoying the smell of warm bread and spicy meat, they'd dined in a glassed-in room off the kitchen, homey with sophisticated touches, and sat there long after sunset sipping flavored coffee and tea. They didn't talk about Lauren's likeness to Dana or Helen Ivie's concern. Instead, they discussed their lives, their dreams. She listened to his parents talk about how they'd met, Vera's medical-school years, the diner Wes bought after he'd retired from fire fighting. And she loved hearing stories about Alex and his sisters, especially since she was an only child. She'd always wished for siblings.

During it all, Lauren was mesmerized by Alex's obvious devotion to his parents. He'd touched his mother's shoulder or arm whenever he walked past her, and playfully headlocked his dad or affectionately socked his shoulder. That, as much as the kiss in the driveway, had her thinking about him all day long.

"I'll follow you home," he'd said when he walked her out at the end of the night.

"Absolutely not. I drove here and I'm capable of driving back to my place." When he looked askance, she said, "We had the locks changed. The police turned up nothing regarding an intruder. And there've been no more incidents. I can't keep depending on you to protect me, Alex. It's not right."

"Aw, shucks. I thought maybe you'd invite me to stay overnight again."

"For the French toast?"

They'd reached her Honda. He backed her up against it playfully and rubbed his thumb over her bottom lip. "No, not for breakfast. For this." Lowering his head, he kissed her searingly. When he drew back, he whispered, "I've been dying to do that since my parents got home."

She'd wrapped herself around him. "Do it again."

Shaking off her thoughts, Lauren left the window and crossed to her desk. She picked up her new drawings and tried to concentrate.

But as Deirdre's face stared back at her, the cartoon character quipped, *You're dead meat, kiddo, like I said.*

Well, at least this time, she agreed with her imaginary friend.

Feel good?

It feels great, Dee. Just great.

ALEX TRIED ALL DAY not to call her. It was just that seeing her watch him from the window, more than once, wreaked havoc with his willpower. So when things slowed down at the station house, he sequestered himself in his office and whipped out his cell phone.

She answered hers on the first ring. "Lauren Conway."

"You know, even your voice has texture. Sometimes, it's smooth as silk, like now. Sometimes, it's raspy." Like an idiot, he grinned into the mouthpiece and whispered, "When you're aroused."

"Who is this?" Lauren asked.

He laughed out loud.

"I'm not getting any work done," she told him.

"No?"

"You're distracting. I should move my office."

"Don't you dare. I like the idea of you watching me."

"Drooling over you, you mean." She sighed and it went straight to his gut—and lower. "You know, I've never seen you without a shirt before."

"Hell. We…were together in that hut…but I guess you're right. We kept our clothes on."

"Did we?"

He loved bantering with her. "Didn't we?"

She giggled.

"I was crazy in there, pretty lady."

"Me, too."

"What time are you done working?" he asked.

"Actually, I'm ready to leave right now."

"I'll come out and say goodbye. I'm on all night." He said it as if he were getting shipped to India.

"I know."

"Meet me in the parking lot by your car."

"All right."

Minutes later, the bright sunshine beat down on him as he headed across the street. He greeted Bud Patchett, the department mechanic, who was fixing a generator on the lawn.

"Hey, Alex. How ya doin'?" Bud asked.

"Terrific."

The mechanic smiled back.

Then Alex's attention was snagged by Lauren, as she appeared in the doorway. She walked to her car and waited by it. "See ya, Bud," he said, and jogged across the street. He met up with her at the Honda, which was parked in the newspaper lot. "Hey."

"Hey." She smiled sweetly and pressed her cute little fanny—hugged by a short tan skirt—against the driver's door. Her peach silky blouse left her arms bare, and they just begged for his touch. He leaned against the car. "So, what will you do, now?" he asked.

"I've got errands to run, then I'll work some more on *Dee and Me*."

He dropped his voice a notch. "What's going on with them?"

"Lily's making some progress. She's taking more risks." Lauren's eyes twinkled. "And she's going to meet up with the muscle-bound boy again. Readers like him—and their budding relationship."

He had to force himself not to touch her, but his gaze caressed every inch of her face. "Glad to hear that."

She looked coyly at him. "It's just a cartoon, Alex."

"Like hell." He chuckled. "What else will you do?"

"I'm having dinner at six with Hannah. We're talking wedding stuff."

Damn, he wished he could be with her today. "Will you miss me?"

"What do you think?" Reaching out, she touched his hand where it rested on the car. She outlined his index finger, then his thumb, with the lightest trace. "I'd like to sketch your hand. It's so powerful. It can tame the elements." She glanced up at him, her gaze hot. "Yet it can be so gentle. I'd try to capture that dichotomy."

"Lauren." His voice came out a croak.

She smiled. "I think I'd better go and let you get back to work."

"I think you'd better." He stared at her mouth. "I want to kiss you."

"Hmm. Me, too." But she stepped away.

He opened the door for her.

She smiled again and slid inside. "See you, Alex."

"Bye." He grinned sheepishly. He felt like such a sap, but he couldn't help it. "Drive safely."

He stood and watched her start the car. She backed out of her parking space and into the road that separated the newspaper parking lot from the firehouse. But instead of stopping and going forward, she continued to back up...and back up...

The rear end of her Honda smashed into the yellow fire hydrant on the other side of the road.

"Lauren!" he yelled, and ran toward the car. Several other firefighters headed for her, too. Forcing his mind to be calm, Alex reached her first and whipped open the driver's-side door. She sat with her head back against the headrest, her eyes staring ahead. She looked dazed.

"Lauren, are you all right?" he asked tightly. He could hear panic edging into his voice.

She nodded, then winced.

He was already checking her pulse and pupil dilation. "What hurts?"

"My neck." She frowned. "I couldn't stop the car, Alex. Something was wrong with the brakes."

THERE WERE SO MANY of them—Alex, the paramedic named Gonzales and Dr. Yube, who'd walked out of the newspaper office building with Perry just after the collision. They hovered over her before they got her out of the car and now again as she was seated outside on a chair one of the firefighters had provided. Alex stayed in the background, his brow furrowed, his faced flushed. "Worried Man," she thought. Though he controlled it, she knew just by looking at him he was concerned.

"She should go to the hospital." Yube had just taken her pulse and examined her neck. He addressed his comments to Perry O'Connor. "It's probably just whiplash, but she should be checked out. She might need medication."

The last thing she wanted was another hospital visit, but she saw Alex staring hard at her. *Don't even think about objecting,* his expression said. He glanced at his watch. "I—" The alarm blared from the speakers, which were set up outside. All she caught was "Ladder One." Alex's rig.

"Hell, I gotta go." He circled around Perry and squeezed her arm. "You okay?"

"Yes, of course."

With an exasperated sigh, he left hurriedly.

She glanced longingly at her car and swallowed hard. The Honda Accord had been her mother's, and she hated seeing the back end squished like an accordion.

The ambulance pulled up. Once again she was loaded into it, brought the short distance to the hospital and given a room in the E.R. She was examined, prodded, poked at and was ready to be released, when she realized she didn't have any way to get home.

Just then, Hannah and Vince rushed in. "Hannah? What are you doing here?"

"Alex called me. I came as soon as I could."

"Thanks, I didn't have a way home."

Vince moved in close to the bed; his craggy face showed lines of worry. "Lauren, we need to talk about this."

"Why?"

"Because you've been in a fire, the victim of two possible break-ins and now a so-called accident."

Lauren swallowed hard. "You think this wasn't an accident?"

"I don't know. When did you last have your brakes checked?"

"About six months ago when the car was inspected."

"Any problems with them before today?"

"No. Not that I was aware of."

"You should come down to the precinct and file an official complaint. I can handle the case."

"You mean somebody..."

"We don't know. It's just too coincidental for my taste."

She closed her eyes. Now she really *was* frightened.

ALEX HAD A HELL of a night. They'd gone on five calls. All the while, he worried about Lauren. He'd phoned her in between, before she went to bed. Hannah had stayed the night with her. And now, here he was at eight the next morning on her porch. Before he could ring the bell, the door swung open. "Hi, Alex," Hannah said. "I was just leaving."

"I just got off work. Everything okay?"

"Yeah, she's fine. Her neck is sore. They gave her painkillers and muscle relaxants."

"Neck injuries can be a bitch." He glanced past Hannah into Lauren's house. "Think it would be okay if I came in and waited till she woke up?"

Eyes twinkling, Hannah smiled. "I think it would be fine." She gave him a once-over. "Lauren and I had a long talk last night. Your name came up."

"Uh-oh."

"You better be nice to her, Alex. She likes you. A lot. And she's had a rough year."

"I will. Scout's honor."

Hannah let him inside, bade goodbye and left.

The house was still, but Alex could hear the birds pecking at the feeder and the subtle tinkle of the wind chimes. The rooms had a unique smell, too. Potpourri, his mother called it. And flowers. The kittens bounded out of the kitchen and nuzzled his legs. Scooping them up, he walked through the house into the bedroom. He stopped in the doorway to appreciate the sight. Lauren was nestled in a big teak bed, surrounded by frilly beige covers, pillow slips and flowered sheets. The walls looked like somebody had sponged them with a deep beige and brown. At the windows, linen shades knocked softly in the slight breeze. A modern-looking teak grandfather clock stood in the corner.

And her paintings hung on the wall, also framed in teak. He crossed to a large one of a man and woman, entwined. It was an abstract, and he couldn't make out their features or even all their limbs as they meshed, but there was a tenderness about the way they came together, an intimacy in the way their bodies touched that made it clear they were lovers. He couldn't drag his gaze from it.

"Alex?"

He turned. She'd awakened and was staring at him, her eyes heavy with sleep. Once again he felt his body respond to the sight of her. But the tenderness and concern that welled inside him were the more powerful emotions. "Hi, sweetheart. I came over to check on you, and Hannah let me in."

"That's nice." She lay back in the pillows. "I've been sleeping for hours."

He crossed to the bed. She smiled and patted the side of the mattress. He sat, gently brushing the hair from her eyes. "You okay? I was so worried..."

"My neck hurts."

"Want a back rub?"

Her eyes widened. "Did Hannah tell you?"

"Tell me what?"

"I'm a sucker for back rubs. They're one of my favorite things in life, besides foot massages."

"No, she didn't tell me." He smiled. "Turn over."

Wincing as she sat up, she started to change positions. "Wait a sec." He touched a strap of the ice-pink camisole she wore with matching pants. "Take this top off."

She arched a brow.

"Your choice. But a back rub's better on bare skin." He leaned over and said in his sexiest voice, "Besides, it's nothing I haven't seen."

Chuckling, she slipped off her top, giving him only a quick sneak peek before holding the top in front of her breasts.

"Heartless," he mumbled as she turned and lay on

her stomach. Even her chuckle was sexy, and he liked making her laugh.

Her skin was velvet and silk under his hands. She must have used a lotion, because he inhaled roses. ''You smell great.''

She moaned.

He kneaded her deltoids.

He heard her groan.

He found the tight muscle that was giving her problems and she flinched. ''I'll be careful, but if I work the knot out, it'll feel better.''

He massaged it until he felt her relax, then his hands traveled to her spine.

''Mmm....''

''Lauren?''

''Yes?''

''Please try not to make those noises, I'm having trouble controlling myself as it is.''

She giggled but it was muted by her face in the pillow. ''All right.''

He kneaded her waist, then her butt, over the tap pants. Beneath the flimsy material, he knew her upper thighs were creamy and smooth, baby soft. Even the backs of her knees felt like heaven.

When he got to her feet, and began a long, luscious, sexy massage, she whispered, ''Alex...''

''Have trouble controlling yourself, too?'' He kissed her ankle. ''I like to keep things on an equal footing, so to speak.''

''THANKS FOR COMING HERE, instead of meeting at your office,'' Lauren said to the security expert Vince had sent over. ''Are you sure I can't get you anything?''

"No, thanks." Hawk Longstreet sat on her couch and watched her like his namesake. He was another big hulk of a man with Native American features and black hair. "Your neck better?"

"Some." She thought of the back rub Alex had given her that morning. God, his hands had felt good.

Right now he was having lunch with his mother; he hadn't known that Longstreet was coming. Her accident had made him even more protective, and he probably would have canceled his date with Vera, so she didn't tell him.

"I needed to see the house anyway." He surveyed the area. "You don't own it, do you?"

"No, but the landlord is sharing the cost of the security system, like he did the renovations." She shifted uncomfortably. "I think installing the system is a good idea. The other stuff Vince suggested...I'm just not sure."

"Being under surveillance is hard. I can understand your hesitation."

She smiled. "Thanks."

He rested his arm on the back of the sofa. "I used to be a detective. I think Vince is right that your four incidents are probably not coincidental. We can take care of the house. But it's harder to keep you safe away from home, if there's a repeat fire or somebody tampers with your brakes."

"Well, the police are having my car checked out. It may have been a fluke."

"Maybe." He stood. "Show me around the place," he said easily.

He made surprisingly astute comments about the way she'd decorated her home, and especially about her art. They were chatting companionably when the doorbell chimed. She left him admiring a piece of sculpture one of her friends had made to answer it.

"Hi." It was Alex. He looked...grim. He'd gone home before meeting his mother and in contrast to his delicious bristle this morning, his face was smooth shaven. His hair shone. He'd changed out of his uniform into khaki cargo pants and a loose-fitting dark blue sports shirt.

His mother stood next to him, at least a head shorter.

"Vera, how nice to see you."

Vera smiled warmly. "Hello, dear." She reached out and touched Lauren's arm. "I'm sorry to hear about your accident." She glanced worriedly at Alex. "George Yube told me at the hospital, even before I met my son for lunch."

"I'm feeling better now." Together they walked into the living area.

"Oh, dear, you have company," Vera said.

Alex gave her a quizzical look.

"This is Hawk Longstreet." She worried the strings on the bottom of the white cotton top she wore. "Vince Wojohowitz recommended he come out to discuss security."

"You didn't tell me." Alex's tone was accusative.

No, we were too busy with the back rub. "I'm sorry. I was pretty out of it this morning."

Longstreet stepped forward. "I'm wiring the house."

"Anything else?" Vera asked, once they took seats on the couch.

Lauren picked up Caramel and began to stroke her. The kitten had pestered the hell out of Hawk, as she did all new people. "We're talking about some surveillance. I think that might be a little excessive, though.''

''Maybe not,'' Vera said.

Alex stood and crossed to Lauren. Dropping down next to her, he grasped her hand. ''Tell her, Mom.''

''I found out some things at Courage Bay Hospital.'' Her gaze narrowed. ''Or rather I couldn't find out some things.''

Her heart speeding up, Lauren fingered the tiger's-eye she'd put on again after the accident and hadn't taken off. ''What does that mean?''

''When I went to check the birth records at the hospital the week Dana was born, they were gone.''

HE STARED at the picture of her that he'd cut out of the newspaper when she'd left Benicia and come to work at the Courage Bay *Courier*. Lauren Conway. Who would have thought…

So it would start unraveling now. Vera Shields had done some digging, which he'd tried unsuccessfully to thwart. Just like he'd failed to scare Lauren back to Benicia, stalking her and setting up accidents where she wouldn't really get hurt. The fire was started in a different part of the building, the car brakes tampered with to fail when she'd be backing out driving slowly. And finally, the forays into her house, all meant to chase her out of Courage Bay.

But she'd stayed. Probably because of that bastard Shields. He gripped the picture. Well, he'd have to knock this up a notch. Someone would have to get hurt.

CHAPTER EIGHT

AFTER HIS SHOWER, Alex donned black fleece shorts, grabbed the paper and a mug of steaming coffee and headed out to his backyard. All the work was finished in his house: the floors and kitchen cabinets gleamed with the sheen of new wood, and the interior painting was finally done. He'd moved back in last night. Settling into a comfortable chair on the grass, he whipped open the paper.

Frame One:

Lily stands peeking into an indoor-pool area. *Maybe this isn't such a hot idea.*

Deirdre is behind her. *Of course it is. Go on, Lil.*

Frame Two:

The muscle-bound boy turns around. *Hey. Nice to see you, pretty lady.*

Alex did a double take. That's what he called Lauren sometimes. He read on...

Lily glances back at Deirdre. Deirdre scowls.

Frame Three:

Lily is now beside the pool. *I, um, don't know how to swim so I signed up for this class.*

I'm the teacher. My name is Adam.

Hot damn! Adam—Alex...

Frame Four:

I'm Lily.

The boy's smile is wide and delighted. *Nice to meet you.*

Frame Five:

All right, Adam yells. *Everybody into the pool!*

Lily faces the reader, her expression panicked. *Oh, no, I hope this is worth it.*

Alex stared out into the trees, which rustled in the light breeze, and sipped his coffee. "Oh, it's gonna be worth it, sweetheart. I promise." He glanced at his watch. Lauren had her second swimming lesson this morning, then was coming over to see his house. He frowned, thinking about what was happening with her.

"This is so unusual," his mother had told him at lunch yesterday. "Medical records just don't disappear, Alex."

"I wish she'd get some protection."

But after the call had come from the garage where her car had been towed, Lauren had put off hiring someone to watch her. The brake fluid was gone, they'd said. So she and Alex had fished out her records and after a lot of searching, found her latest automotive receipt. The brake fluid had been checked at that time.

Hawk Longstreet, the security expert had shrugged. "Well, it could drain out on its own. Did you see any puddles in the driveway?"

"Yes, as a matter of fact, twice. I was going to take it back to the garage, but then all this creepy stuff started happening and I forgot about it. I never saw the fluid again, though."

Alex frowned. That could have been coincidence. Still, it seemed like too much.

"Hi." He turned to see Lauren standing in the

yard, looking like a flower again. She wore a pink top that showcased her curves, green shorts and the cute pink Nikes on her feet. He thought of the cartoon. ''Hi, pretty lady.''

She threw him a sideways glance at his use of the term but said nothing about it. ''I rang the bell, but no one answered. Your car was in the driveway, so I came around.'' She glanced out at the small yard. ''Nice trees back here.'' She scanned the area. ''Where are your flowers?''

''My flowers?''

She walked over to a two-feet-high stone wall that rimmed the perimeter of his property. ''Alex, this yard begs for flowers. And you should have a swing.''

He'd never thought about it. Rising, he crossed to her. She seemed so small, standing with her back to him, inspecting his yard. He slid his arms around her waist and drew her to him. She even smelled like flowers. He buried his face in her hair, then kissed her neck. She was warm from the morning heat. ''I have a great idea. Why don't we do a flower garden together? I gotta tell you, I know nothing about perannuals or whatever the hell they're called.''

She chuckled. ''Annuals and perennials.''

''See?'' He drew her closer. ''God, you feel good.''

''So do you.'' She turned in his arms, stood on tiptoe, kissed him. And practically leveled him with her heat. ''I'd love to do your garden.''

He drew in a breath. ''Well, okay, I'll…'' He pulled her back, as she started to walk away. ''You can't kiss me like that and expect me to talk about flowers.'' He lowered his head and took his time. When he was somewhat satisfied, he drew away.

"There, that's better." He brushed back her slightly damp hair. "How was the swimming lesson?"

"Excruciating." Her eyes brightened. "I put my head in the water, this time. Well, my face, but I did it."

For some reason a flash of him and Dana surfing came to mind. "Great."

"I don't like it," she added.

"But you're doing it."

"For you, Alex. But for me, too. Living in California, I should know how to swim."

"I have a reward for your bravery."

She lay her head on his shoulder. "You do?"

"Come inside. I'll show you."

He took her hand and led her through the open French doors off his kitchen, to stand in front of a chrome-and-glass table. Oak floors sparkled at their feet. "This is beautiful."

He stared at the state-of-the-art appliances, granite countertops and sleek black cupboards. "But it's not your taste."

"That doesn't matter. It's still lovely." She crossed into the adjacent living area. Lots of windows, a high ceiling, entertainment center, more hardwood floors. She ran her hand over a glass étagère. "Your place has flair."

"It's so different from yours."

"Now there's a surprise."

He grinned and went to the built-in desk in the corner. He drew something out and handed it to her.

"What's this?" she asked.

"Tickets to a Picasso show in Los Angeles."

Her eyes widened. "*The* Picasso show? At the LACMA?"

He felt like a kid who'd done something to please the teacher. "Yeah."

She fingered the envelope as if it contained precious artifacts. "I saw the Modigliani exhibit there last fall. It was terrific." She took out the tickets then looked up at him, still startled by his gift. "They're for tomorrow night. I tried to get tickets and they were sold out weeks ago."

"Yeah?"

"How did you get them?"

"A woman we dragged out of a burning car a while back stays in touch with us because we saved her life. She works at the gallery."

"So you called in a favor? For me? For something you won't enjoy at all?"

Her pleasure did funny things to his insides. It was another unfamiliar feeling, wanting to make this woman happy. He took her in his arms. "I'll enjoy being with you. I took some furlough so I'm off."

She wrapped her arms around him. "Thank you so much."

His heart swelled. "You're welcome." Other parts of him swelled, as well.

She fitted herself to those parts. "Alex, do you still want to wait? We don't have to."

He grasped her hips and nestled her against him. "Sometimes I don't want to wait at all. But getting to know each other is…right. And the anticipation's kind of fun."

"Okay, show me the rest of your house. It's so you. That'll speed things along, I think."

He grinned. "Yeah, I wouldn't mind speeding things along." He grabbed her hand, kissed it and, holding on to her tightly, he took her on a tour.

LAUREN HAD TO GIVE Alex credit, he was really trying. Inside the big stone-and-glass building that was the Los Angeles Museum of Art on Wilshire Boulevard, he'd stood before Picasso's Cubist paintings, read the descriptions, listened to the headset and even squinted his eyes to make out the figures.

His own picture would be titled "Man Out Of His Element."

He'd been partial to "Paulo as a Harlequin" and "Woman in Blue," Picasso's more traditional work, though he'd thought they were depressing.

Now, the two of them approached "Les Demoiselles d'Avignon." As he'd done before, he read and listened, then just stared at the naked women portrayed through the master's mind. Finally he turned to her. "I like this one."

"Do you really? It's my favorite of his work."

"See, I've got some taste." He tugged her close. His scent—something really sexy, not what he'd worn before—filled her head. She leaned into him, nestling against the long-sleeved red-and-black-checked shirt he wore with black pants. The material was soft. Through it, she could feel the muscular wall of his chest—all hard planes and sinew. Because she couldn't resist how he felt, she let her hand rest on him. "Tell me what you like about the painting."

"I probably don't understand it, but the plaque says it's his rendition of the prostitutes in Avignon. It's sad."

"I think so, too."

"Their faces look like masks."

"He did that on purpose."

Alex shifted. "Sure. He'd see the women as putting up fronts, not showing who they really were as women of the night. That's why he posed them like he did.''

"That's exactly what I think." She shot him a sideways glance. "Are you quoting the books you read?"

His look was Boy Scout innocent. "No, honest, ma'am, I've never seen this painting before." He nodded to the women again. "I can't imagine doing what they do for a living. Picasso felt sorry for them."

Just a little bump in her chest, that's all it was. But she rarely had that reaction to men. It was as if her heart was reaching out to Alex. She said only, "Picasso frequented prostitutes."

"Doesn't make him less sympathetic." He nodded to the painting. "Maybe more so."

They walked through the high-ceilinged rooms to the section that housed Picasso's sculpture. "Thanks for bringing me here today. I can't say when I've enjoyed myself more."

He stopped dead in his tracks. His earlier sensitivity was replaced by a look of pure male affront. He thumped a hand over his chest. "You wound me, woman."

"Oh." She felt herself blush. It had become a game with them to refer to that night, but still, sometimes she got embarrassed. "In the hut, of course, it was a terrific time…it was good for me…" She shook her head, closed her eyes.

He laughed and put an arm around her shoulders. "I know, love."

They were seated in the Plaza Café sharing a piece of carrot cake, and Alex was staring at her mouth, watching her lick the creamy frosting off her lips when a shadow fell over the table. They both looked up.

"Lauren." James Tildan stood there, his face angry.

A sense of unease swept through her, like a chilling wind on a summer day. She swallowed hard. "Hello, James."

He shot Alex a withering glance, then focused on her. "I asked you to come to this show with me. I went out of my way to get tickets for you, Lauren."

Across the table, Alex looked surprised, but he said nothing. "James, I wish you'd stop calling and leaving messages. I'm not going anywhere with you. Ever again."

"That's not true." He faced Alex, who peered up at him mildly, but Lauren wasn't fooled. She could see a muscle tick in his jaw. "You can't have her, Shields."

Reaching across the table, Alex grasped Lauren's hand. Her throat felt tight. It was exactly the right thing to do. As was his low-key reaction. "Give it up, Tildan. You and Lauren are through."

James's face darkened. "That remains to be seen." He stalked away.

Alex's gaze followed him for a minute. Then he turned to Lauren. "You okay?"

"Yeah."

"I didn't know he was bothering you like that."

"It…I…" She pushed back her hair. "I didn't want to make a big deal of it."

He turned her hand over and laced her fingers in his. "It's a big deal. Do you think his coming here was coincidence?"

She startled. "How could it not be?"

"If he's following you, keeping tabs on you, he'd know you were here."

"Oh, God, no. I don't think that's happening."

Alex shook his head. "And you don't have to keep things from me. I won't go huntin' him down with my daddy's shotgun."

"You won't?"

"Nah." He grinned. "'Cuz he was wrong."

"Wrong?"

"Uh-huh. I'm gonna have you, sweetheart." His eyes danced with sexual suggestion. "Slow and quick, easy and hard—lots of ways. I can't wait."

Her heart swelled this time. "Thanks for distracting me."

He flashed a big boyish grin. "Did it work?"

"Oh, yeah, it worked."

WILL BEGAY'S HOUSE PARTY the next night was a raucous affair. Underneath a sky so cloudless it almost looked fake, with warm air swirling around them, people played games, visited and joked good-naturedly. Razzing and black humor, the staples of rescue personnel, abounded. Alex stood by the volleyball net set up in the yard, sipping an ice-cold draft, and kept an eye on the path that lead to Begay's backyard.

He was worried about Lauren. For two reasons. One was because of the phone call from his mother today.

"Alex, I found out some interesting things. The medical records the week of Dana's birth are the only files missing from the hospital during that time period. But they do have employment records. I've asked a friend of mine to help me sift through which nurses and doctors might have been working labor and delivery that week.''

"Who's the friend?"

"George Yube." Perry O'Connor's friend, too.

"Mom, this sounds ominous."

"I know. Keep an eye on Lauren."

Which he wasn't exactly doing, because she was taking a freakin' *private* swimming lesson.

"Cal said I have a lot of potential. He offered to give me extra lessons. Isn't that great?"

Great? Hell, the guy was putting the moves on her, for sure. Who wouldn't? Alex shook his head, still unable to believe the jealousy that sparked inside him so uncharacteristically.

"You're wearin' your heart on your sleeve, Shields."

Alex looked up to see Will. "Yeah, I guess."

Will scowled. "What's wrong? You worried about her being here tonight?"

"No. I'm worried about her, period." He explained the accident and other related things to Will, but kept the stupid jealousy stuff to himself. All he needed was for the guys to find out. They'd bust his chops till kingdom come.

"If it was Mareeta, I wouldn't let her out of my sight."

"I'm beginning to feel that way." He checked his watch. "She had a swimming lesson this afternoon, and said she'd meet me here."

"She can't *swim?*" A tough firefighter married to an even tougher nurse, Will's dark eyes reflected his disbelief.

"No, she can't. It was a childhood trauma."

"She really is different from you. And the women

you usually date. She may be Dana's double physically, which is still odd in my book, but she's not like Dana personality-wise, is she?''

"No, not at all."

He nodded to the court. "Not like Julia, either."

"I know. Hey, what can I say? When it hits, it hits."

Will glanced beyond him to the gate. "She's here." His expression was strange. "With some guy."

Alex turned to see Lauren enter the yard with a man he'd never met. She looked terrific in pink cropped pants with lacy cutouts at the bottom and a delicate white top that was made for her curves. The guy had a swimmer's body, tall and lean, light brown hair, and was dressed in jeans and a Hawaiian shirt. Who the hell was he?

Catching sight of Alex, Lauren said something to the guy and they headed over. Her smile was thousand watt as she came close. "Hi, Alex. Will." Alex noticed she didn't kiss him, or touch him. Turning, she laid her hand on the other man's arm. "This is Cal Smith, my swimming instructor."

Smith smiled. "I hope it's all right I stopped in with Lauren for a few minutes."

"Sure," Will said easily. "The more the merrier."

Alex folded his arms over his chest and cocked an eyebrow at Lauren. She shifted from one pink-sneakered foot to the other. "I lost the directions to your house, Will, but I had the address written in my day planner. When I asked Cal how to get here, he offered to drive me out, since it was on his way." She faced Alex. "I thought I could ride back with you."

Plausible, but damn, she didn't even know this guy. It was dangerous.

"Cal's a friend of Toby's," she added, as if she read his objection.

"Hmm."

Will said, "You guys want a brew? We got wine, beer and margaritas."

Casting a worried glance at Alex, Cal hesitated.

"Sure. I'll have a glass of wine," Lauren spoke up. "Cal?"

"Okay, I'll have the same."

Alex stewed as they made small talk. When another volleyball game was called, and good old Cal hadn't left yet, Alex excused himself to join the group. He was pissed about feeling like this. He tried to stifle the jealousy, not let anybody see it, by throwing himself into the game.

Ramirez came up to him as they were moving the line. "Your girl bring another guy, Cap?"

"Shut up."

"Ow-ee. The great Shields is jealous. This is a first."

"Bite me," he said, and spiked the ball hard into the grass on the other side of the net.

He tried not to, but he kept looking over at them. Finally the swimmer appeared ready to leave. He spoke to Lauren, his expression clearly interested. Hell. Then they found Will, Smith said something to him and at last took off.

Lauren stayed talking with Will and Mareeta. After a bit, they all headed to the house.

He wouldn't go after her. Instead, Alex concentrated on the play, on the sweat that poured from him, on how his heart pumped with the serves. When the game ended, he looked around. She still wasn't back. Alvarez must have caught his expression when they gathered at the big icy tub that held beer. "What's the matter, Alex?" He winked at Ramirez. "Worried about your lady?"

"Don't fret. You coulda taken him," Kellison put in.

Son of a bitch. This was just what he wanted. "I don't have a jealous bone in my body," Alex snarled, tipping the cup, letting the cold liquid drench his throat.

"Oh, good, 'cause I heard Will ask her if she'd like to try some Ping-Pong in the basement. He thought it might be more her speed."

"Good for her." Alex watched the court, wanting to go down to Will's basement. "I'm in for another game," he said, refusing again to run after her like a lovesick pup. "What about you guys?"

He didn't think much about it when his crew started bowing out—there were others still playing—until several minutes later when every last one was missing. It took forever to finish the game. Then he went in search of them.

Will's basement had recently been redone; all the guys had pitched in to tile, drywall and paint. At the bottom of the stairs, off to the left, was a room filled with Native American art. To the right was a game room. He could hear them before he saw them.

"My turn."

"No, it's mine."

Alex reached the doorway. Nobody seemed to notice him.

"Shut up." Ramirez practically tripped over himself crossing to Lauren, who stood at the far end of the Ping-Pong table.

"All right, *querida,* that last shot was good. But let me show you how to hold the paddle so you can get better aim." He moved close enough to her to make Alex's blood pressure rise, but not enough to be rude.

"Oh, sure," Lauren said, laughing.

She hit the ball pretty well, though Ramirez seemed to think she needed more *adjustment*—touching her hand and fixing her stance in the process.

Her opponent held back, Alex could tell, letting Lauren return it easily. They played for a while. Until Alvarez muscled Ramirez out of the way. "My turn."

Alex leaned against the doorway. They were busting his chops—he saw their glances at each other and at him—but they seemed to like her, too. In their own way, they were making her feel accepted. When LaSpino came to take Alvarez's place, Lauren protested. "No more. I'm going to take a break."

They practically surrounded her. "I'll get you wine…come on, let's hit the chow table…"

Alex strode into the room.

"Aw, shucks, the boyfriend," said Ramirez.

"Party pooper."

Lauren laughed again.

He reached her and grabbed her hand. "Come with me, I'm gonna show you Will's art collection."

"Oh, okay."

"Don't believe him, Lauren," Ramirez called after them. "Showing you etchings is the oldest line in the book."

Good-natured mockery followed them out. Alex closed the door on the sitting area that housed Will's collection, locked it and leaned against the knotty pine wall. "You're a pretty popular gal, tonight."

She studied him, biting her lip, obviously in an attempt not to laugh. "Your friends are nice."

"They were flirting with you."

"Were they?" She scanned the artwork. "Oh, this is beautiful." She started toward a colorful wall hanging. She didn't get far before he grabbed the back of her shirt and spun her around.

"Not so fast." He pulled her to him. Up close, he could see her deep brown eyes glimmer with mirth. They reminded him of warm chestnuts just out of the fire. "I can handle those clowns. I wanna know about the one who brought you here."

"I told you what happened."

"Yeah, sure, you lost your directions. He didn't go home with you, did he?"

"No, I'd walked over to the Y. I showered and changed there."

Alex bent his head and nuzzled her neck. "First he offers you a private lesson, then he comes here with you." He took a nip at her jaw. "I don't like this."

"No?"

"No." She sucked in her breath when his hands slipped under her white top. "You think he's attractive?" His fingers roamed her back, flirted with her bra. Then slid around front.

"Who?" she whispered throatily.

"Mark Spitz."

She chuckled. "I don't know, I'd have to think about it."

"We'll see about that," he said, cupping her breasts.

When she moaned, he knew she wasn't thinking about the swim teacher, or anybody else but him.

"WANT TO COME IN?" Lauren glanced at the dashboard of his Blazer. "I know it's late."

He hooked his wrist on the wheel. The cocoa-brown T-shirt he wore had teased her all night, clinging to him, especially when he was sweaty. "I'd love to come in, you know that. But I have to be at the station house by six."

That was a disappointment. She had the morning off. She'd been thinking maybe...

He stared at her in the dim light cast from the streetlamp in front of her house. "What are you thinking? A million emotions just flitted across your face."

She slid over as close as she could get. "I'm disappointed." Her hand went around his neck. It was damp with the warm night air that filtered in from outside. She curled into the crook of his shoulder. Breathed in the musky smell of him.

"You know, when you do that...you seem to absorb me; it makes me hard in about two seconds."

Her hand went to his lap. Pressed gently. "I wanted to be close to you tonight."

"Damn it, Lauren!" In a flash, he jerked the seat back, tilted the steering wheel and dragged her over the gearshift. It was awkward but she managed to snuggle into him. He was full and firm against her bottom. One of his hands slid under her shirt while the other tilted her head back. He devoured her throat, teased the lacy band of her bra with deft fingers, then closed his big, masculine hand over her straining breasts. His kiss was wild, long and thorough.

"There," he said, his voice husky. "Now, you'll be as frustrated as me until we can do this right."

It was a struggle to open her eyes. All she wanted was to languish against him. "What do you mean?"

"I gotta work in about five hours. And I'm not rushing this again."

A Deirdre comment popped out of her mouth before she could stop it. "Let's do it here, in the driveway. Like in the hut."

"No way, sweetheart. We're gonna be in a bed the next time, and I'm gonna have hours to do all the things to you I've been dreaming about."

"What are they?" she whispered, her face buried in his neck again.

By the time he had cataloged all of them to her, she was squirming. His hand went to the front of her pants. "I could take the edge off for you, now," he offered.

Chuckling, she arched into his palm when it cupped her. "Can't say I'm not tempted, but fair is fair. I'm waiting, too, lover boy."

He laughed.

It was so easy with him, teasing, sex…everything. Why hadn't she seen that before. "When?" she asked sexily.

"I'll be on till Sunday morning. Let me go home, grab some sleep. I'll come over about noon."

"I'll fix you something special."

He sobered. "All I want is you, Lauren."

This time, it was the emotion that almost did her in. "Alex." She kissed him again.

By the time he kissed her at the door—after a quick sweep of the house to make sure nothing was amiss—and said, "Think of me," she wasn't sure she'd ever get sleep.

CHAPTER NINE

THE NEXT DAY, Lauren woke late, and decided to go shopping for something naughty to wear for Alex when they made love again tomorrow. Something really sexy. In the lingerie store, she bought a peach-colored slip of a thing, with scalloped lace on the plunging neckline and hem, some sinfully sexy-smelling lotion and massage oil that claimed its formula came from a harem.

She was on her way home when she heard the siren behind her and pulled off the road. Alex's truck sped by her down the street.

On impulse, she followed it, thinking of the time she'd watched him lay the foam blanket. There was something about the bravery, the heroism of his job that excited her. Aroused her.

Just what you need, she thought, but followed the rig anyway, to a small side street. Orange flames burst from a two-story Victorian house. She parked across the street as Alex bounded out of the truck. Two other trucks arrived within minutes. Alex had told her a one-alarm blaze called in one company, a two-alarm was two companies, etc., depending on the seriousness of the fire. He'd also explained to her that many times he, as senior captain, conducted Incident Command—directing the operation—while other times he went inside. There was an official vehicle at the scene, and she watched as Alex approached the white-shirted guy, the battalion chief. Alex donned his gear as they talked. Turnout coat. Air-pack. Helmet. A face mask dangled from his hand. He held an ax, which she knew from her research for the cookies, was called a halligan. She'd paint him now as "America's Bravest."

In minutes, he was across the narrow porch and at the door of the house, behind guys going in with a huge hose. Then he disappeared inside.

Her heart catapulted with admiration and awe. And with worry.

THE INTERIOR of the house was cloaked in a curtain of black smoke. The pumper guys had gone in with a three-inch hose, suspecting the seat of the fire was in the basement. Alex had just crossed through the front door, taken two steps into the room—when the floor beneath him gave way.

He dropped straight down.

Grabbing for purchase, his hands connected with the joist.

His helmet flew off his head.

His air bottle hit the wood, pushed up and dislodged his face mask.

His face mask—with the breathing hose—fell off into the hole where the floor opened up.

And then his turnout coat slid up, exposing a strip of his lower back above the bunker pants.

"Cap!" Ramirez's voice sounded tinny through his air-pack.

Alex gripped the joist. On either side of him, Ramirez and Alvarez raced over and each grabbed one of his arms.

"Pull me up," he said calmly, feeling the heat at his back. He'd be burned for sure.

They yanked.

LaSpino swore. "You're pinned by the splintered plywood at waist level."

"Son of a bitch."

"Get a chain saw," Begay yelled, taking out his ax. Meanwhile, Alex could hear the guys in the basement searching for the seat of the fire.

"It's getting hotter." He began to cough and the room was getting dim.

Ramirez whipped off his mask. "Here." He gave Alex oxygen.

Alex gulped it in, then pushed the mask back to his engineer.

"I'm going out to look for another entrance to the basement," Begay said, "I don't like the feel of this." He disappeared.

Alex heard the explosion first. Then the heat intensified, and stabbing pain assaulted him. As if in slow motion, the beams he gripped gave way...his men lost their hold on him.

And Alex fell through the floor.

SENSING SOMETHING was wrong, she'd come closer to Incident Command and caught snatches of conversation. "Shields...pinned by wood...fire really rolling...lost his air mask...holy mother of God, what was that...?"

Standing by a tree off to the side, she saw a firefighter race around the house. The name on the back of his coat was Begay.

A chain saw rent the air.

More trucks arrived.

And Lauren stood by, her arms wrapped around her waist, praying.

THOUSANDS OF TINY PINPRICKS in his back... coughing, choking on the black smoke...the basement blurred...would they get to him in time?

A figure emerged in the darkness. It loomed over him. Two people. He felt himself lifted, and moaned in pain. A mask was fitted over his face, and he sucked in the clean air. He was being dragged. His eyes closed. His head lolled. He saw a window being pushed up. More pain. Swearing. Then he was outside.

"Lay him on his stomach," somebody barked. "His back's burned."

The mask was off. He was placed on something cushioning.

"Get the medics," he heard.

Then he passed out.

SHE'D BEEN IN THE EMERGENCY room waiting area for over an hour with all of Alex's crew, who'd refused to return to the station house. If another call came, they'd go from here, though she couldn't imagine how they'd manage. Their faces were covered with grime and their expressions were grim. Their huge shoulders slumped with fatigue and fear, while their eyes darted to one another, avoiding her. They were seasoned firefighters, and they were worried.

Lauren wanted to weep. She didn't, though. Someone handed her coffee. She looked up. "Thanks, Will."

He sat next to her. Nobody offered platitudes. She didn't ask for them. She guessed, if you were involved with a firefighter, you had to toughen up fast. And right now, she knew without a doubt that she was involved with a firefighter.

"Did someone call his parents?" she asked Will when he sat beside her.

"They're out of town for the weekend with the Ivies."

Maybe that was for the best. How could you be a firefighter's mother? she wondered idly. Or his wife? Or even his girlfriend?

Don't start down that road, Deirdre said.

I won't. She was in this now, and wasn't going to run scared. If only he'd be all right. *Please, dear God, let him be all right.*

It seemed an eternity before the doctor came out from the same emergency area where Lauren had been. Young and harried, he approached the men where they'd gathered by the coffee machine. Will helped her up and led her over to the group.

"He's fine," the doctor told them. "Smoke inhalation was pretty bad, but the burns on his back are only second-degree."

"That's a miracle," LaSpino said.

"He was hanging onto the joist with his back exposed for a hell of a long time," added Ramirez.

Lauren moaned. She insisted on being told everything, but the pictures taking shape in her head were making her ill. She was grateful when Will slipped his arm around her.

"How long will he be here?" Will asked.

"I'm keeping him overnight. He's not a happy camper."

They all snorted.

Chuckling, the doctor ran a hand through his hair. "Good thing you warned me."

"Warned you?" Lauren asked.

Alvarez rolled his eyes. "Shields is a big baby when he gets hurt. Grumpy. Mean. Snaps at everybody except his mama. And only then because she won't let him."

That drew a smile from Lauren.

"And he won't take pain pills."

"Who's gonna stay with him?" Will shook his head. "Vera's out of town."

The guys backed away.

Will said, "We'll draw straws."

Lauren knew their reluctance was sham. Firefighters took care of their own. "I'll stay with him when he gets out," she offered.

They jumped on her suggestion.

"Ah, darlin', you just made our day."

"Way to go, Lauren."

"You don't know what you're in for, girl."

Overcome with relief that they had this to joke about, she willed back the moisture in her eyes. "I'm just glad he's all right."

"You won't be sayin' that come Monday."

Lauren didn't censor her response. "I can handle Alex."

"Just wait."

"YOU KNOW, your buddies were right. You're a baby. A cranky one."

A sheet draping his torso, Alex buried his face in the pillow and mumbled something.

She adjusted the blinds, as he'd *ordered* her to. "What was that?"

"Nothing." He coughed, a hoarse bark creeping up from his chest. He'd slept most of the time since the guys helped bring him home yesterday—he'd stayed overnight at the hospital Friday—but he'd been awake for about thirty minutes and had done nothing but complain. Seeing the strip of raw, red skin across his back—though it looked remarkably better today—she guessed she would, too. She softened her tone. "If you'd take the pain pills regularly, it wouldn't hurt so much."

Gripping the pillow, he came up on his elbows. "It's not just that."

"What, then?"

"*What,* she asks. How quickly she forgets."

Crossing to him, she sat on the edge of the bed. His back was bare but really dry. She reached over and began to knead his neck. He groaned, and put his face in the pillow again. Hmm. Maybe this was the key. "I didn't forget what we were supposed to do yesterday. I'm disappointed, too." She bent over and kissed his spine. "But you're healing great. Only another day or so and you'll be up and around."

She heard more incoherent mumbling. She rose, then, and shook out a pain pill. "Here, take this, and then I'll give you a proper massage."

He gulped the pill. His beautiful amber eyes were completely bloodshot; his hair matted. They'd cleaned him up at the hospital but he couldn't take a shower. Grabbing her hand, he kissed it. "I'm sorry."

"I'd be a bear, too." She dropped back down. "Now just relax."

After she had massaged his upper back, he slept again. She worked on the drawing she was doing for his backyard until he awoke.

"I wanna get up for a while. I gotta use the head. And this is a damned uncomfortable position."

"Okay." Getting out of bed without rolling onto his back was a challenge. He was unsteady on his feet, so she helped him to the bathroom. "I wish I could clean up better." They'd given him a sponge bath in the hospital, but she knew he felt grimy.

"You can." She squeezed his arm. "With a little help. Take care of business and I'll wait out here."

"Why?"

"I'm going to give you a bath."

"I can't go in the tub."

"Not that kind of bath."

He raised his eyebrows. "Yeah?"

"Yeah. It'll be fun."

While he went inside, she dragged out the three-foot stool she'd spotted in the kitchen. He opened the door and she went into the bathroom.

"Want to wash your hair first?"

"Uh-huh. How, though?"

"Kneel down, if you can, and bend over the tub.

He groaned so loud, she said, "I'm sorry, if it hurts…"

"No, it'll be worth it to get clean."

She used the detachable sprayer on the shower to wet his hair. It was thick, coarse. She washed it quickly but took an extra minute to massage his scalp.

"That feels good," he murmured.

Toweling his hair dry so water didn't drip down his back, she helped him up. "Sit on the toilet till I'm ready."

She ran some water in the bottom of the tub, and set the stool in it. "You can sit there and I'll wash you."

His eyes narrowed on the stool.

"I promise I'll be careful." She grinned, and said flirtatiously, "You can take your boxers off."

The corners of his mouth turned up. "I can, huh?"

"Yep."

He dropped them to the floor. He was so perfectly formed she found herself gawking. And he swelled under her perusal. He must be feeling better.

She reached up and kissed him. "Let me help you so you don't slip." With some fancy maneuvering, she got him seated, then reached for her jeans.

"What are you doing?"

"I'm getting in with you." She stripped off her jeans, revealing lacy pink panties. She started to get into the tub.

"Wait." She did. "Take your shirt off."

"Why? It won't get wet."

Mischief lit his eyes. "I know."

Grinning, she reached for the hem of her T-shirt. His gaze sparked something hot and delicious in her. She pulled the shirt over her head. "Want a shave first?"

"If you can handle that."

She arched a brow. "Oh, I think I can handle just about anything." God, he freed her from her inhibitions in so many ways.

Retrieving what she needed from his medicine cabinets, clad only in her undies, she climbed into the tub.

His jaw was bristly from two days of growth. It was so sexy, she reached up and kissed him first. Then she lathered it and drew the razor down one side, again and again...then the other...finally his jaw.

He rubbed his hand over his face when she was done. "Feels good."

Just wait, she thought.

Next, she took the washcloth and wet it. Soaped it. The clean scent filled the small space. On her knees, she started with his chest. She rubbed the cloth over the whorls of hair, gently abrading his nipples. He let out a very male groan. She washed his throat…his arms…each finger. Then she rinsed him with warm water from the tap.

She did each leg. Slowly. Sensuously. Relishing in the muscle, in the sinew of his calves, his thighs. "Hmm," she said, kneading him as she worked.

"Sweetheart, don't *do* that."

"Sorry." But she wasn't. Bending her head, she kissed each knee.

His hand went to her hair. Smoothed it down.

Adding some warm water to the tub and abandoning the cloth, she soaped her hands. Then she took his penis in her palms. Washed him. Caressed him.

He growled, "That feels so good."

"Just relax."

"Relax, hell." He grasped her shoulders for balance. "Oh, God, Lauren…" His voice, hoarse from the smoke, was even hoarser from her ministrations.

"Shh, Alex, just let me…"

"No, honey, you wouldn't let me…in the car two nights ago."

"I wasn't hurt. And in pain." She rinsed him with the spray, then kissed the tip of his pulsing erection. "Please."

"Oh, Lord."

Her mouth closed over him.

He was in a good mood the rest of the night.

WHISTLING, Alex set out champagne glasses, white cloth napkins and the colorful dishes and mugs his mother had gotten him in Mexico. He rummaged through his cupboard for a frying pan. The pain in his back had abated to a dull ache, and he'd slept well, thanks to the medication Lauren had forced him to take—along with her other personal remedy. He'd slept alone, though.

"Stay with me," he'd said as he climbed back in bed after having something to eat.

"I will. In the spare bedroom, like I did last night."

"Here. I'm better."

"No."

"Why?"

She'd flushed. "I'm a cuddler, Alex. I'll be all over you in my sleep. I won't be careful of your back."

Though he hated thinking of her in bed with any other man, he'd liked the idea of her *all over him* on the nights he planned to spend with her. Many of them. "Hell."

She'd kissed his cheek, and he'd reached out for her hand. "Thanks, sweetheart. For earlier."

"My pleasure."

"No, all mine. But tomorrow…"

And now tomorrow was here. The smell of coffee told him the pot was done. He poured a mugful and, mindful of his back, went to the table and sat. Lauren had left a sketch there. It was of his backyard, or what his backyard could be. Off to the left was a brick patio. Behind that, there was a flower bed with a profusion of colors spouting from the ground and the pots surrounding it. To the right was a swing; next to that, a grill. She was something else—as was her vision. The strokes were strong yet delicate. Like her.

Staring down at the drawing, he admitted some things to himself.

He was falling for her, hard and fast. What she'd done for him last night wasn't anything new to him, but there was a giving in the act, a simple joy in making him feel better that had affected his heart as much as his groin. He grinned, thinking of her in that sexy bra and how her breasts plumped over the lacy tops...

"Hi."

He looked up as he lifted his coffee cup. His hand froze partway to his mouth.

She stood in the doorway, her auburn hair tousled and kissed by the sun streaming through the window. Some silk thing the color of apricots clung to her every curve. She'd painted her toenails and fingernails the same color.

"Good morning."

"You look great." Her voice was husky. "Feeling better?"

He stood. "Much." He swallowed hard. "You are so beautiful."

Her dark eyes glimmered like hot coals. "Thank you, Alex."

"Hungry?" God, he hoped not.

Her smile was Jezebel's. "Just for you."

"That does it." He rose and strode to her. "I was going to give you some tea, let you wake up. But I can't wait any longer." He stood over her, brushing wayward tendrils from her face. "I want you, Lauren. In bed. Us, together this time."

She grinned and leaned into his chest. "I want that, too."

He slipped his arm around her and they made their

way to his bedroom. It was cool in here, with a slight breeze wafting in from the open window. Gently he pressed her down on the bed. There was surrender in her eyes, a slight tension in her body. He put his hand on her throat. "You look so delicate here." He brushed his knuckles across her cheek. "And here. But you're not. You're strong."

"I'm as weak as my kittens right now." She took his hand and kissed it. "You make me feel like no one ever has before."

"I like hearing that, pretty lady." His hands slid along the peach silk, traced the scalloped top. "This is gorgeous, but it's gotta go." He lifted it while she sat up so he could slide it off her.

And there she lay, totally exposed to him. But he was the one who felt vulnerable. "Your breasts are so perfect," he said, cupping them. He kissed the small patch of freckles on her chest. His fingers kneaded her taut waist. His palms caressed her smooth, sleek legs.

Eyes locked, he lowered his hand to the auburn curls at the juncture of her thighs. She practically purred at his touch, arching into it. "I want to do everything to you, Lauren. Look at you all over. Touch you everywhere."

She ground against his hand. "No, I can't wait."

His grin was all male. "Ah, love, you don't have to." Kneeling beside the bed, he closed his mouth over a nipple while his hand worked lazy circles on her.

"Oh…Alex…" She gripped his neck. "Alex…"

With tiny kisses, he made his way to her navel. Her abdomen. She squirmed on the bed. He took his time going lower, then removed his hand and replaced it with his mouth.

She came almost immediately. His heart constricted as he brought her over the climax, intensifying the aftershocks with his tongue. It was the sweetest thing, fulfilling in an unfamiliar way. When he raised his head, she was smiling like a woman in love. He supposed his grin matched hers.

She said simply, "I want more."

"So do I." He stood and dropped his navy boxers to the floor.

"Adam Reincarnated." That's what Lauren thought he looked like, naked, eloquently aroused. Still buzzing from his touch and the mind-numbing explosion of her body, Lauren held out her hand. He took it, kissed it and then knelt on the bed while she scooted over. "How shall we do this? I don't want to hurt your back."

"On my side. But lie flat for a minute."

Gingerly he stretched out on his side, bracing himself on his elbow. Then he began to explore her. Tracing her earlobe. The curve of her jaw. Leaning over and inhaling her scent. "I've never touched anything quite so soft, so silky."

His hand closed over her waist, went to her thigh. Again his knuckles brushed her there, everywhere. She drifted into a state of pure sensation, letting herself wallow in the experience. Her eyes opened when he spoke.

"Lauren, I can't wait any longer."

"Don't, then."

She turned to her side.

He scissored her legs apart.

And, as Adam had to Eve, he slipped into her and altered her world forever.

"You feel so good." He did. Firm. *Hers.*

"You, too." He buried his face in her neck. "Mine," he whispered as he began to move.

It happened impossibly fast again. She spiraled upward, the heat was so intense. He began to thrust. Behind closed lids, colors swirled. The crimson red of passion. Silvery heat. The depths of indigo and mauve. They mixed together as he increased the pace, intensified the force of his thrusts.

Then every color in her head crystallized into its own bright hue, combined into one and burst like fireworks around her.

He came, too, in a shattering climax, repeating, "Lauren, Lauren, Lauren." He gripped her shoulder, holding on to her. It was nothing she'd ever experienced before.

The aftermath was like a rainbow. She bathed in its soothing glow. Crooking his arm, he braced his head. His eyes spoke to her, but he said nothing. She couldn't talk, either, just raised her hand to his jaw. She knew in her heart she'd just done something irrevocable.

His expression said he knew it, too. "Lauren, I know it hasn't been that long. But I think I—"

A door slammed outside the cozy cocoon of the room. "Alex? Alex? It's me."

The call jarred Lauren. What was going on?

"Oh, no," she heard him say. He grabbed the sheet, got them covered, and positioned his body to block hers. She couldn't see who he turned to at the door. It took Lauren a minute for it to sink in that a woman had a key to his house. And it didn't sound like his mother.

It wasn't.

Alex said, "Dana, what are you *doing* here?"

CHAPTER TEN

"Oops." Dana's grin was mischievous and teasing. "Sorry, buddy. I'll…um… I'll be in the kitchen." She backed out of the room.

Damn it. Alex turned to Lauren. At least he'd shielded her from Dana's view. "I'm so sorry." His heart was full to bursting with feelings for the woman next to him. He wanted to savor her, talk about what she meant to him, make…promises. "I don't know what to say."

Her face was scarlet. "I…this has never…oh, God."

Clasping her head to his chest, he chuckled. "First the hut…then the bath last night…now this. I know what you're thinking about me…about us."

Raising her face, she cupped his jaw and gave him a smile that could've melted stone. "I'm thinking this was the most wonderful experience of my life." She closed her eyes. "I just wish we had time to bask in it."

Emotion clogged his throat. "It was the same for me, too, love." He sighed. "But instead of basking in it, or a repeat performance, I think you're gonna have to meet your twin."

Her face grew serious. "She's not my twin, Alex."

"I meant your look-alike." He rolled away, wincing when his back hit the sheets, and got out of the bed.

She turned on her side. "I'll be right out."

Bending over, he kissed her nose. She needed to regroup. "Take your time." He braced his arms on either side of her. "Lauren, I—"

"Go, we'll talk later."

Slipping into his fleece shorts and forgoing a shirt, he headed for the kitchen. Dana was sipping a cup of tea, leaning against the counter. The sun slanted in through the windows, accenting her features. His first thought was how different she looked from Lauren. And it wasn't just the long hair, though that was identical in color to Lauren's. She was about equal height, but much more muscular. In denim shorts and a tank top, her honed body revealed arms that could wrestle the guys at the firehouse to the floor, and legs that could descend a ladder with a grown man over her shoulder. "Well, I blew it," she said, looking up at him.

"No, it's okay." He crossed to her and kissed her on the cheek. "Welcome back."

"I stopped by the firehouse and they said you'd gotten hurt." She touched his arm. "I was worried so I came over, came in without thinking."

He brushed his hand down her hair. It wasn't as silky as Lauren's. "I'm fine."

"Turn around, let me see."

He knew enough not to argue with her, so he pivoted.

"Wow. That's brutal."

"It's a lot better this morning." He felt her cheek on his upper back. They'd always been physical with each other, even after they'd stopped sleeping together, but her closeness felt odd today. He turned around and got a mug from the cupboard. "So, tell me about the seminar."

She grasped his arm. "I will, but wait a sec." He stopped. She nodded to the breakfast stuff lined up on the counter—it was obvious what he'd been planning by the champagne flutes and white napkins. "You into something here?"

"What do you mean?"

"Is, like, this thing with her—who is she anyway?"

"The woman I told you about."

"The one who looks just like me?"

He didn't like the way that sounded. As if that was why he was interested in Lauren. Before he could respond, Dana said, "Alex. The look on your face." Her eyes widened. "Don't tell me this is serious."

He shifted to one foot. "It's not—"

Dana looked past him and gasped.

Turning, he saw Lauren in the archway. She simply stared at Dana, her mouth slightly open, a dazed look on her face. Reaching out, she gripped the archway. The atmosphere seemed charged. Almost electrical. Neither woman moved—except for the eerie shiver that rocked Lauren.

His gaze swung between the two of them. Dana had frozen, too, but as he watched, the same kind of shiver passed through her. Her hand clutched the cup, and her cheeks were pale. She was also wide-eyed.

Alex squeezed Dana's arm, then crossed to Lauren and kissed her forehead. "You all right?"

Staring at Dana, she bit her lip and nodded.

The silence was becoming awkward. He coughed. "Lauren, this is—"

Dana recovered first. She shook off the daze and strode across the room. Up close, the two women looked at each other quizzically—and he was reminded of somebody studying an image in the mirror. Again, the perusal went on long enough to make Alex shift on his feet, though the women's obvious curiosity kept them from being uncomfortable. Finally Dana said, "Holy hell."

Lauren just watched her. Her face was also pale, and her lips trembled.

"I can't believe it," Dana added.

Still, Lauren said nothing. Her grip tightened on the doorway. Alex wanted to enfold her in his arms and reassure her.

Dana stepped back and shrugged. But she never took her eyes off Lauren. "Except for being thinner, and the short hair, you could be my twin."

When Lauren continued to stare, Dana shot a look at Alex. "Um, Alex?"

Reaching out, Alex squeezed Lauren's arm. "Honey, are you all right?"

Finally Lauren seemed to emerge from the trance. "I—I don't know what to say."

Feeling ridiculous, Alex nonetheless said, "Lauren Conway, meet Dana Ivie."

Dana shook her head. "This is spooky."

"I guess."

"Why don't we sit? I'll get coffee." Alex went to the stove, pouring mugs for him and Lauren and retrieved Dana's tea. The two women made their way to the table.

When he placed the coffee in front of her, Lauren looked at it strangely. Fidgeting, Dana picked up the sketch on the table. She frowned. "What's this?"

"I'm redoing my backyard."

"You are?" She examined the drawing. "Why?"

"It's time, is all."

"Alex, you don't know a gladiola from a tulip. We used to joke about people who liked to dig in the dirt." When he said nothing, she cocked her head. "Where did this sudden interest in horticulture come from?"

Alex looked at Lauren. The three sat through another silent, awkward moment. Alex was just about to defuse the situation, when the doorbell rang. Torn, he got up, made his way to the foyer and whipped open the door. On the stoop stood his parents and the Ivies.

He let them in, wondering how the *hell* the morning had turned into such a circus.

THEY WERE LIKE one big happy family—the Ivies and the Shields—Dana flanked by her parents, Alex across from his. Lauren sat at the end of the table feeling like the interloper that she was. It was so familiar, this sense of not belonging, it stunned her. She'd said almost nothing since the four parents had arrived.

Dana kept up a string of commentary, fascinating everybody, making them laugh. "No kidding, Mom. The guy was supposed to be our pseudovictim during the seminar, and he had an angina attack right there on the floor."

"What did you do?" Wes Shields asked. He looked at Dana like a father would a daughter.

"Mouth to mouth." She winked at Alex. "He was yummy, too."

As Dana expounded on her exploits at the EMS

seminar, which were exciting and interesting, she touched Alex's arm frequently, and often directed her comments to him. Lauren had a flashback to when she'd come out to the kitchen: Dana was standing with her cheek against Alex's back. Her face was obscured from Lauren's view, but Lauren could see that it was an intimate, loving gesture.

Alex had turned toward Dana, who was shielded from Lauren's view. She heard Dana say, "Don't tell me this is serious."

His answer had been, "It's not."

"Lauren, are you all right? You went pale again." Alex's tone was concerned.

"Yes, I'm fine."

"Is your coffee cold, dear?" Vera asked. "You're not drinking it."

She glanced down at her mug. "I don't drink coffee."

"Hell. I forgot." Alex blushed. "I'll fix some tea."

Dana threw her chair back. "No, sit. I'll get it. I know my way around."

She knew more than that. *Alex, you don't know a gladiola from a tulip…we used to joke about people who liked to dig in the dirt…*

As she fussed at the microwave, Dana asked, "So guys, what do you think of Lauren looking so much like me?"

Helen rose and crossed to the stove. "It's startling." She ran a hand down Dana's hair and kissed her head. It was such a loving, motherly gesture it made Lauren want to weep. Sara Conway had been demonstrative just like that.

"We missed you so much, dear." Helen obviously

wanted to change the subject. "I hope you don't have to go away again so soon."

Dana hugged her mother, took the tea out of the microwave when it was done, and brought it to Lauren. Standing over her, she addressed her comment to everybody. "I think there are differences between us, don't you?"

When no one responded, the loom became tense. Tim Ivie finally jumped in. "You're more robust, kiddo."

Translated, Lauren had thought, staring up at the other woman who belonged in this kitchen and in this family, it meant Dana was more voluptuous, vibrant and sexy.

Dana laughed, made some comment about beating her dad in arm wrestling and crossed to hug him from behind before she sat again.

Suddenly Lauren needed space. She was suffocating from the tension and the all-too-familiar feeling of not belonging. And she still felt disoriented about her uncanny resemblance to Dana.

Politely she sipped the tea, listened to a bit more small talk, then pushed back her chair. "I've got to go, I have a swimming lesson at nine." She'd called and told the Y she wasn't coming, but now she changed her mind.

Dana's face blanked. "You can't *swim?*"

Well, she was right to be shocked, disgusted, by that. Lauren felt stupid and incompetent and worthless...just like Lily.

She managed to say goodbye and get away from them. Her purse was in the spare bedroom, so she stopped there on her way out. Her breathing was coming fast and she was shaky. *Let me just get out of here,* she thought. *Go home. Think this through.*

In the spare room, her things were scattered all over. She spotted her purse in the corner, picked it up and turned to make her escape.

Alex stood in the doorway. "What's going on?"

She shook back her hair and summoned her pride. "Nothing, I told you I had a swimming lesson."

"Skip it. Stay here with us."

"I don't want to."

"Why?"

Because it's not serious to you. "I'm embarrassed by being caught in bed with you." But it was more than that. "And I'm thrown by how much Dana looks like me. I need time to process this."

His eyes flared with anger. "I thought we were past you running away when you're upset."

"Alex, please." She nodded to her things. "I'll get this stuff later."

He didn't step aside when she reached the doorway. He grasped her shoulders lightly. "Lauren, don't go."

Resting her forehead on his chest, she was flooded by his scent, his presence. He'd changed into shorts and a Courage Bay Fire Department T-shirt. The cotton was soft against her face. "Please, Alex. Just let me go."

He kissed her head. "All right. I'm not happy about this, though."

No, she thought dryly. *Neither am I.*

She left without kissing him goodbye, drove home, changed into her suit and grabbed her stuff for class. But her mind kept drifting back to the scene she'd just left, of people who'd known each other for years, loved each other, belonged together.

She arrived at the Y on time for her lesson. In the pool area, the chlorinated air enveloped her. Cal's face lit up when he saw her. "Hey, I thought you weren't coming."

"Change of plans." She stepped into the water, which didn't scare her anymore.

"Today, we're going to practice rhythmic breathing." He grinned at her. "Come over here, Lauren. You can be my guinea pig."

The lesson went well, and Cal's praise managed to raise Lauren's spirits. After she'd showered and changed in the locker room, she found him waiting for her outside the door. "You did great today," he said.

"Thanks."

"You had breakfast?"

She thought of the champagne and kisses she'd planned to share with the man she had made love with last night. "I haven't, no."

"Wanna hit the diner with me?"

"Why not?" she said, pushing away thoughts of Alex.

They'd reached the Y parking lot when Alex's truck pulled in. He got out of the car gingerly, and she could tell by the stiffness of his gait that he was in pain. He came toward them. His face was pinched and his coloring pale. The sun beating down on his head emphasized how vulnerable he looked.

"Alex, what are you doing here? You're not well yet."

He glanced from her to Cal. "Where are you going?"

"We're having breakfast," Cal said, affectionately tousling Lauren's hair. "Our girl here did great in her lesson, so I'm treating."

Lauren saw Alex's fists curl at his side. "*Our* girl, huh?" he said silkily.

"Yep." Cal smiled.

"Well, that's just great." He didn't mean it as a compliment. With one last look, he turned and strode away.

Go after him, Deirdre urged.

But Lauren didn't.

Lily-livered.

SLAMMING THE DOOR of his house, Alex walked back inside with fire in his eyes. His back hurt and he was exhausted from the short, frustrating trip to the Courage Bay Y. Whipping off his shirt, he lay down on the bed.

That was a huge mistake. Her scent clung to the pillow. Flowery. Female. The scent of them, together, making love, encompassed him. He punched the pillow. The hell with it. He was sick of the seesaw. If she could walk out on him after what they'd shared last night, then she couldn't feel the same as he did. He'd been poleaxed by their lovemaking and had been about to tell her he cared for her—a lot.

He was behaving like a high-schooler with his first girlfriend. He forced himself to think sanely. What the hell had happened?

Well, first, idiot, Dana had a key to your place and Lauren could have mistaken what was going on. And of course she'd been totally rocked by her similarity to Dana.

Did that give her reason to have breakfast with another man? Especially when Alex had planned a sexy little meal with her, after which they would probably have made love again?

His visitors—all of them—had spoiled everything.

He tried to sleep but kept seeing her watch him when he touched her. Kept hearing her whisper his name, holding on as if she couldn't get enough of him.

And then there'd been last night in the tub. Her actions had not been those of a woman cavalierly having sex.

Damn it. He wasn't going to blow this. And he'd be damned if he'd let her go after all that. Abruptly, he got up, put on his shirt and headed for his car.

This wasn't over by a long shot.

LAUREN PULLED INTO Alex's driveway and her heart sank. His car was gone. She'd come back as soon as she could after the interminable breakfast with Cal. All she could think about was Alex, driving into her, calling her name as he loved her. And the way he smelled, how bristly his jaw had been, how his eyes glittered with sexual intensity and with something much more. She concentrated on those images instead of the hurt look on his face when he saw her with Cal this morning. That she viciously pushed from her mind.

She sat in her car a minute, then decided to wait for him. She got out and, after ringing the doorbell just to be sure he wasn't home, she circled the house. His backyard was small but private. She dragged the big chaise into the shade and dropped into it. She was going to deal with this now. And if he came home with Dana, or anybody else, she'd tell him she needed to see him alone. He owed her that much.

Tired, she closed her eyes. She wasn't giving up on Alex. This morning had been a big misunderstanding, and she was going to clear it up as soon as possible.

DAMN IT, Alex thought, driving back home. His earlier hard-won sanity had deserted him. Where the hell was she? It had been two hours since she went to breakfast with the swimming teacher. Alex had freakin' dozed off in the car in her driveway as he waited for her to return. When he'd awakened, sweaty and frustrated, he'd stuck around even longer before deciding to come home.

Where, as he pulled up to his house, he found her car. He shook his head. She'd come here? *Been* here?

He barreled out of the Blazer and hurried into the house. It was quiet, of course. She couldn't have gotten in. He crossed right to the French doors that led to the backyard.

And there she was. Asleep under the tree. His own little Goldilocks. His heart seized up at the sight of her. At the fact that she'd come to him, too.

He pushed the door open and stepped outside. When he reached the chaise, he looked down at her. She was partly on her side, her cheek nestled in the old cushions. She wore a denim skirt and a lacy camisole top, which left her shoulders and upper chest bare. Her skin gleamed in the noon light filtering through the trees. Carefully he sat next to her and brushed a wayward lock of hair out of her face. She stirred. Opened her eyes. "Alex." She took his hand and brought it to her chest. "Mmm."

He flexed his fingers. Leaning over, he kissed her cheek. "You're still sleeping, pretty lady."

She came awake slowly. It was a joy to watch how her skin flushed, how her eyes reached awareness, how her body lost its relaxed pose. She turned her head slightly. "Where..." Then she seemed to remember. She looked up. "What time is it?"

"Almost one."

"Oh." She shook her head and sat up straighter, the action pulling the cotton tightly across her breasts. "I came over as soon as we finished breakfast." Quickly she grabbed his hand tighter. "Alex, I'm sorry."

"Me, too—"

Her hand went to his mouth. "No, let me say this. I...something happened this morning when I met Dana. Some kind of jolt—of awareness or connection. It threw me. Then, you two seemed so close, she seemed so at home here. And when your parents came...you *all* seemed so close, I felt like an outsider...so I left."

"I know, honey. I'm sorry for all that." He stared at her. "But you can't keep running from me when things get tough. I hate it. And there always seems to be another guy waiting in the wings for you—first Hanson, now Smith."

"I wasn't running from you. I just need time to process things."

"All right. I'll work on my patience. But don't leave me like that when you need to do it." He kissed her fingers. "It hurts."

"I'm sorry." She cradled his jaw in her palm. "As long as we're being honest, I need to know some things."

"Anything."

"And I need the truth, Alex."

"I'll tell you the truth."

"I heard Dana ask you if this thing between you and me was serious. You said it wasn't. If that's the case, I have to pull back some. Because—" she bit her lip "—it's serious to me. Just like I knew it would be." Her voice cracked with the last admission.

He replayed the conversation with Dana in his mind. Dana had asked if it was serious between him and Lauren, and he'd started to say, *It's not any of your business.* But she'd interrupted him. "I didn't mean it wasn't serious. She cut me off when I was going to say it wasn't any of her business. You misunderstood, Lauren."

Lauren looked confused. He could see she wanted to believe him.

"It *is* serious, honey. I was going to tell her that when Dana barged in this morning." Reaching out, he brushed back Lauren's bangs. "How could you think anything different after what happened this morning in my bed?"

"I guess, deep down, I don't. But I got confused when I heard…" She sighed. "There's more. I need to know something else. How involved with Dana are you?"

He knew in his gut this was going to be tricky. He also knew he needed to handle it right or Lauren's insecurities would kick in. She could draw the wrong conclusion as to why he wanted *her* now. She might think, as a few others had suggested in veiled hints, that he was interested in her because she looked like Dana. No, he decided firmly. He couldn't risk it now.

He'd tell her, but later when the relationship was on safer ground.

"Alex? You drifted off."

"I'm sorry. Dana and I are friends, sweetheart. That's all." He smiled, though the omission stung. "We have been since we were children."

"You don't have any male-female feelings for her?"

At least he could answer that truthfully. "No, none. I swear to God, I don't."

"You seem so close."

"We are. But not that way."

She bit her lip. "This is hard for me. After James…I don't trust easily."

James…the art exhibit at the LACMA…the show on the pier…

You don't like this, do you? she'd asked.

He'd been teasing. *Should I lie?*

Never lie to me. Or not tell me something.

He banished the memory, concentrating on the fact that he would do what he had to in order to keep her in his life. And now wasn't the time for complete honesty. "Lauren, I swear to God, I have no romantic feelings for Dana." He brushed his knuckles down her cheek. "Don't you realize last night, this morning, in the hut…it meant everything to me. I want you in my life. I care about you. A lot. Already."

"I care about you, too."

He drew her close. "Then come to bed with me. I want to be close like that again. We connect there. We're good together there."

"I know."

But as he led her into the house, guilt niggled at

him, and his conscience warned him that he should
have told Lauren he and Dana had been involved.

And that Dana had dumped him.

THE ROOM was dark, except for the light over his
desk. He stared at the two pictures tacked up on his
bulletin board. One was of Dana Ivie, dressed in turnout gear, a jaunty smile on her lips. Next to it was a
somber Lauren Conway. No smile. But those eyes and
the depth of emotion they revealed was stunning. For
a minute he wished he was somebody else, that he
could court her, explore the layers he saw in the picture.

But of course, he couldn't. The problem had to be
eliminated. And soon. He was unable to stop the train
of events from happening. He couldn't get them back
on track. He'd have to derail them completely. And
maybe, just maybe, he'd get out of this.

CHAPTER ELEVEN

As HE EXITED his Blazer and headed for the firehouse, Alex reveled in the crystal clear morning. The temperature was already high for Courage Bay, with a soft breeze stirring the air. Inside the station house, he thought it odd that no one was in the bay. He strode to his locker and stopped dead. Lauren's cartoon from that day's *Courier* had been blown up and taped to the front of his locker.

Frame One:

Lily in the bleachers, watches the muscle-bound boy, Adam, up at bat. She sighs dreamily. Adam, muscles flexed, cracks the bat on the ball.

Frame Two:

Adam slides into first. *Ouch!*

Frame Three:

Lily sits next to him on the bench. *Does it hurt?*

Adam turns his face away, tears in his eyes. *Uh, no.*

Frame Four:

Lily touches Adam's shoulder. *It's okay to cry.*

Adam is clearly torn. *Boys don't cry.*

Frame Five:

Both sit on the bench. Lily looks sympathetic. *I could kiss and make it better.*

Charmed, Alex smiled broadly. Like hell he and Lauren weren't Adam and Lily. Even the guys at work got it or they wouldn't have put the cartoon up. Though he knew he was in for some razzing, he was lighthearted as he stored his goods on the truck and made his way to the kitchen. Where he was once again stopped in his tracks.

Hell. Copies of the cartoon were plastered all over the fridge and cupboard doors. Ramirez and Kellison sat at the table. "Hey, Shields," Ramirez said, glancing up from the paper.

"Morning, gentlemen."

"How's the burn?" Kellison, the paramedic, asked around his own section of the *Courier*.

"Great. I'm feeling super."

Snickers.

"I'll bet," Ramirez said.

The smell of strong coffee, just brewed, drew Alex to the other side of the room, where he poured himself a mug and ignored their innuendos. He leaned against the counter, sipping the hot, bitter liquid.

Three more firefighters came in. Alvarez, LaSpino and Dana. Greetings all around.

Dana dropped down on a chair and propped her feet up on the seat next to her. "So," she said, winking at LaSpino. "Did she?"

"You talkin' to me?" Alex did his best Robert DeNiro imitation.

She chuckled. "Yeah, Adam, I am."

Snorts from everybody.

Dana's dark eyes widened in sham innocence. "Did she kiss and make it better?"

Shaking his head, Alex didn't take the bait. "The comic is just a cartoon, Ivie." He thought of Lauren's denials of the parallels between her and him and the characters in the strip. Soon he'd get her to admit that truth. His mind drifted to delicious ways to do that. She'd still been asleep when he left her bed this morning. He'd awakened at five to get to work, and taken a few minutes just to watch her. Her delicate features had been relaxed in the early-morning dawn. Her breathing soft and even. Before he left, he'd leaned over and inhaled the flowery scent of her shampoo.

Dana dragged him from his thoughts. "If you're not Adam, I'm the Queen of England."

"Well, Your Majesty," he said, pushing himself off the counter, "I hope you do housework. I'm gonna go put together the assignments." He tossed her an evil grin. "I'll bet I can find a downright nasty chore for you." As he brushed past her, he ruffled her hair. Then he added, "Good to have you back."

He was in his office, where they'd pasted more cartoons on the computer screen and bulletin board, when Dana meandered in. Sitting on his desk while he worked at his computer, she kicked her legs back and forth. "It's serious, isn't it?"

He didn't look at her. "Yeah, I guess."

"Alex?"

"Hmm?"

"Can I ask something without you getting mad?"

"When did that ever stop you?"

"I mean it."

"Okay. Shoot."

"Is it because she looks like me?"

He whipped around in his chair. "No!" He ran a hand through his hair, stung by the comment he'd fully anticipated, probably because he felt guilty keeping their former relationship from Lauren. Besides, it wasn't true. "Hell, Dana, how could you ask me that?"

"I never saw you get sappy over somebody so fast before." She studied the bulletin board. "Actually, I've never seen you sappy." Then she faced him. "I'm not sure I like it."

"I'm not sappy over her." The denial made him feel even more guilty. He sure as hell was sappy.

"You ran after her the other day like a puppy chasing his master."

"She was upset." He studied Dana, noting again the subtle differences between her and Lauren. But there were so many identical features. "Dana, did you feel anything when you met her?"

"Like what?"

"Some connection, maybe."

"Just because we look similar, doesn't mean we're, like, related. *Twins separated at birth,*" she quipped with theatrical flourish. Angling his chair, he leaned back and put his feet up on the desk. Dana stood and began to rub his neck.

"Your mother tell you about the photographs?"

"Coincidence."

"How about the missing birth records from Courage Bay Hospital when you were born?"

"Computer glitch."

"Seems pretty coincidental to me. Mom's worried."

"Vera's a scientist—she can't stand unsolved puzzles. She won't leave the house until she finishes the crossword in the morning."

"I'm worried, Dana."

"Yeah, 'cause of Lily." She kneaded his shoulder blades. "Is that why your muscles are so tense?"

"I…this thing about you looking alike, I feel there's more to it."

"Alex—"

The PA crackled loudly before Dana could finish her comment. "Vehicle accident on freeway exit ramp at Washington Avenue. Truck One, Engine One, Paramedic One, go into service."

Agile and fast, Dana bounded out of the office like a knight charging into battle, while Alex waited for the printout. When it came through, he raced to the bay. Everybody was on the rigs. Kicking off his shoes, he dived into his bunker pants and boots and hopped into shotgun position on Truck Two. As Ramirez sped out behind the medical vehicle, followed by the engine, he paraphrased the report. "Woman and baby trapped in two-door sedan. Apparently she lost control of the car and crashed into the cement wall on the exit. There's a warning about a compromised gas tank. Car's nosedived into the wall and tipped at a ninety-degree angle."

Above the roar of the sirens, Dana asked tightly, "How old's the kid?"

"Police report a car seat, so little, I'd guess."

Everybody was silent. Losing a child was one of their greatest fears.

At the scene, lights flashed from two police black-and-whites, as officers directed traffic around a teal-blue, two-door Cavalier butted up against the cement wall supporting the freeway. It was tipped up at an angle, with the trunk in the air. Alex bounded out of the truck while Dana and Ramirez began to remove air bags, chocking and Hurst tools from the back. He jogged quickly to where a police officer stood by the wreck. "Hank, any signs of life?"

The young beat cop was chalk-white. "Lady's

moaning." He gulped. "Kid in the back seat was crying, but no more."

Traffic whizzed by them while all the firefighters and paramedics approached Alex and awaited orders.

"Get chocking and air bags under the back end," he told LaSpino and Ramirez. "Robertson and North, start the generators and get ready to pop the doors if they're stuck. We can't try them till the car's braced." He faced Begay. "Will, your men should get the water ready in case the gas tank goes." Two guys were already pulling a hose out of the rig. "Kellison and Gonzales, stand by for the victims."

He turned to Dana, an EMT and the smallest among them. "Get ready to go in."

"If the guys just held up the back end, I could hop up now." Dana looked at him searchingly. "The kid's in there."

"Wait till it's secured, Ivie. That's an order."

Dana sometimes rushed headlong into things, executing heroic acts of bravery without concern for her own safety. When the wooden blocks and the inflated air bags were finally in place, each crew member took a section of the car to brace it further. If the chocking slipped with Dana inside, she and the passengers could be injured. Alex checked the doors first. Stuck. Then, donning heavy gloves, he hopped up on the slanted hood and picked most of the glass out of the front window. He hoisted Dana up and watched her crawl through it.

After a minute, she said, "Woman seems okay. ABCs—" airways, breathing and circulation "—are in safety range. We need a headboard and backboard."

While the two paramedics got the equipment, Alex

said, "Check the kid," but she was already climbing over the front seat. After another minute, she called out, "Baby's breathing slow. Pulse low. We need to get her out of here, Alex."

Kellison told her, "Do a jaw thrust so the kid'll breathe easier."

"Already am."

The sound of a generator split the air. In minutes the door was popped. Kellison leaned in. "Give me the collar." Though it took time, it was important to stabilize the victim before moving her to prevent spinal injury that could result in paralysis. Meanwhile, the baby began to cry.

"Shh, little one," Dana crooned over the grating sound.

As Kellison worked, Alex yelled, "What do you need, Dana?"

"A knife so I can spring the car seat. The belt won't budge. Kid's lungs are in good shape."

"We'll have to take the roof off and lift her out." Alex was frustrated. "The car seat won't fit through the front bucket seats and we can't risk removing the baby without it." He gave orders to LaSpino. "As soon as we get the mother free, we'll pop the hood."

The engine crew assisted with the backboard and, when the mother was out, turned her over to Gonzales.

Alex felt the car shift under his feet as he took the Jaws of Life from Ramirez and began work on the roof. Dana had already covered herself and the baby with a Mylar blanket, which would protect them from flying fragments. With the added noise of screeching metal, the baby cried louder.

It took long minutes and backbreaking exertion before Alex had the roof cut and peeled back. Dana held up the baby seat, and Alex hoisted it out. The kid was still crying.

Begay and LaSpino took the child from Alex before he gingerly climbed off the hood. "Okay, Ivie, come on."

Slowly Dana climbed out of the car onto the hood and jumped down—right into Alex's arms. He held her tight, feeling her heart pounding, the same tattoo as his. Anything could have happened to her, or to him—the gas tank exploding, the car falling…

Dana pulled away, the rush of adrenaline bright in her chocolate-brown eyes. "We make a good team, Shields. We always have."

LAUREN WIPED the sweat off her face with the hem of her T-shirt. She was glad she'd dressed in shorts and a tank top, since noonday the sun had elevated the temperature to at least eighty. A small tree partially shaded her, thank goodness, but she was afraid she'd burned her nose and arms. She'd sweated off her sunscreen.

The rich topsoil, which Alex had dumped in the garden section of his backyard, felt moist in her hands. On her knees, she worked in fertilizer and peat moss as he drifted in and out of her mind all morning. Things couldn't be better between them. He'd been so attentive in bed last night, so tender yet insistent. Her heart skipped a beat remembering how he touched her. As she finished with the last of the soil, she smiled. Men usually treated her like spun glass. Alex treated her like a woman. Actually, she acted more like a strong, independent woman with him.

Like in the hut. Or the bathtub.

"Lauren?"

She glanced over her shoulder to find him in the arch of the open French doors, wearing denim shorts and a white T-shirt. She'd title him "Sexual Magnetism, Personified." She smiled. "Hi."

He leaned against the jamb. "What are you doing here?"

"I decided to come over and work on the garden. I got up early and went to buy the plants." She glanced to the side at the array of geraniums and marigolds and begonias, spread out for placement in the garden. Their sweet scent had kept her company all morning.

"Didn't you go to the paper today?"

"No. I'm working all day tomorrow on some layouts for Perry." Looking up at him from the ground, she shaded her eyes with her hand. "How was your shift?"

Sauntering outside, he dropped down into a chair. "Super. We were called to a car accident and saved a baby." His face lit from within and there was a special glow about him. She wondered briefly if all firefighters got to feel that kind of satisfaction.

"How wonderful."

"If I knew you'd be here, I would've come right home after I got off work."

"I didn't expect you to do that. Though I thought you might be here sleeping."

"I was too pumped. Dana and I went for breakfast, then I helped her do some stuff at her house."

Lauren tried to quell the spurt of reaction she felt in her stomach. He'd been with Dana all morning. She looked down at her hands.

We joked about people who liked to dig in the dirt.

Leaning over, he brushed a finger down her nose. "You got a burn. How long have you been in the sun?"

"What time is it?"

"Almost one."

"A while, I guess." Hours, actually. Again she glanced at the garden. "I got a lot done."

"Yeah. It looks great." He swiped at her arm. "You're burned here, too, honey."

She smiled at his endearment.

He frowned. "You had any water or anything all morning?"

"Um, I guess not. I love gardening and I didn't think about it."

"Well, the door was locked, so you couldn't have gotten in anyway." The frown deepened to a scowl. "I don't like that you might get dehydrated or need to use the john, and you can't."

Shrugging, she laid a hand on his knee. "I'm fine. I'm just going to finish with these geraniums, then I'll stop."

He stood. "All right."

She turned back to the garden and put in the last of plants. Before she could do any more, she saw a plastic cup in her line of vision. "Here," he said, "drink this."

She sat back on her heels and took the cup. The ice water felt frigid on her throat. She hadn't realized how parched she was. When she finished, she handed him back the glass. He dropped down onto the ground with her. A tube in his hand, he squeezed out some green gel. Its scent was flowery.

"What's that?"

"Aloe vera." He rubbed it on her nose and worked a little into her cheeks. It cooled her face in seconds.

"Ahh."

He smiled, then rubbed some on her arms. The ointment took the sting away almost immediately.

"Thanks."

He capped the tube, set it on the ground and reached in his pocket. Taking her hand, he placed something metal in it, then closed her fist over it and kissed her knuckles. Puzzled, she opened her hand. A key nestled in her palm.

Surprise—and something else—made her heart catapult in her chest. It didn't mean that much, just that she'd be working in the garden and might need to get into his house. But it felt big. Very big. She'd never had a key to a man's house before, not even James's.

Still she quelled her reaction. "Oh, thanks. I can use this when I work out here and you're not home."

He tipped her chin. The expression on his face was soft and tender. "It's not just for that, love."

"No?"

He shook his head.

Huge powerful feelings for this man swelled inside her. From her knees, she launched herself at him. He hugged her tight, telling her he felt them, too. Letting her know that he meant the gesture to be significant. "Lauren." She felt his hand smooth down her hair.

She nuzzled into him. They stayed that way, relishing in the feel of each other, in the new level their relationship had just reached until her cell phone rang.

"Don't get it," he whispered softly.

"All right."

Standing, he drew her up. Took her hand. Without speaking, they went into the house.

It wasn't till later, after exquisite lovemaking, that she checked her messages. One was from James. A disturbing same old, same old.

The next was equally disturbing. "Lauren, this is Vera Shields. It's about one o'clock on Monday. I was wondering if I could see you, Alex and the Ivies today. Something's happened." Her voice cracked, making Lauren tense. "I have some news…I found out something…oh, hell, this needs to be shared in person. I'd like to meet at the Ivies' home before suppertime. Please try to come. It's important."

A chill coursed through Lauren.

Something was wrong. She just knew it.

LAUREN GRIPPED Alex's hand as they entered the Ivies' house around five. Vera's phone call had really upset her and she needed Alex as her anchor. Like the last time, they went inside without ringing the doorbell. Again, everyone was assembled on the back porch. The Ivies sat together on the love seat. Dana, dressed in tight white jeans and a peach scooped top, paced off to the side. Alex's dad sat on the couch. His mom was standing by the sliding doors. Alex let go of Lauren's hand and went to kiss his mother. Vera's pretty face was strained. "Mom?" he said softly.

"It's okay, sweetie. Just sit down."

Alex's father scooted over on the opposite couch. "Come sit here, buddy. You, too—"

Before he could finish, Dana dropped onto the cushion next to Alex. Lauren noticed she sat very close to him. Alex's gaze flew to Lauren's, and she smiled weakly, then took a chair alone on the opposite side of the room.

Vera clasped her hands together and faced them. "You all know I was going to look into this uncanny resemblance between Lauren and Dana. You also know I couldn't find the hospital records of Dana's birth here in Courage Bay. What you don't know is that I did get some information on births at Los Angeles Hospital. Five baby girls were born that week. Only one was in the hospital on Lauren's birthday. She was born a month early."

"It was me," Lauren said automatically.

Vera gave her a shaky smile. "Let's hope so. But," she looked sympathetically from Lauren to Dana, "there were three girls born in Courage Bay on your birthday, Dana."

"Not uncommon." Tim Ivie's voice was gruff.

"No," Vera said. "Except two were twins. Identical."

The air seemed to leech out of the room. No one spoke. They all stared at Vera. Finally Helen Ivie broke the silence. "That doesn't mean much. We can get in touch with the twin girls and put an end to this speculation." She frowned. "Did you find the records of who they were?"

"No. I tracked down a nurse who worked here then. The records are still missing. But she remembered the three babies, especially the twins, because they were a month early and she was assigned to care for them."

"Is she sure of the dates? If it was that long ago?" Alex asked.

"Yes. The twins were born on her daughter's birthday."

"We'll find the twins anyway." Helen sounded confident.

"You can't, Helen. I'm sorry. They died a few days after they were born. The nurse remembers all this because she was heartbroken over such a surprising and shocking turn of events. Both babies, she said, were healthy despite being born early."

Helen stood. "Well, I know I had one child. I was awake during the birth, and Tim was there. I couldn't possibly have had two babies. What are you thinking, Vera? That I had twins and someone took one of them away and said I only had one? That's ludicrous."

"And I've got the videotape of my birth," Lauren put in. It *was* ludicrous, but nonetheless scared her. "I'm certain I was a single birth, too."

"I know this is upsetting," Vera said. "But given the facts that Lauren and Dana look so much alike, that twins were born on Dana's birthday and that the birth records are missing, I don't see how we can ignore all this."

Lauren felt like the world was spinning. But damn it, she was going to stay in control. She tossed back her head and straightened her shoulders. "What would you like to do about this, Vera?"

"Well, we could take a look at your videotape and the first birth photos of both of you." She hesitated. "But I'd also recommend DNA testing because it's the only sure way to know anything."

Dana, who'd been silent, bolted off the couch. "What the hell are we looking for? You can't possibly assume that babies were mixed up." She shot her mother an anxious look. "These are my parents, Vera. And I don't want to know anything else."

Helen stood, and so did Tim. They started to cross to her.

Dana held up her hand. "No, Mom, don't. I need

some air.'' Reaching down, she took Alex's hand and tugged on it. ''Come with me, Alex, I want to talk this through with you.''

So did Lauren.

Again, Alex looked over at her.

Dana stepped in front of him, effectively blocking his view. ''Alex, please!'' Her voice rose and she began to tremble.

Looking torn, Alex got off the couch and followed Dana out.

Quietly Wes Shields stood and crossed to Lauren. ''Are you all right?''

Still staring after Alex, trying to calm her thrumming heart, she shook her head. ''No, actually, I'm reeling from Vera's news.'' And from the fact that now that Dana was back, Alex's priorities seemed... different.

CHAPTER TWELVE

ALEX SAW HER about a hundred yards ahead and picked up his pace. Even from a distance, he could tell by the set of her shoulders and the downward tilt of her head that she was upset. When he'd returned from calming Dana down, Alex's mother had told him Lauren had gone for a walk with his dad.

When he was close enough, he called out, "Lauren, wait up." He sucked in his breath. They'd been making such progress in overcoming their differences and her fears, and he was afraid this would make her backtrack.

Stopping in the muted six o'clock light, she turned and gave him a sad smile. She looked even more fragile in the white eyelet sundress she wore with strappy sandals too delicate to be walking in. He jogged up to them.

"Hi, son." His father rested his hand on Lauren's shoulder. The tender gesture made something inside Alex shift.

"Dad." He zeroed in on Lauren. "Hi."

"Hi."

His father coughed. "I'll be heading back." He smiled at Lauren. "Remember what we discussed, young lady."

"Thank you, Wes."

With his dad gone, she faced Alex. "I wasn't running away. I just needed to clear my head."

Reaching out, he cradled her face in his palm. "I'm so sorry, honey."

"It's okay."

"No, it's not." In front of the old Manson house, he tugged her close. Briefly he reveled in the scent of her lotion and lemon shampoo. Clean, womanly.

"I didn't want to leave you," he told her.

"I know." She mumbled the words against his chest.

"I'm glad Dad was with you."

"He was worried about me being alone out here, after all that's gone on. And your mother's discovery upset me." She looked up at him, worry in her eyes. "This isn't good, Alex. Something's wrong. I can feel it. Actually, I think I sensed it all along, especially after I met Dana."

He took her hand and they started walking back toward the house.

"How's Dana?" she asked without rancor.

"A total wreck." He hesitated, wondering how much to tell Lauren, knowing he needed to give her some explanation. "I'm sorry I left with her, but she was really freaked, and it's…a pattern with her."

"A pattern?"

"Uh-huh. All our lives, since she was five and I was seven, whenever something went wrong, we'd go somewhere and hash it out." He smiled, remembering. "Our tree hut when we were little. The woods later on. She used to come down and climb in my bedroom window when were teens."

"You have a history, I know. But…" She stopped. "I have to be honest. I felt bad when you left with her." She shook her head. "God, this sounds selfish. But I was upset, too. I needed you, too."

He liked hearing the last part. "I'm so sorry. Dana gets clingy when things aren't going well."

Her eyes narrowed at that, then she shook it off. "Let's drop it. I understand, really I do." They began walking again, and he grasped her hand more firmly in his, loving the suppleness of it, the hidden strength of it.

"What did you and my dad talk about?"

"You, mostly. My parents. He thinks maybe Dana's handling this worse than me because she loves Helen and Tim and doesn't want to ever consider that they aren't…" She stopped. "They're suffering, too, I know." She drew in a breath and smoothed her hair with her fingers. "I wish my parents were here to help sort all this out. They were always good at these kinds of things. Supportive whenever I had a problem."

It made him feel worse, hearing about how alone she was in the world. He brought their clasped hands to his mouth and kissed her fingers. "I'll be there for you through this, I promise."

"You already have been. I appreciate it." A man walking a dog trundled past them. After he got by, Lauren cleared her throat. "Alex, your mother's right. The simplest way to solve this is through DNA testing."

"I know."

She sighed. "I wish this was over."

"You probably wish you'd never set foot in Courage Bay."

They walked for a long time and she didn't say anything. Finally she let go of his hand and slid an arm around his waist, nestling her head against him. "No, Alex, I don't regret coming here. How could I?"

He let out a relieved sigh.

A jogger approached them from the other direction. It was Dana, dressed in running clothes. When she got close, she shook back her hair. Her gaze dropped to where Lauren hugged Alex's waist. "Am I interrupting?"

"No," Lauren said. "Walk with us. We can talk."

"Uh-uh. I'm just out for a run."

Lauren reached out to her, but Dana shrank from the contact. Still, Lauren asked, "Are you all right?"

Dana looked at Alex. "No, I'm not." Her voice was tremulous. "Your mother said…the DNA testing…" She stared back at Lauren then. "Identical twins have identical DNA. I can't believe it, I don't want to believe it. Mom and Dad—they mean everything to me." She glanced around wildly. "Never mind." And she took off at a dead run.

Alex stared after her. "Goddamn it. She's losin' it."

"Go after her."

"*What?*"

"Go after her."

He shook his head. "No, I won't leave you again."

"Like I said, I'm doing better with this than she is." She gestured ahead. "We're not far from the Ivies' house. I'll walk back there. I'll be fine." She gave him a brave smile. "Go after her. You'll never forgive yourself if you don't and something happens to her."

"Do you have any idea how special you are?"

"You can tell me later. Now go."

After a moment he took off. The woman was amazing, he thought, as he ran after Dana. He wanted to stay with *Lauren*. Comfort *Lauren*. God, he hoped she understood that.

LAUREN STARED at the blank cartoon fields. It was time to give Lily more in her life.

Frame One:

Deirdre finds Lily on a bench. *Hey, girlfriend, where's the muscle-bound boy?*

Lily sticks her chin out. *I don't know. I don't spend all my time with him, you know.*

Deirdre raises her eyebrows. *I would.*

Lily faces the reader. *He'd like her better anyway.*

Disgusted, Lauren balled up the paper and tossed it at the wastebasket. She glanced at the clock on the living-room wall. Seven. And Alex hadn't come over or called. She'd gone back to the Ivies and asked Wes to take her home since she didn't have her car. Fibbing, she'd told them Alex knew she'd be leaving. They'd invited her to stay for dinner, but she said she wanted some time alone. Since the Shields had walked from their house to the Ivies, Wes had driven her home in Alex's Blazer.

She really wanted to be with Alex.

And he was with Dana.

The doorbell rang. *Thank God.* She flew to the security system and disarmed it, then whipped open the door. Only to find Toby Hanson on her porch. "Hey, Lauren."

"Toby? What are you doing here?"

He shrugged. "I don't know. I was driving by and saw your lights on."

"You live on the other side of town."

"It's a nice night. I went for a drive." He jammed his hands in his pockets. Sometimes he was really shy, but tonight he seemed…jittery. "Can I come in for a while?"

"Um, sure, I guess."

For some reason she felt uncomfortable letting him into her house. She fixed him tea—he liked it as much as she did—then they sat in the living room.

When the cats came in to join them, he sneezed. "I'm allergic."

"Sorry." She picked up the kittens, shut them in her bedroom, then returned. "You seem upset."

"I had a run-in with Perry. About my career path."

"Oh, dear."

He pushed up his glasses with his finger. "I don't know. People…sometimes…they underestimate me."

"You're a nice guy. That happens a lot to people like you."

"You're like that."

"Yeah, and people underestimate me, too."

They talked a while longer but she was relieved when Toby finally left. Pacing, she decided this was stupid and called Alex's cell phone. His voice mail came on. "Shields. Leave a message."

Briefly she told the machine she was worried, then disconnected. Crossing the room, she dropped down into the hammock with the phone cradled in her palm. In the next half hour, she tried two more times to reach him. Then she put the phone onto the floor and closed her eyes. Though it was only nine, she felt drained by the events of the day.

She awoke, startled, to pounding on the front door. The room was dark, but she could make out the clock on the TV. Midnight.

Her heart thundered in her chest. She slid out of the hammock. Had she locked the door after Toby left? Put the alarm on? Her gaze rested on the system. There was no red light to indicate she'd set it. In the darkness, she crept to the door and saw that the new dead bolt wasn't in place. Damn. Gingerly she reached out and flicked the lock.

"Lauren?" she heard from outside. "It's me, Alex."

She exhaled with relief and yanked open the door. He stood before her. His face was drawn, his hair disheveled.

"What happened? Where have you been? I tried your cell phone several times."

"I've been at the hospital. My father was in a car accident, driving back in my truck after dropping you off. He's okay, but he swears the Blazer was run off the road."

LAUREN WENT WITH Alex to visit his father in the hospital the next morning—he had a concussion so they kept him overnight—and stayed with Wes while Alex took his mother home to get cleaned up and pack a change of clothes. They expected him to be released in a few hours.

"I feel terrible this happened to you after you took me home," she told Wes when they were alone.

"Don't feel bad, Lauren." The older man's bushy brows knit over his dark eyes. Alex had told her he'd been a tough firefighter who never slowed down even when he was injured. "It didn't seem like an accident."

"Alex told me that." She reached out and squeezed his arm. "I don't know what to think."

"I'm not the most popular kid on the block, but can't say I got any enemies who'd wanna do me harm." He chuckled. "My diner's taking business away from the one down the street, but hell..." He jammed his hand through his hair, a mannerism Alex had inherited. "Doesn't make a lot of sense to me."

"I'm sorry." There was a knock at the open door. Dr. Yube stood in the entrance. "Am I intruding?"

Alex's father stiffened. The reaction was subtle, but Lauren caught it. "No, George, come on in."

Lauren smiled. "Hello, Dr. Yube."

Dr. Yube's return smile was warm and fatherly. "Call me George, please." He crossed to the bed. "What happened, Wes?"

In a surprisingly curt tone, Wes explained the situation. Lauren remembered that George and Vera Shields were friends and that he was helping her track down the missing hospital records. But Wes obviously didn't like the man. "Anything I can do?" Yube asked.

"Not that I know of. Except maybe light a fire under my doc to spring me earlier."

"I'll see what I can do." Yube excused himself and left, just as Dana raced like a whirlwind through the door.

"Oh, my God, Wes?" Dana hurried to the bed and elbowed Lauren out of the way. "Are you all right?"

"Yeah, honey, of course I am." He kissed her forehead.

Dana looked up. "What are you doing here?"

"I came with Alex."

"Where is he?"

Forcing herself to be patient, Lauren told her. Then, purposefully, Lauren guessed, Dana turned her back to Lauren, sat on the side of the bed and began talking softly to Wes.

Feeling as excluded as she was meant to, Lauren stood. "I think I'll get something to drink."

Outside Wes's room, she bumped into George Yube. "Lauren, hi."

"Hello again."

"You look like you could use some coffee. Or tea, perhaps." He took hold of her elbow. "Come on to the lounge, I'll get you some there."

"That's not necessary."

"You seem distressed." He checked his watch. "I have a few minutes." He edged her down the corridor into the staff lounge, which was empty. It smelled like toast and eggs. A breeze wafted through the open windows. "Sit." He made tea and sat with a cup of his own. "Are you close to the Shields, Lauren?"

"Not really. I know their son best." She sighed. "Dana's practically like their daughter."

"You...do look like her." He scowled. "It's got Vera upset. That and the missing records from this hospital."

"Tell me about it."

He arched a brow. "Do you want to talk about anything? We don't know each other, but I have two daughters, and they tell me I'm a good listener. You look like you could use a friend."

"Truthfully, there's not much to tell. Everything keeps pointing to Dana and me being related. Only, we're both sure our parents gave birth to single babies, so it's confusing..." The thought of Sara and John Conway not being her real parents hit her with volcanic force. Her eyes filled. "I'm sorry, I just can't believe my parents aren't..." She couldn't finish.

He grasped her hand and squeezed it. "You don't know anything for sure. Maybe it's just some bizarre coincidence."

"Vera thinks we all should take DNA tests."

"Hmm." He scowled. "Are you going to?"

"I don't know. I wish my parents were alive. They'd know how to advise me."

"I'm here, Lauren, if you need an unbiased opinion."

"What do you mean?"

"Well, the Shields are involved in this because of their friendship with the Ivies. Maybe everybody's too close to the situation and not thinking straight."

"You don't think we should do the DNA testing?"

"Sometimes it's best to leave things alone. Not stir the waters."

This seemed like an odd comment from someone who was helping Vera locate the missing information. "Maybe." But she didn't see how that was ever going to happen.

It was nice, though, to have someone so concerned about her. Even if he was almost a stranger.

AS THE SEXY SOUND of reggae music blasted from the speaker system, Alex watched Dana throw herself into the dance steps. It didn't take an Einstein to figure out what she was doing. What she *had* been doing all week.

"What's gotten into her?" Will Begay asked from beside him. "She's been as wired as a junkie jonesing on crack."

Alex let out a heavy breath. "It's this thing with Lauren."

"Dana's jealous." It wasn't a question.

Alex had been hoping Dana's possessiveness was a result of the situation. But Will's somber honesty elicited his own. "Yeah, maybe."

Hesitating, Will rested a hand on Alex's shoulder. "Be careful, my friend." He scanned the area. Night had fallen and tiny pinpricks of stars twinkled down on them. "Where's Lauren?"

"She went for a walk with your wife. I think they're talking Native American art."

Just then Dana, wearing a bathing-suit top and skintight white shorts, jogged over and tugged at Alex's arm. "Come on, buddy. Let's do the *but-ter-fly*." Tilting her hips, thrusting them forward, she mimicked both the Jamaican accent and the dance step. It was something they'd learned on a trip they'd taken together to the Caribbean. He'd been opposed to coming to this beach party some of the cops were throwing because he thought the Jamaican theme might remind Dana of their trip and make her even more clingy. He also worried that Dana might upset Lauren, as she had all week.

"No, thanks, you go ahead."

"Party pooper," she said, taking a swig of his beer.

He got irritated at her surliness. "Lay off, Dana."

Her eyes lit with fire. He used to think it was sexy when she got mad like this.

Now he backed away. "I'm going to look for Lauren."

"When did you get so pussy-whipped that you won't even dance with your friends?" she snapped.

"Can it, Dana." He turned and walked down to the beach, letting the soft lapping of the ocean calm him.

Things weren't going well all-around. The DNA

thing had upset everybody, especially Dana, so it had been put on hold. But overriding that was his dad's accident. Vince Wojohowitz had visited Alex at the firehouse two days after it happened...

His friend had settled his big frame into a chair in Alex's office. "I don't think this was an accident."

"Well, Dad thought maybe he was run off the road, so you're probably right. I've tried to rationalize that Dad could have enemies, but it doesn't make sense, does it?"

"No." Vince's tone was gentle. "It makes more sense that somebody was after you."

"Because of Lauren, right? You think they knew Lauren was in the car."

"Good chance of that." He hesitated. "This all adds up, Alex. The fire. The brakes. Now a car accident. Hawk Longstreet should be watching her."

"I'll talk to her about it..."

And so Lauren was to be put under surveillance, starting tomorrow when Hawk and his partner could be freed up. Meanwhile, a cop was shadowing her when Alex wasn't around.

Dana's comments hadn't helped...

"Somebody's watching her?" she'd said when she found out about the surveillance. They were cleaning up in the bay. "Jeez, she's a weak little darling, isn't she? Can't even take care of herself."

"What's with you, Dana?" She sounded like a jealous shrew.

"I'm not crazy about her, is all." She shrugged. "She's not your type anyway, so I don't understand why you're so hot over her."

He'd stalked away before he told her off, knowing

she was hurting over the Ivies' worry and her own. He didn't want to make things worse.

He was distracted by Lauren coming down the beach with Mareeta, and the cop trailing behind. He smiled. The two women were deep in discussion, their heads close together. Lauren had been a trouper through all this, bravely facing up to Vince's conclusions, giving Dana some slack. Especially at the boating party two days ago, held down by the marina. The fund-raiser was put on every year by local businesses and organizations to support different projects around the community. There had been competitions all day long…

"Take me skiing in the next heat," Dana had said when he and Lauren were heading for his father's boat.

"Don't you have somebody else to do it? We're going for a cruise."

"I want you, buddy." She socked his arm. Then her eyes widened at Lauren. "Oh, I forgot. You can't swim. Would you be…*scared* if Alex was driving fast enough for me to ski?"

"I wouldn't be scared, Dana. And I'd love to see you compete."

Once on the boat, Lauren stared back at Dana slaloming behind them, doing every fancy twist and turn she knew. "She's good at everything."

"Yeah, she's pretty athletic." He'd studied Lauren, loving the way the sun had turned her nose and cheeks pink and the way her eyes glimmered in the afternoon light. The breeze played havoc with her hair. "Feeling okay?"

"Hmm. The motion sickness medicine works like a charm." She glanced down at her foot, revealing her pink sneakers. Then she yanked on her life jacket. "Soon, I'm not going to need one of these."

With his free arm, he yanked her close by the straps of the vest. "You look adorable." He kissed her nose. "Besides, everybody needs one in a boat."

"No, everybody wears one, but they don't need one like me." She touched his hair. He loved how she always did that—felt him, smelled him, experienced him. "You're going to ski, aren't you?" she asked.

"I might not this year."

"Please, don't back out because of me."

"I wasn't." He'd grinned. "It's just that every time I leave you alone, I come back and some guy's sniffin' around you." He pretended affront. "Especially Hanson and Smith. They're both here today." He rolled his eyes. "And pretty soon I gotta worry about Longstreet."

She punched his arm lightly. "Don't look for excuses. I'd really like to see you ski. Please, Alex."

And so he'd competed, and won, and Lauren had cheered him on all the way—and congratulated Dana for her victory, too.

"Looking for somebody, sailor?" Lauren had reached him. Tonight she wore a flowing dress that gradually changed from deep pink at the top to lighter pink at the hem. Mareeta was by her side. The cop following waved to Alex to let him know Lauren was now in his charge.

He'd grasped Lauren around the waist. "You, pretty lady."

"I like that."

"I like you." He kissed her hard.

"Don't mind me, guys," Mareeta quipped. "I'll be on my way."

When Will's wife left, Alex kept Lauren close. "Let's go for a walk on the shore."

"To the hut?" she whispered, her voice satiny in the starry night.

"The hut? Oh, God, don't mention the hut. You know what that does to me."

She stepped in closer and brushed a hand down his front. "Uh-huh. Come on, let's go find our place. It'll be fun." She patted his fanny. "You got a condom in there?"

"Um—yeah." She made him stutter like a probie.

They took their time meandering down the beach, joking, teasing, stealing kisses. But when they got inside the infamous hut, and her fingers went to his shirt, he grasped her hands. Held them close to his heart. "I want to talk a minute."

She put her mouth near his. "After."

"No, love, now." His tone was grave and she stepped back.

"What?"

His hand trembled as he lifted it to her face. There was just enough moonlight through the open slats to reveal her expression clearly. "I want to tell you something."

She looked at him expectantly and his heart did a little two-step.

"Something's happened to me."

"It has?"

"Uh-huh. And you gotta help me."

"Alex, of course. I'd do anything for you."

"I'd do anything for you, too."

She smiled.

"Because I've fallen in love with you, Lauren."
When she stilled—completely—he kissed her. "I just
wanted you to know."

Starlike tears sparkled in her eyes. "Oh, Alex."

"I know it's only been a few weeks and it's too
soon to tell you this. And I don't expect any declarations back. But I want you to know what's going
on inside me. With all this mess happening…things
are tough…but…" He shrugged. "I…"

She raised shaky fingers to his mouth. "Shh. Let
me talk."

He held his breath.

"I love you too, Alex," she said simply.

HE WATCHED from behind the trees. His plan had
backfired, and now she had a bodyguard—a goddamn
cop had been tailing her all night. He could still try
to eliminate Shields, but he might be better off chang-
ing tactics. His fist curled. He had to do something,
couldn't let this happen. He pounded the bark with
his fist. He wouldn't lose now. Not after all this time.

CHAPTER THIRTEEN

"I LOVE YOU, Alex, so much." On his bed, in the dark, she leaned over his chest and brushed back a stray lock of hair from his forehead. It was damp, his skin was sweaty, his cheeks ruddy. And his amber eyes glowed with emotion. Clearly this picture would be "Man In Love."

"Being together is different, isn't it?" he said hoarsely as he ran his knuckles over her bare shoulder.

"Yes. I..." She hesitated. "I've said I love you to men before. But it never meant *this* to me, Alex."

"Me, too, sweetheart. I've said those words, too, but I didn't feel like this." He closed his eyes and sighed. "It affects the sex."

Rolling off him, she lay back into his navy-blue pillows, and smiled. "Tell me about it. The whole thing was incredible." She nudged his shoulder. "You're incredible."

His chest rumbled. "Me? Where'd you learn how to do that last thing with your mouth? I thought I was going to go up in smoke."

"Nowhere. It just came naturally, felt right."

He eased over and braced himself on his elbow, looking down at her. His jaw had been scratchy on her body. "Does the whole thing feel right for you now?"

"Yes, it does. I'm so glad you didn't give up." She batted her eyes. "You bring out a whole new side of me."

"How is that?"

"Mischievous. Sexy. Adventurous."

"More like Dee."

Rolling her eyes, she said, "It's just a cartoon, Alex."

He laughed. "I like how you are with me, too."

"Oh, good, because I want to know."

"Know what?"

"Who else you told you loved."

He stiffened, almost imperceptibly. If his body hadn't been aligned with hers, she wouldn't have caught it.

"Does that make you nervous, Alex?"

"No, but, I, um…"

"I'll tell you first. James of course. Since we were engaged. And a guy in high school."

"High school?"

"Yeah, after the senior ball. We, you know, *did it.* He said he loved me. I said I loved him. We'd been going together for a year."

He smiled. "I wish I'd known you then."

Her finger traced a little scar on his arm. "Don't try to sidetrack me. Who were they?"

She saw him swallow and couldn't fathom why on earth this would be hard for him. Finally he said, "I've had a few serious relationships in my life. But I only told one woman I loved her. In my twenties. We were involved for a long time."

"What happened?"

"We grew bored with each other."

"Who broke it off?"

"Hell, I don't want to talk about this while I'm in bed with you, woman."

Giggling, she reversed their positions. "I can't believe it. Somebody dumped you?"

"I didn't say that."

"She must have been crazy. You are so sexy."

"Yeah?" He nuzzled her neck. "Show me."

"All right." She began to kiss her way down his body. "I'd love to."

"OH, THERE'S A WORM." Wearing gardening gloves, Lauren picked the squirming thing up, walked to the fence and set it in the grass. "There you go, little guy. Live long and prosper."

From where he worked, installing the swing he'd ordered, Alex watched her. "You're something else, you know that?"

She faced him. Dressed in navy gym shorts and a white tank top, she looked cute as hell. Her skin was lightly tanned, her hair was mussed and her face was shiny with sweat. Alex almost couldn't contain his feelings for her. "Don't laugh at me," she said. "We're all God's creatures."

"So I heard."

Returning to the plants, she chuckled. "Hey, he deserves a life." She threw her arms out and looked up at the sun. "Besides, I feel so good today, I want everything and everybody to be happy."

He grinned, at her words and at the delightful view he got when she bent over. He could see pink lace under her shorts.

"So," she said, continuing to plant the flowers and a few bushes. "What was her name?"

"Who?"

"The woman you loved."

It was like dousing fire with water. His whole mood evaporated into guilty steam. He needed to tell Lauren that the woman she'd been asking about was Dana. That he'd kept his involvement with Dana from Lauren out of fear she'd stop seeing him, that she'd think she was some kind of surrogate for Dana. And now he was keeping it from her because he wanted to enjoy, just for a while, the undiluted happiness he felt since she said she loved him.

But he knew he couldn't keep this secret any longer. Rising, he crossed the yard and sat next to her as she finished putting an azalea bush into the ground. "I need to tell you something, honey."

She glanced at him. "Nothing could be better than what you told me two days ago." She smiled. "You make me so happy, Alex. I've never felt quite so loved for being who I am. I told you about my parents, and how different we were. How I felt like an outsider. But now, despite what's going on, I feel so special, like I belong." She cleared her throat. "With you."

Hell!

"So what were you going to tell me?"

"Just that I love you."

"SIT STILL."

"How can I when you're looking at me like that."

"I'm drawing you."

"Naked."

"Oh, yeah."

He shifted and willed himself to stay in pose. But she was looking at him...

"Alex!"

"Honey, I can't control *that*. I know you told me not to move, but *he* doesn't obey me ever. Anyway, my condition's your fault."

"Sorry."

"Are you?"

"Of course not." She flicked the pencil across the paper. "There, the sketch is done."

"Let me see."

She came to the bed. She was dressed in the peach thing she'd worn that morning after he got burned. Handing him the paper, she winked. "The drawing's one of my best, if I do say so myself."

He studied it. Lounging on the bed, he looked big and strong and…what was the word…virile. His muscles were so well-defined, he thought the figure might leap off the page. His anatomy was well portrayed, though not aroused, thank God.

"I look like that Greek statue you showed me."

"The Discus Thrower."

"It's your favorite work of art, you said."

"Until now." She threw herself at him. "Now, you're my favorite work of art."

He sighed. "Come on, your reward for flattery is a back rub."

Flipping over, she settled into the pillow. As his fingers dug into her, she sighed. "Ah, that's perfect. Everything is perfect."

Not quite, Alex knew, thinking about the secret he was keeping. But things would be better soon. He planned to tell her about Dana after his twenty-four-hour shift the next day. He just hoped she'd understand.

Massaging his way down her body, loving the feel

of her, he wondered what he'd do if this tore them apart. No, he wouldn't consider that. He wouldn't let that happen.

SHE FELT SO LIGHT. Free. Happy. She simply couldn't contain it, and decided to tackle the job she'd been dreading—going through her parents' things, which were stored in boxes in the spare room. Caramel nudged at her feet as she bent over the first box, in his usual nosy way, trying to see what she was doing.

Rummaging through silverware that had been in Sara Conway's family for generations forced Lauren to wonder if she was the rightful heir. Or was she somebody else's child? Damn it. Was Dana her sister? *Dana,* who was still treating her like dirt, trying to show her up in front of Alex. Lauren knew they'd been friends and she tried to tell herself Dana was just watching out for her buddy. But she couldn't convince herself. Dana's behavior smacked too much of jealousy.

"Think about something else."

She reached for a second box marked Clothes. Lauren knew her mother had saved some of her old things for her. She opened the flap. Inside, she found her baptismal gown, stowed away in soft tissue paper. She brought it to her nose, inhaled the scent, ran her finger over the crisp lace. Under it was the pink gingham dress with *Lauren* stitched on a white placket that her mother's friend MJ had bought her on Lauren's first birthday. And there was the blue velveteen dress. She remembered her father picking her up and swinging her around, telling her she looked like a princess in it. Though her throat clogged with emotion, she smiled at the memories.

A third box was marked Drawings. "Oh, Lord."

Inside were scribbles she'd done when she was one and two years old. And some real drawings. They were a child's, of course, but even then she'd shown promise. She found several of her and her parents— she remembered sketching them when she was ten, twelve, fifteen. She ran her finger over the slight arch of her mother's eyebrow, the sturdy girth of her father's shoulders, which she'd cried on often enough. "I miss you," she whispered, tears trickling down her cheeks. They'd always made her feel safe.

She decided to go through one more box marked Miscellaneous. In it she found a music box a boy had given her, a pair of particularly pretty shoes she and her mother bought for a prom. Her hand connected with a smaller box inside the large one. It was marked Tapes and Videos. *Videos.* She found the one labeled, in big letters, Lauren's Birth.

Her throat felt as if somebody had stuck a sock in it. What would she do if she found out Sara and John Conway weren't her parents?

She saw Alex's face shining with love. She saw him tell her how strong she was. How brave she was to face her fears—of water, of taking risks, of him. Confident now, she stood, grabbed the cassette and the cats and went to the living room.

She pushed the tape in the VCR.

Her parents came up on the screen. Her mother, smiling at her dad. Telling him she was a mess, not to tape this. Her dad said he loved her, he thought she was beautiful.

And Lauren began to cry again.

She was still crying when she saw the baby—her— slip out of her mother. A red, bloodied, squalling infant.

There was more tape of her mother. Shots of her dad cutting the umbilical cord. And then the nurses taking the child to the isolette, cleaning her up.

The video returned to her mother holding the baby. "Oh, John, she's gorgeous."

"Just like her mom."

"I want to count her fingers and toes."

"Go ahead. I'll film it."

She watched Sara unwrap the tiny pink blanket. A close-up of the ten fingers her mother counted. Then the ten toes.

Lauren was still crying when she put the VCR on Pause. But not out of nostalgia anymore.

The video was focused on her left foot.

Where, clearly, there was no birthmark like the one Lauren was born with.

ALEX STOOD under the showerhead and let the hot spray pummel his aching muscles. They'd made several runs the night before, one where he'd wrenched his back lifting a king-size man. Maybe Lauren would give *him* a back rub this time.

He chuckled and sang the oldie that had been blaring from the CD player in his bedroom. The Turtles, "So Happy Together." Damn right, he thought. He was happy with her. Happy with just a back rub. Happy to sleep with her today, tonight, every night, whether they made love or not. Briefly he wondered if she'd move in with him if he asked her. God, he'd never wanted a woman here permanently before.

The only blight on the horizon was the secret he was keeping from her, which he planned to clear up today. He told himself she trusted him now, and he trusted her enough to tell her the truth about Dana.

There was a maturity and an inner strength about Lauren that he admired. He could still see her bravely facing the news that her entire childhood might prove to be a lie. His pretty lady was a knight when she had to be. She could handle what he had to tell her.

Stepping out of the shower, he dried off and still singing—now the old Sonny and Cher song, "I Got You, Babe"—he walked into his bedroom towel-drying his hair. "What the hell?"

Dana lay on his bed. She was dressed in a skimpy black tank top, with spaghetti straps, and black spandex shorts. The outfit almost looked like underwear. Her hair was down and flowing over her shoulders, unusual for her, since she almost always wore it tied up. "Hey, buddy."

"Hell, Dana, I'm naked."

She gave him a typically Dana impish smile. "Nothing I haven't seen before. You're lookin' good these days. Been working out?"

He took the towel he'd been drying his hair with and wrapped it around his waist. He thought about asking for his key back right then, but as he moved closer, he got a good look at her face. "What's wrong?"

Tears glimmered in her eyes. He couldn't remember the last time he'd seen her cry. "Lauren came to see me."

Uh-oh. "Why?"

"She…" Dana smushed the pillow over her face and screamed. "God, I can't do this!"

Alarmed, he sat on the bed and pulled the pillow away. "What is it, kiddo?"

"She watched the video of her birth. She says she

doesn't think she's the infant that was born to Sara and John Conway.''

"Why?"

"The baby in the video doesn't have a birthmark. Apparently Lauren has one on her left ankle like the one I have on my right ankle.''

"Was she upset?"

"Hell, no. She's Miss Calm and Cool about all this and I'm the wreck.'' Dana grabbed his hand. "Alex, do you think…God, could something really have happened, when I was born? If she's my twin, then Mom and Dad aren't my parents. Except for you, they're the most important people in my life. I can't bear to think of anybody else as my parents. I love them so much.''

"I know that, Dana. We'll get through this. Whatever it is. But you've got to cooperate, find out the truth for sure.''

She brought his hand to her face. Held it there. "I know. I've handled this really bad. But I'm going to do better. Will you be with me through it?''

"Sure, but we need to talk about some things.''

"I think so, too.'' She looked him in the eye. "Us.''

"Dana, there isn't any us. I'm in love with Lauren.''

"Don't say that. I always thought we might get back together. Didn't you?''

"At times. But things have changed. You're just running scared. You know in your heart, nothing would be different. You'd be bored with me. I'd get restless. Just like the last time.''

"Maybe not.''

He brushed her hair out of her eyes. "It doesn't matter anyway. Lauren's in my life now."

Lying back on the pillows, she sighed. "You're probably right. I guess I knew it all along."

"That doesn't mean I won't help you through all this. Both of you."

"Okay."

"And ease up on Lauren, will you? You haven't been very nice to her."

"I know. I'm sorry."

He leaned over and kissed her on the cheek. A brotherly kiss.

As he did, the CD player stopped suddenly. He looked up to see Lauren standing at the door. And Alex knew he'd go to his grave remembering the expression on her face.

Utter desolation.

"Well, I guess you didn't hear me come in, with the music on."

"Lauren, this isn't what it looks like."

"No?" She shook her head. "You're sitting there in nothing but a towel, on a bed with a woman in her underwear—kissing her, to boot—and you expect me to believe it isn't what it looks like?" Though she sounded angry, her voice trembled. She swallowed hard. "I just don't understand, Alex. You told me you loved me. You said there'd only been one other woman…" She clapped a hand over her mouth and tears welled in her eyes. Her gaze shifted to Dana. "Oh, no. You're the one, aren't you?"

He had to stop this. "Lauren—"

"Let her answer, Alex. Maybe she'll tell me the truth."

That stung. But before he could say anything more,

Dana straightened. "Look, Lauren, Alex is right. Nothing's going on between us."

"Alex was in love with you in the past, wasn't he?"

"Well, yeah. But we weren't rekindling that."

"You were kissing!"

Alex stood, grasping the towel. Lauren's attention dropped to his hand and her expression became even more pained. "Lauren, I can explain." He faced Dana. "Would you leave us alone?"

Climbing off the bed, Dana put her hand on his arm. "I'm sorry." She looked at Lauren. "I've been acting crazy, and I can see I've made things bad for you two. I've been a mess, but I'll get my act together."

Lauren's laugh was full of disbelief and disgust. "Don't bother on my account. You know, I really hope you aren't my sister." She started to sweep past Dana, but Alex grabbed her arm.

"You aren't going anywhere," he said.

"Don't touch me."

Holding firm, he repeated, "You aren't going anywhere." He looked at Dana.

She gave him a sad smile and left.

Alex crossed to the door and closed it. Blocking the exit, he snagged his shorts off the nearby chair and put them on. Then he turned to face Lauren, who leaned against a dresser as if she needed the support.

"You know, it all makes sense now," she said.

"What does?"

"Your immediate attraction to me. How fast our relationship developed. I was just a stand-in for Dana, wasn't I?"

"No, you weren't."

"She dumped you, didn't she? You said that earlier."

"Well, yes, but Lauren, please…it's not what you think at all."

"No? Then why didn't you tell me you'd been involved with her when I asked you directly? Why did you lie to me instead?"

That stopped him. How did he explain it to her?

"Never mind, I know. Because *you* knew I'd think exactly what I'm thinking."

He didn't answer her.

Her voice rose a notch. "Didn't you?"

"Yes. At first, I was afraid you'd think I was attracted to you because of your similarity to Dana. Then, when things progressed, you were so up and down about me, I didn't say anything. I was afraid you'd leave before we could cement our relationship."

"That is the worst kind of manipulation."

"If it was, I'm sorry. I was going to tell you today."

"Oh, sure." She shook her head. "I told you about James. I told you I didn't trust easily and that I needed you to be honest."

"I know. You're right. As I said, my only defense is that I was afraid you'd leave me."

Briefly she closed her eyes. "It's partly my fault. There were clues. You said some things the night of the fire, called me sweetheart, said you thought you were over me." She swore harshly. "And after we started going out, I overheard some comments people made about my resemblance to Dana, and your interest in me. I ignored them."

"None of this is your fault. It's mine. I'm sorry."

She stared at him, her throat working convulsively. "So, does she outshine me in bed, too? Like she does everywhere else?"

He felt his eyes sting. "Don't say that. You know how special making love with you is for me."

"I thought I did." She started to cry in earnest. "But how can I ever believe what you say again?" She put her head in her hands and turned away from him.

Coming up behind her, he grasped her shoulders. "Give me another chance. I'll prove what I feel for you is real."

She shook her head. He turned her to face him and tugged her to his chest. Resisting at first, she eventually relaxed in his arms, sobbing quietly. It broke his heart. He crooned to her. Apologized. Held her until she was spent.

Finally, she pulled back. Her face was swollen from crying, her eyes still swimming with tears. "I'm all right." She wiped her face. "I have to go."

"No, Lauren. You can't go. Stay and talk this out."

"There's nothing more to say."

"Are you telling me it's over between us?"

"Of course it's over. How could I ever trust you again?"

"I don't believe this."

"I've got to go."

"Listen, you've had two big blows. Finding out about me and Dana. And the video. Let's at least talk about that."

"No. I don't want to talk about that with you or anyone else."

"What do you mean?"

"I'm going to leave town. I'll go back to Benicia.

I'm going to forget all about you and everybody else in Courage Bay."

He grabbed for her arm but she shook him off.

"Please don't," she said. "If you care for me at all, don't try to stop me."

He didn't. Instead, he watched her walk away, then sank onto the bed, feeling as if he'd just lost something rare and precious that he'd never find again.

CHAPTER FOURTEEN

"THANK YOU FOR SEEING ME, dear. I know this must be uncomfortable for you."

"It's fine, Vera. You said it was important, and that we wouldn't talk about Alex." Lauren could barely say his name. In the three days since she'd walked into his bedroom and found him with Dana, she hadn't talked to him, or to anyone about him. He'd done as she'd asked and stayed away from her, too. She felt as if someone had cut off one of her limbs.

Against the backdrop of the dining room of the Courage Bay Bar and Grill, Vera's face darkened. "May I say I'm sorry that things didn't work out for you two?"

"I am, too." Lauren hesitated, grasping the tiger's-eye she wore. "How is he?"

"More miserable than I've ever seen him in his life."

"Has he told you anything?"

"Just that it's his fault you're not seeing each other anymore." She shook her head.

"What?"

"Ever since Alex was little, when he was inconsolable, he'd isolate himself. As a child, he'd practically live out in his tree house. As a teenager, he'd barricade himself in his room."

"And now?"

"He's gone camping."

Oh, God. With Dana? "Alone?"

"Yes, of course, dear. He's in love with you. He wouldn't go with another woman, if that's what put that look of horror on your face."

Lauren bit back the pain and tried to conceal her reaction by taking a sip of her iced tea. "Did he tell you he was in love with me?"

Vera smiled fondly. "Yes. I hope that's all right. He came over a few days ago to help his father with something, and his feet weren't touching the ground. His feelings for you just bubbled out of him." Reaching across the table, she squeezed Lauren's hand. "It's why we're so shocked about you two ending it."

Tears welled in Lauren's eyes. "I'm sorry. I can't talk anymore about this. I know I brought it up, but I..." She shrugged. "I just can't."

"You obviously love him, too, Lauren. And that makes it even more of a shame." Vera watched her for a minute then picked up the menu. "Now, let's order first, then I'll tell you why I asked you to lunch. I may not have a lot of time. I'm on call for a special case I'm consulting on."

After the waiter took their selections, Vera faced her squarely, as Alex often had. Her amber eyes reminded Lauren of him, too. "I'll cut right to the chase. Dana's agreed to DNA testing. I've set up a lab appointment for tomorrow for all three of the Ivies."

I really hope you're not my sister...

"Oh."

"They'd like you to be tested, too. Alex said you probably wouldn't agree, but I don't understand why he'd think that.'' She furrowed her brow, making her look like a befuddled scientist. "You've been so co-operative up until now.''

"I said some things a couple of days ago. I was angry and upset. I told Alex I didn't want to pursue this with the Ivies."

Vera's eyes widened and she fiddled with the jeweled neckline of the teal blouse she wore. "I hope you didn't mean that. I'm really concerned about Helen. She needs closure on this."

I'm going back to Benicia...

"But what if we find out...that they're my parents? Then I'd have to stay."

Alex's mother paled. "Oh, Lauren, you're not thinking about leaving town, are you?"

"I—" She looked away, her attention landing on the Remembrance Wall. It was a poignant reminder that real tragedy could happen any time to the people you loved. It made her search more honestly within herself. She'd not only had second thoughts about what she'd told Alex, but third and fourth thoughts. Now she was just confused.

"Hello, ladies."

Both women looked up to see George Yube standing at their table. Once again, Lauren was struck by the kindness in his eyes. Vera smiled warmly. "George, hello."

He patted Vera's shoulder.

Lauren gave him a welcoming smile, too. "George."

"Lauren, how are you? I've been thinking about you since our little chat."

"Thanks for caring. I'm fine."

His eyes narrowed. "You don't look it. But I'm

intruding.'' He faced Vera. ''Any luck with the hospital records?''

''No, I'm afraid those are gone for good. We're pursing other avenues. Thanks for your help, though.''

''Other avenues?''

Vera nodded. ''The Ivies want answers. They're going to have DNA tests.''

''Ah.'' He scrutinized Lauren. ''And you?''

''I—I don't know what I'm going to do.''

''Well, remember what we talked about. And know that I'm here.'' He nodded and left.

''He's so sweet,'' Lauren said.

''Yes, it's a shame he never had children of his own. He'd make a good father.''

Lauren frowned. ''He has two daughters.''

''No, he doesn't. His wife died a few years ago. They were childless.''

''Could he have children by another marriage?''

Alex's mother looked puzzled. ''Maybe, but I never heard a word about that.'' She shrugged. ''I—'' Then her hand went to her waist. ''That's my pager.'' Vera checked it. ''I have to get back to the hospital. As I said, I'm consulting on a difficult pregnancy and the parents are upset. I told my colleague I'd be available today.'' Over the table, she touched Lauren's hand. ''Please, think about what I asked.''

''What time is the testing tomorrow?''

''Nine. At the hospital lab. I'll be overseeing the procedure myself so there'll be no error. It's noninvasive and only involves taking a swab of cells from the inside of your cheek.''

''How long before the results come in?''

"Usually a few days. I can make sure this gets top priority so it might be less."

"I'll think about it."

Vera left and Lauren sat where she was, sipping her iced tea. Just after her food was delivered, a shadow fell over her table. It was George again. "Did Vera get called back to the hospital?"

"Yes."

George nodded to Vera's food and snagged a waitress. "Wrap that up. I'll take it back to her." He looked at Lauren. "Would you mind if I joined you?"

"No, I'd like the company."

"Well, good." He took a seat and smiled. "Now. Let's talk about this testing. Shall we?"

HUNCHED OVER, Alex sat in the hospital waiting area, his hands linked between his knees. He didn't know if Lauren would show up today, but he was here for the Ivies, in any case.

Lauren. On the chair beside him was the Courage Bay *Courier.* He'd been studiously avoiding the comics, so he had no idea what was going on with *Dee and Me* or if Lauren was even writing it.

I'm going back to Benicia.

What did it matter? He picked up the paper and opened to the comic section.

Frame One:

Lily stands in a row of people, with a certificate in her hand. Dee claps from the sidelines. Adam smiles. *You did it, Lily.*

Yeah, thanks for all your help.

Frame Two:

Adam's face turns red. *I'll miss seeing you every day.*

Lily turns away, shy. *Me, too.*

Frame Three:

Dee behind Lily, whispers in her ear. *Tell him you want to keep seeing him.*

Lily stands frozen.

Frame Four:

Lily and Dee on the sidewalk. *What am I going to do with you? Haven't I taught you anything?*

You can't teach an old dog new tricks. Some things weren't meant to be.

Alex dropped the paper to the chair without reading frame five. Well, there it was. She hadn't changed her mind. Hadn't decided to give them another chance. "Damn it to hell." He'd had some furlough coming, so he'd gone camping. It was there, he'd realized he was mad at Lauren. How could she give this up?

Because you lied to her, asshole.

"Alex?" Dana had arrived and stood over him, looking more fragile than he'd ever seen her. "Thanks for coming back."

Rising, he gave her a quick hug. "I told you I'd be here for you."

"We won't get any results today."

He squeezed her arm. "I know. But this will be hard for all of you." He looked over her shoulder; Dana stepped aside. "Helen, Tim." He hugged the couple.

He could practically see the nerves dancing around Helen's eyes. She glanced at her watch. "It's almost nine. Do you think Lauren will show?" she asked Alex.

"I'm not…"

Someone came through the doors. And there she was, standing about ten feet away, dressed in plaid cropped pants and a teal-blue sleeveless blouse. Alex's heart started to pound at seeing her again after an absence that seemed like drought to a thirsty man.

Before anyone else could react, Dana crossed to her. "Thanks for coming, Lauren. My parents really appreciate it."

"It's fine. We all have a right to know." She looked over at Alex.

Tracking the direction of her gaze, Dana said, "Come on, Mom, Dad. Let's go to the lab. Vera said she'd be in when we got here."

Helen and Tim spoke briefly to Lauren on their way out. Alex stared at Lauren, and she stared back, neither able to look away.

"I hope my being here doesn't make it harder for you."

"No, of course not. You're close to them. They need you."

He jammed his fists in his pockets. "What about you? How are you doing with this?"

"I'm worried."

"I don't blame you." He reached out to squeeze her arm, but she stepped back. It felt like somebody had punched him in the gut. He fought to keep his voice even. "I'm surprised you decided to do this. You said you were leaving town, that you didn't want to know."

"I was upset. I said some mean things. I'm sorry if they hurt you."

"Hurt me?" He tried to keep a lid on his emotions. "Of course you hurt me. I'm leveled that you ended this relationship."

"Me, too." She shook her head. "Seems like we've been through this before."

"Yeah, that day at the marina."

"I guess I should have followed my instincts then."

"How can you say that? After what's happened between us?"

She stared at him. "Look at us. You're miserable. And I'm miserable. Which means I was right that day. We shouldn't have let things get this far." She turned away then and headed for the door to the lab.

"Lauren?" She glanced over her shoulder and he saw the tears in her eyes. Instead of making this test easier for her, he was making it more difficult. "Never mind. Good luck."

He watched her walk away—the gentle sway of her hips, the feminine slope of her back. When she was gone, he sank onto the vinyl chair, put his head in his hands and wondered how he was going to survive the loss of her.

Three days later he was no better off as he sat next to Dana in his mother's office, flanked by the Ivies. Lauren, having refused a seat, stood behind them, leaning against the wall. She seemed so…breakable in her white top and pink crop pants. Mauve smudges under her eyes testified to the fact that she wasn't sleeping well.

His mother faced them. "Let's get straight to the facts. The twin zygosity DNA testing reveals that you, Lauren, and you, Dana, are identical twins."

Dana started and clasped a hand over her mouth. Alex heard Lauren moan behind him.

Then Vera faced her friends. "I'm sorry, Helen. Tim. The paternity and maternity tests show that neither of you are the girls' biological parents."

Helen Ivie began to weep softly and Tim grasped

her hand. Dana bolted from her seat, and dropped down in front of Helen. "It doesn't matter, Mom. In every way that counts, you're my mother." She grasped her father's hand. "I promise this won't change anything." Her voice broke when she said, "I didn't want this to happen but we'll deal with it."

Both parents clung to Dana. Alex had a feeling they'd be all right. He wished he could say the same for the woman behind him. Standing, he turned to see how she was taking this.

But Lauren was gone.

WITH RELENTLESS ZEAL, Lauren turned up the dirt, added fertilizer and peat moss and planted the last of the daisies. She glanced up at the sun. She had no idea how long she'd been out here. Her arms were sunburned and she was sweating like a marathon run- ner in the desert, but she kept working until she fin- ished with the flowers. Sinking back on her heels, she studied the garden. It was done. *Fini*. Like a lot of things.

Sniffling, she glanced back at the house. And saw Alex appear at the French doors off the dining area. "Lauren, oh, God." He took in a breath. "You're here? I didn't see Longstreet's car."

The tears, kept at bay all day, moistened her eyes. "I…" She nodded over her shoulder. "I finished the garden."

He strode out into the yard and knelt next to her. "How long have you been here?"

"I don't know."

"Why didn't you change your clothes? Your pants and top are all dirty."

"I don't know."

Reaching up, he pushed the hair back from her eyes. "Honey, what's going on? Why are you gardening out here in the middle of the day? After the news you've had?"

"I don't know."

His eyes narrowed.

She bit her lip. "I didn't come here to garden."

"What did you come for?"

"To see you. To find you." She ran a hand through her hair, then realized it was filthy. "Where have you been?"

"I've been *looking* all over for you."

"For me? When you didn't come home, I assumed you were with Dana."

"Why would I be? I was frantic about you. Everybody is. I drove to your house, waited there, went to the *Courier*. I even checked out the Y and questioned Smith. And Hanson at the paper."

"You did?"

He studied her carefully, then stood. He grasped her hand and pulled her up. When she wavered on her feet, he slid an arm under her legs, one around her back and picked her up. Gently he held her close as he strode into the house. The feel of him, the smell of him, being near him, triggered something inside her.

And finally she began to cry. All the fear and anger and sorrow poured out from her as she sobbed into his shirt. A gulf of darkness and pain enveloped her. When she came back to awareness, she looked up at him. He'd sat with her in the living room, and the fan overhead was cool on her heated skin. "I—"

He tugged her close. "Shh, it's okay. You needed that."

"I guess." She nestled into him again. His hand felt wonderful on her hair, soothing on her back.

"Want to talk?"

She nodded. "What could have happened, Alex? I don't get it. If anything, I expected the Ivies to be my parents."

"Mom figures that, of the three babies born here in the hospital the day of Dana's birth, two of them were you and Dana. The other one born here—the Ivies' child—and the one born in L.A. must have died." He cleared his throat. "Somehow they were switched with you and Dana."

"So we went to two different sets of parents."

"Yes."

"And the person who switched us had connections with the hospital in L.A. and with the facilities in Courage Bay."

"It would seem logical. Mom's betting on that."

Lauren laid her head against his chest. Being close to him seemed the only thing that comforted her. "Was there foul play?"

"A switch like this would have to be covering up something, I'd think."

"Unless it was accidental." Her tone was hopeful. "I've seen movies about that."

"I doubt it, honey. One baby came from Los Angeles Hospital. That had to be intentional."

"I guess. I'm not thinking clearly."

"Why would you? You've had a terrible blow."

Her hand tightened on his shirt. "Dana's my sister."

"Yes."

"My identical twin."

"Uh-huh."

"Who could our parents be?"

"Some poor unknown couple the nurse my mother interviewed remembers. The ones who thought they lost their twin girls." He swore under his breath. "I feel so sorry for them."

"The nurse doesn't remember their names."

"No." He sat very still. "Do you want to know who they are?"

"Of course." She drew back. "Doesn't Dana?"

"I don't know. She seemed pretty intent on helping Tim and Helen cope."

Lauren sighed. "I knew all along she was resisting this, acting as she did, because she was scared for them."

"Right now, it's you I'm worried about. You're exhausted."

Glancing down at her hands and clothes, she said, "And grimy."

He stood. Still cuddling her next to his heart, he strode to the bathroom and set her on the toilet. Then he bent over the tub and turned on the taps. Testing the water, he reached up and got her the bubble bath he'd purchased for her on a visit to a boutique in town. It smelled like raspberries when he put it in. Alex stood and removed a tube of ointment from the medicine cabinet. "Put this on after you bathe," he told her, and started to leave the bathroom. "It's the aloe."

She grabbed his hand. "Where are you going?" she asked, panicked at the thought of being alone.

"I'll be right back." He kissed her nose, left and returned with a T-shirt and a pair of her panties. "You left these here." He knelt in front of her. "Get undressed, get in the tub and try to relax."

She grasped his hand. "Don't go."

"I'm not going anywhere, sweetheart." He nodded to the bedroom. "I'll leave the door open and be right in there when you're done."

"Okay." She sighed. "Alex, I...about us..."

He placed his finger over her mouth. "Shh, not now. I love you, Lauren, I just want to help you through today and as many of the upcoming days that you'll let me. No strings attached."

She nodded. "All right."

ALEX STRETCHED out on his bed and stared through the window at the birds gathering around the feeder Lauren had helped him put up. Her favorites were blue jays, and he watched one pick at the seeds. Listening to the soft sounds of her bathing, he felt a sense of joy. That would be short-lived, he knew. When she felt better, maybe even as soon as she came out of the tub, she'd leave him again. But at least she'd let him take care of her for a little while.

He'd called the Ivies and his parents and told them he'd found Lauren—he couldn't believe she came to him—and was thinking about the bizarre circumstances that brought them together again when she appeared in the doorway.

Her face and arms were ruddy from the sunburn. But that wasn't what caught his attention. She was wearing the big green towel he'd left on the vanity.

"Honey, what..." He scanned her from head to toe. "I brought you clothes."

He watched her studying him. Slowly she raised her hand and undid the knot of the towel. It fell in soft folds to the floor. And then she stood before him, naked, perfectly formed, so female and alluring his breath caught in his throat. He said nothing as she came toward him. Knelt on the bed. And started unbuttoning his shirt. He stayed her hands. "Lauren, what…what are you doing?"

"I want to feel good again. I've been miserable for days. I miss you so much. Now this stuff with the Ivies. I want to be with you, lose myself in how you make me feel. Just for a little while?" Her words were a question. Would he do this for her?

"All right." He pulled her down on top of him. "Whatever you want, love. Whatever you want."

THE BEDROOM WAS DIM, cocooning them against the world…

"Touch me, Alex, please."

"Here? You're so full, so feminine."

"Ah, yes…ohh."

"I love being close to you."

She arched into his palm. "Harder."

His own breath quickened. "Like this?"

"Yes. More, please."

"I'll give you whatever you need, Lauren. Always…"

"STAY INSIDE ME while we sleep."

"All right."

She inhaled him. "It calms me."

He stroked her back. "I know. There's a sense of peace when we're together like this. I never felt it before you."

She nuzzled into him. "Me, either."

He was still holding her when she cried out in sleep.

"Honey, wake up."

She opened her eyes and sat up, clutching the sheet. "I had a dream. There were all these women, looking just like me...."

"It's okay, I'm here."

She lay back down, snuggled into him. "Don't leave me, please."

"I won't. Ever."

ALEX AWOKE to darkness. He reached over for Lauren, but she wasn't there. He heard a rustle and glanced over at the window. She was standing in the shadows, staring outside. He said, "I thought maybe you'd left."

Turning she watched him for a minute. She had his shirt on. "No." She cleared her throat. "I don't want to leave. I want to stay here for a while, Alex."

"Tonight?"

She shook her head. "For a few days. Maybe more."

He wanted to leap out of bed and drop to his knees and thank God. But he said only, "I'd like that."

"I have to be honest. My staying here won't change what's happened, what's going to happen from now on."

Like hell. "Meaning?"

"I'll go back to Benicia as soon as I can see this thing through with the Ivies."

Over his dead body. "If that's what you want."

"You'll let me stay, on those terms?"

"Of course. I told you, I'd do anything for you, Lauren."

Unspoken was that she'd once said the same words to him, but she didn't repeat them now.

"All right."

He reached out his hand. "Now come back to bed."

Slowly she approached the bed. Climbed in beside him. And nestled close.

That night as she slept, Alex made a promise to himself and, in a way, to Lauren. He'd be here for her through this, take care of her, do whatever it took to make her feel better, without putting any pressure on her.

But he wasn't letting her go.

SITTING IN HIS CAR, he stared at Shields's house. So the test results had come in. He'd tried to stop them but failed. This was not good. And now he couldn't even get to her. He needed to get her away from that bastard. He heard voices…

Why do you want to? What's to gain? He silenced them, and tuned in to the other voices… *Cover this up…don't let them find out it's you…*

It had affected so many lives. And it wasn't even his fault. The circumstances were bizarre.

Fury rose in him at the thought of everything being uncovered, all the shame, the end of his chance to make his mark on the world. He hadn't accomplished what he'd wanted to yet, though he'd tried. And now…faces swam before him…Vera Shields…Perry O'Connor…Dana Ivie and, mostly, Lauren. No, he had to find a way to stop this.

CHAPTER FIFTEEN

LAUREN SAT in Sam Prophet's office next to Vince Wojohowitz, who'd been put in charge of her case. Clustered around the desk were the Ivies and Alex. They'd all met at the arson investigator's office because it was housed in fire department headquarters and Alex and Dana were on duty. If a call came, they could leave from here.

Vince took charge of the meeting. "From now on, this is an active case for the Courage Bay Police Department. The results of the DNA tests have made it obvious something happened thirty-two years ago. We'll determine if it was criminal, or just negligence."

From behind his desk, Sam Prophet steepled his hands and scowled. "The arson at the newspaper office makes the situation criminal."

"Yeah, it relates to the case if Lauren was the target, which we still don't know. But given the failure of her car's brakes and then Wes's accident, we're pretty sure something criminal's going on here." He nodded to her. "You've got protection, Lauren, so you should be safe enough now."

She nodded and moved closer to Alex, within touching distance, as she did every time they were together. She needed the physical contact; his sheer presence calmed her. Surreptitiously she cast a glance at Dana, who she caught staring at her, too. Quickly Dana looked away. They were acting like little girls sizing each other up on the playground. This woman was her sister, yet they hadn't talked alone since finding out two days ago they were identical twins. When the Ivies arrived, it had been excruciatingly awkward. Lauren fingered the tiger's-eye beneath the lace at the top of her white eyelet blouse, wondering if anything was ever going to feel right again.

"What's the next step in investigating this case?" Vera asked, sitting forward in her seat.

Vince shook his head. "I really can't go into it with you all."

"What you should do," Vera said as if he hadn't spoken, "is get the employment records from Courage Bay Hospital and Los Angeles Hospital at the time the girls were born. Cross-match them to see if there were any common staff."

Lauren grabbed Alex's hand. Out of the corner of her eye, she saw Dana grasp Helen's fingers.

"We've got that in the works, Vera." Vince's eyes narrowed. "But I want you to stay out of this from now on for your own safety."

Wes touched Vera's arm. "She will."

"Fine, I'll keep you informed."

Everybody stood. Vince asked Alex to stay back about something to do with his wedding. Again, it was awkward bidding goodbye to the Ivies. Lauren felt compelled to say something more than "see you around," but couldn't come up with the right words. They seemed equally at a loss. Vera kissed her cheek and said they'd talk soon.

"I'll wait for you out in the bay," Lauren told Alex.

She'd noticed Dana hesitating, looking back at her, but she'd gone out with the rest of them. With some vague notion of finding her, Lauren left the office. Rounding the corner, she caught sight of Dana going into the firehouse proper. On impulse, Lauren followed her.

Will Begay was cleaning the counters in the kitchen alone. "Hey, Lauren. How you doing?"

"As well as can be expected."

"Alex told me about the DNA tests. It must be hard, but good, too, knowing you have a sister. A twin, at that."

Good? Could this in any way be good? "Where did Dana go, Will?"

"Into the bunk room, through there."

"Is it all right if I go back?"

"Sure. I'll take you. If anybody else is around, I'll kick them out so you can have some privacy."

Lauren followed Will, who, when he saw Dana was alone, squeezed Lauren's arm and left.

On the far side of the bunk room near a window, Dana sat on a bed, with papers spread out around her. She looked strong and competent in her dark blue fire department shirt and navy pants. *Just like Dee.* Slowly Lauren crossed to her sister. When she reached the bed, Lauren could see Dana had clippings from the Courage Bay *Courier* spread before her. On closer examination, it was obvious what they were.

Dana looked up. Her eyes were moist. "You sensed it all along, didn't you?" She picked up what appeared to be Lauren's first *Dee and Me* comic. The rest remained on the bed.

"I think so, way down deep. Unconsciously."

Staring at the comic, Dana shook her head and smiled. "Dee's pretty pushy. Know-it-all."

Dropping on the bunk facing Dana, Lauren smiled. "I think she's brave and strong and admirable."

Dana's head snapped up. "You do?" Again she reminded Lauren of a little girl trying to make friends. Dana swallowed hard. "I can be all those things, especially when life gets tough. I'm sorry for how I treated you the past few weeks."

"I'm sorry for what I said about hoping you weren't my sister."

It was awkward again. Dana picked up another comic. "I read all of them. Lily's made a lot of progress."

"I thought she had." Lauren sighed, knowing she wasn't seeing things clearly with Alex. But every time she tried to figure out what she was feeling, she just got sadder.

"The muscle-bound boy?" Dana asked. "What's Lily going to do about him?"

"She doesn't know. Too much has happened to make any decisions now."

"Can I tell you something? Two things really."

"I guess."

"I'm sorry if I caused trouble with you and Alex. There's nothing romantic between us." She brushed back hair almost the exact color of Lauren's own. Under her short sleeves, Dana had a spattering of freckles on the opposite arm from Lauren. Identical twins often had mirror images of birthmarks, freckles, that kind of thing. "Alex and I drifted into a relationship that never should have gone further. We drifted out of it, too."

"You ended it, Dana."

"We both got bored."

"In any case, it's hard to accept that I'm not just a substitute for you."

"I'm sorry, because in my heart I know you're not. I believe he really loves you."

"I don't want to talk about this anymore." She couldn't. She didn't want to talk at all. All she wanted was to be with Alex and shut out the world. Yet she'd come here. She must need something from Dana. "What was the second thing you were going to tell me?"

Dana bit her lip. "No matter what happens with my mom and dad, you and I are, we'll stay...we're sisters, Lauren. No matter who our parents are." Her voice cracked at the word *parents*.

"I know. I can't bear to think about Sara and John Conway not being my mother and father. They weren't yours, so they can't be mine. It hurts so much."

Dana glanced at the window. "And out there are two people who thought their little girls died at birth. That's so sad. Why would somebody do that?"

"I don't know."

"Think they're alive? And if they are, will we ever find them?"

"Do you want to?"

"I don't know."

"Me neither."

"I'm scared, Lauren. I don't want to face this."

"I'm scared, too." Rising, Lauren pushed the comics out of the way and sat next to Dana. And for the first time since they left the womb, she touched her sister. She picked up Dana's hand.

All the things people speculated about twins were true. "Do you feel it?" Lauren asked.

Dana's eyes were wide and wondrous. "The connection? Yes. I felt something the first time I met you, too. I just wouldn't admit it."

Lauren held on tight. Dana did the same. "No matter what we want, Dana, we have this connection."

"I know."

"It's good, isn't it?" she asked tentatively.

"Yeah, it's good." Dana sidled in close, just as Lauren did the same. "This feels right," Dana said.

"Yeah."

They didn't talk after that. Just sat there, on Dana's bunk, until the noise of others coming down the hall broke them apart.

SORE, EXHAUSTED and frustrated, Alex grabbed a pint of chunky cheesecake ice cream from the freezer and headed outside. He sank onto a chair and opened the sweet confection. They'd had two calls tonight, which, on top of everything else, had drained him. The paramedics were out yet again, but at one in the morning, the rest of his men were hunkered down for the night.

He couldn't stop thinking about Lauren. And it brought no joy. She'd completely distanced herself from him, even as she physically tried to get inside his skin. She'd made love to him over the past few days like a courtesan out to please her master, snuggled into him in private and public every chance she got, touched him constantly. But she wouldn't share what was going on inside…

"Sweetheart, please, tell me what you're thinking.'' They'd been in bed, after lovemaking that sky-rocketed his blood pressure.

''That this was great.''

''No, I mean where your head's at.''

''I won't talk about that.''

''You won't talk about anything,'' he said with ex-asperation.

She'd cuddled closer so he could feel her heartbeat. ''Please, don't push this. I can't bear that now. I just need to be close to you.''

So he'd let it go.

He looked up at her office window. They'd moved back into the east side of the building and had almost completed work on the charred section. Alex was surprised to see a light go on, its sudden brightness startling in the dark building. A figure skulked past the window. The light went out. Minutes later, somebody exited the building. The paper was printed during the night, so there were usually comings and goings, but this wasn't a typesetter. It was Toby Hanson.

Alex stood, drawing Hanson's attention. The man paused before loping over. Pushing up his glasses, he said, ''Hey, Alex.''

''Toby.'' He nodded to the window. ''What were you doing in Lauren's office?''

''I wasn't in Lauren's office.''

''No? I saw a light go on there.''

''My office is on the other side of the building, so I didn't see anything.'' He glanced up. ''Well, it's dark now. And late. See you,'' he said and beat a hasty—too hasty—retreat.

Damn it. Alex rubbed the back of his neck, swore and dropped back down to finish his ice cream. It was silent out except for the cricket choruses. He studied the *Courier* building. He wondered if there'd be a *Dee and Me* episode today. Thinking about the comic made him even sadder.

Lily was becoming pretty independent these days. She'd mastered swimming and now went into the ocean with Dee all the time. She'd gotten a full-time baby-sitting job.

Adam, the muscle-bound boy, was nowhere in sight. She'd left him in the dust. Would Lauren really do that to *him?*

A car came down the street, and Alex was shocked to see it was his father's. Wes parked in front of the paper and hustled over to the back of the firehouse. "Hey, buddy."

"Dad, what…oh, God, what's happened?"

Wes put a strong hand on his shoulder. "Nothing, son. I just woke up and couldn't go back to sleep. Knew you were on tonight, so I decided to take a ride."

"Yeah?"

He sat in the chair next to Alex. "Your mother and I are worried about you."

"Well, I'm worried about you two. First your accident and now Vince telling Mom to stay out of this investigation for her own safety. Jeez, Dad, how did all this cloak-and-dagger happen?"

"Lauren Conway came to town."

He sighed. "And turned my life upside down."

"That's pretty obvious." Wes stretched out his legs. "Your mother and I have tried not to pry, not to interfere with your life. But…"

"Now you're gonna pry."

"Yep. Way I figure it, father-son relationships are like doctor-patient, lawyer-client, priest—"

"I get the point, Dad."

"What I'm saying is I wanna know what's going on between you and Lauren. Maybe I can help. If not, at least you'd get it off your chest."

Alex set the ice-cream carton down and stretched out his legs, too. "Things are a mess. I blew it, Dad."

"How?"

"I never told her Dana and I were involved. No, it's more than that. I lied directly about it when she asked me. Then she caught us in a compromising position."

"You and Dana? I thought that was a thing of the past."

"It is. Nothing was going on, but it didn't look good."

"So Lauren thinks there's still something between you?"

Hell, this was complicated. "Actually, I think she believes me that there isn't."

"She can't forgive you for lying?"

"No, I think she could get past that, too. What she doesn't believe is that she's not some kind of surrogate for Dana."

"Ouch!"

"I know. It's gotta feel awful."

His father didn't answer for a minute, then he said, "It does. I know."

"Huh?"

Wes offered no explanation.

"Hey, Dad, doesn't this doctor-patient, lawyer-client thing work both ways?"

"It does." His father hunched forward. "Remember I told you your mother and I were really different, should probably never have gotten together?"

"Yeah."

"I found out a long time after we hooked up that she'd been on the rebound from a guy who'd dumped her. I was pissed as hell."

"Dad, that kind of thing happens all the time."

"Yeah, but it doesn't get rekindled years later."

"Mom had an affair?"

"Not like you think. The guy, a doctor, came to work at Courage Bay Hospital. Wanted to start over again. Your mother was…tempted."

"Tempted? Did she do anything?"

"No. I never knew if it was because she had you and the girls by then, or if she really didn't want to go back to him."

"Did she tell you about this?"

"Nope, which made it worse. I found some letters he wrote to her. Her feelings for him were implied."

"So you confronted her. What did Mom say?"

"She admitted she was tempted, but she knew she loved me."

"Oh, Dad."

"I chose to believe it. After a while. But it sucks, big-time, son." He swore, using a four-letter word Alex rarely heard him use. "I hate even thinking about it."

"You know who the guy was?"

"He never signed the letters. And your mother wouldn't tell me. But I think maybe it was George Yube."

"Really? He doesn't seem Mom's type."

"Who knows. I can't stand the guy, anyway. Take it from me, this is a tough nut to crack. Give Lauren some time. Maybe she'll take the risk, like I did."

His smile made him look young. "I'm glad I did, if it's any help."

Alex put a hand on his dad's shoulder. "Thanks for telling me this."

"Yeah, sure. Just remember that your mother and I love you."

After his father left, Alex sat there thinking a while longer. When he was about to go in, he heard a call from the darkness. "Help us, please," somebody called out.

Alex froze. Usually firehouses were safe from crime and vandalism, but he had cautioned his men numerous times that you couldn't be too careful. Damn, he realized, he shouldn't be out here so late, alone.

A man and a pregnant woman emerged from the darkness.

"You gotta help us, *señor*. My wife, she's about to—"

"Alonzo, help me!" She gripped her very big belly, crying out harshly.

Alex hurried over to them and helped the woman's husband carry her into the firehouse. They barely got her to a chair before another contraction hit. Minutes apart, Alex thought, going into EMT mode.

Calmly he said, "I'm Alex Shields, captain of this firehouse. What's your name?"

"Rosa," the mother got out. "The baby's coming."

"Is this your first child?" he asked, checking her vitals as he spoke.

"No, my fourth. He's coming, I know it."

Alex faced the husband. "Alonzo, go to the bunk

room back down that hallway and wake up my men. I don't want to leave your wife."

After he left, Alex sat across from the woman. "How far apart have your labor pains been, Rosa?"

"About two minutes," she told him just as another hit.

"Breathe," Alex said calmly.

"We were gonna go to the hospital but the car died right down the street from the firehouse."

Begay came running out. "What is—holy mother of God."

"She's too close to get her to the hospital," Alex told Will. "Get the sterile delivery pack out of the truck."

The rest of the men joined them. "Gonzales, put some padding on the table."

Behind him, he heard his team go into action. In minutes, he'd been helped into surgical gloves and somebody had tied eye and mouth protection on him. Out of the corner of his eye—as he talked Rosa through yet another contraction—he saw foam being placed on the table and covered with a sterile surgical sheet. Robertson laid out towels, gauze pads, a rubber bulb syringe, cord clamps, tape and surgical scissors.

"Okay, let's get her up." Rosa managed to stand and then four of them lifted her onto the table. As Alex eased her onto her side to reduce blood flow to the heart, he issued instructions. "Go to her head and hold her hand, Alonzo. North, you monitor her vitals from there." He'd also watch for vomiting. To Begay, he said, "You stay here with me to cut the cord. Gonzales, set up the stuff for the baby. You'll be in charge when it comes." The remaining firefighters faded into the background to give the mother privacy, but standing by in case they were needed.

Another contraction hit. "Breathe, Rosa." Alonzo's voice was stern but comforting.

After the pain subsided, Alex straightened. "I'm going to examine you now to see if the child's crowning. Will, get ready to assist." Gonzales and Will had each taken universal precautions, too.

"A full head of black hair, Rosa," Alex told her calmly.

She started to smile when another spasm of pain went through her.

"All right, Mom," Alex said. "Push."

In seconds the baby's head was out. Alex felt a rush of adrenaline. Positioning his hands to avoid the soft spots, he supported the baby's head. He checked that the umbilical cord was not around the neck— thank God it wasn't—then said, "Don't push again, Rosa. Take short breaths."

Begay handed him a syringe, and he suctioned the baby's mouth. "Okay, Rosa, another push." The shoulders eased out. With yet another push the baby's trunk slid out. Then the feet.

A sense of awe overwhelmed Alex, eclipsing everything. As Will cut the cord, Alex marveled at the miracle of life. So much of firefighting dealt with destruction. Beauty and vitality like this were rare.

"There we go, Rosa." He held up the child. "Here's your son."

"Dio mio," she whispered. "My son. I told you, Alonzo, this time it was a boy. We have three girls."

Alex smiled, joy suffusing him. As he watched his men clean up the baby and give him to the parents, he was hit by a wave of longing so intense he practically choked on it. He wanted a child. With Lauren.

He wanted to call her right then and tell her. He wanted to make her see they could overcome anything to get to this point.

But he didn't. Alex was done talking her into a relationship. "Even for this," he whispered, staring at the beautiful baby boy he wished like hell was his.

LAUREN BOLTED UPRIGHT in bed. She didn't know where she was, only heard the noise outside. It sounded like shuffling, a grunt, knocking against the side of the house. She took a deep breath. She was at Alex's house; he was on duty.

Minutes later, she heard the doorbell ring. At five in the morning? Wait! Hawk Longstreet was outside, so it would be okay. Still she crept slowly out of bed, put on a robe and headed for the front door. She could see Hawk through the peephole. "Yes?"

"It's me, Lauren."

She opened the door and there he stood—with James Tildan. Her ex-fiancé's arm was yanked behind his back, his eyes wild, his clothes a mess. "What's going on?"

"This guy's stalking your house. He says you know him. He's your fiancé?"

"Lauren, call this clown off me." James's words were slurred.

"I was engaged to him. You and I talked about him, Hawk." She faced James. "What are you doing here?"

"I came to see you. Why're you at this guy's house?"

"How did you know where I was?"

"Come on, Lauren, I'm your fiancé."

"James, I told you, it's over between us. What I do is none of your business."

"He's drunk," Hawk said. "I think we should call the cops, have him brought downtown."

James came alert. "You're kidding, right?"

Lauren felt anger bubble inside her. "Go ahead, Hawk, call the police."

An hour later, Lauren sat having coffee with Hawk Longstreet. "Thanks for everything."

The tall, lanky man eased his legs out in front of him. "You're gonna get that restraining order, right?"

"Yes. Today. I'm sick of all this. Him. Whoever's been doing these other things."

"You've had a rough few weeks." He smiled. "You're pretty tough, though. I've never once seen you crumple."

"What's going on here?" Lauren looked up to find Alex in the doorway. She hadn't heard him come in.

"Hi. We had a problem this morning, but Hawk took care of it."

Alex's face darkened. The lines of strain around his mouth were marked, and his eyes were heavy lidded. He looked as if he had a headache; he'd told her all firefighters got them regularly from inhaling smoke.

"Did you have a fire?" she asked.

"No. I delivered a baby, though."

"Oh, Alex. How wonderful."

His expression was profound but tinged with sadness. Then he shook it off and crossed to her, rested his hand on her shoulder. She covered his hand with hers. He faced Hawk. "What happened?"

"James Tildan showed up at five o'clock. Drunk. We called the cops, and Lauren's getting a restraining order against him."

"Doesn't that son of a bitch give up?"

"Apparently not." Hawk stood. "Thanks for the coffee. My relief's coming about now." He nodded to Alex and left.

Alex dropped into a chair and rubbed his face with his hands.

"Want some coffee?"

"No, I need to sleep. We had a hell of a night."

"I'm sorry."

"You okay?"

"Yes. I was scared though."

"Longstreet's a good guy."

"He is."

He fiddled with the *Courier* on the table. "Is our comic in today?"

"Um, yeah. Why don't you sleep now, though." She stood and reached out her hand. "Come on, I'll lie down with you."

For a moment, he watched her through bloodshot eyes. Then he picked up the copy of the *Courier*, opened it to the comics and scanned it.

With barely restrained violence, he crumpled the newspaper. Standing abruptly, he said, "I'm going to bed. Alone." Then he walked out of the kitchen.

She stared down at the comic. They'd gotten a lot of reader mail about the muscle-bound boy. Perry wanted him back in the picture. She studied it.

Frame One:

Adam and a girl are sitting in a store. The glass front reads "Soda Shop." He and the girl are sharing a soda with two straws.

Frame Two:

Lily and Dee look in from the outside. *Oh, dear,* Lily says.

Frame Three:

Dee spins her around. *It's your own fault. Do you expect him to wait forever till you come to your senses?*

I don't expect him to wait at all.

Frame Four:

I give up on you. You're a lost cause.

Frame Five:

Lily stares at Deirdre's retreating back. *I've been trying to tell you that all along, Dee.*

Lauren closed her eyes, sick of this whole thing, just as she'd told Hawk. She wanted the mystery solved and she wanted to get out of Courage Bay. She stared at the hallway leading to Alex's bedroom. It would be better for everybody when she left.

She really was a lost cause.

CHAPTER SIXTEEN

"WHERE THE HELL is that oil? I told North I needed it now."

Bud Patchett, the mechanic, looked up from the rig he was working on with Alex in the bay. "I've got a new guy. He probably can't find his way around the supply room." Bud wiped his hands on a cloth. "I'll go check." Then he shrugged. "Why don't you take a break? I can finish this."

"If we get a run, the rig needs to be in top shape."

Patchett bristled. "The truck's in shape. Oil's only down a half." He shook his head. "What's with you, Alex?"

Alex wiped a smeared rag over his filthy fingers. "Not sleeping well," he grumbled. "Didn't mean to bark at you."

"Go get some coffee. I'll finish up here."

"Yeah, sure."

Instead of taking a break, though, he headed for the bunk room and had just changed into shorts when his cell phone rang.

It was Dana. She'd wrenched her shoulder on a call early in the week and the doc had told her to take this shift off. "Is Lauren okay, Alex?" she asked without preamble.

"Far as I know. Why?"

"I'm not sure. I've had this bad feeling all day." She cleared her throat. "About her."

Twin affinity. "Well, she probably moved out of my house today. Maybe you're sensing that."

"Really? Why?"

"A thousand reasons."

"Think I should go over and see how she is?"

"You're not exactly her favorite person."

"We're getting along better."

"Sure, go ahead, then."

After he hung up, he was in an even fouler mood. He strode to the workout room, where two of his men were just finishing up. "Damn it, guys, your shit's all over the floor."

Ramirez looked to Alvarez, who shrugged, then said, "Yeah? When did *you* start to think this place should look like Martha Stewart's living room?"

Ramirez bent down and picked up his gear. "Come on, gringo, maybe the cap here can outrun his demons."

Alex thought about apologizing yet again, but hopped on the treadmill instead, ratcheted it up to seven and began to run.

He tried to blank his mind but he couldn't escape the images...Lauren refusing to talk to him...Lauren silencing his concerns with physical attention...and, of course, *Dee and Me*.

Pushing the speed up to nine, he ran faster. Maybe he could wear himself out enough to sleep tonight. He'd been up and down the night before. She'd come into the kitchen once...

"Alex, what are you doing out here?"

He stood staring out the French doors at the garden

she'd brought to life. He liked it. "Nothing. Sorry I woke you."

She'd come up from behind and circled her arms around his waist. Her fingers flirted with the drawstring of his fleece shorts. "Come back to bed. I want us to be together."

"Is there an us, Lauren?"

He'd felt her stiffen and draw away. He spun around. "Answer me."

"You told me you only wanted to help me through this, no strings attached. That you'd stick by me as long as I let you."

"It's harder than I thought it would be."

"Would you like me to leave?"

"No. I want to help you. I love you."

She turned and started to walk away. "Tell me one thing." His words stopped her.

"All right."

"The cartoon. It's us, isn't it?"

"Yes."

His throat closed up.

She said, "Maybe I should move back to my place."

"Maybe you should, if this is how you feel…"

The way Alex figured it, he'd go home tomorrow after his shift and she'd be gone. And when this case was solved, she'd probably leave town for good.

"Shields, I wanna talk to you." Alex turned to see Will in the doorway.

"I'm busy."

Will walked over to the treadmill and unplugged it. "There, now you're not."

Alex picked up a towel and wiped the sweat from his face.

Will stood in front of him. "I drew the short straw."

"For what?"

"To tell you what a bastard you've been all day."

Expelling a heavy breath, Alex met Will's gaze. "I'm in a bad mood, so what? All the guys have grumpy days."

"You make Scrooge look like a saint."

Alex tossed the towel down and dropped onto a mat.

Will leaned against the wall, his arms crossed. "Spit it out, it'll make you feel better."

His face still dripping with sweat, Alex shook his head. "It's not working out with Lauren."

"She still staying with you?"

"Who knows? My guess is she's moving out today."

"How come?"

"Because I can't accept her shutting me out of what's going on with her."

"Maybe that's the only way she can cope. A lot's come down on her lately."

"Maybe. But *I'm* not coping."

"You got it bad."

"Damn it, Will, what am I supposed to do?"

"Give her space until this whole twin thing is solved."

"I tried that."

"Well, try a—"

The PA crackled and a call effectively cut off their conversation. Alex jumped up and followed Will out the door.

FROM HER WINDOW, Lauren watched the rig race down Fifth Street. Alex was on call. She hoped it was an easy one. He'd be exhausted. He hadn't slept well in days. She'd paint him "Miserable Man."

Your fault.

I know, Dee.

Do something about it.

She looked down at the cartoon. *I am.*

Frame One:

Adam comes running down the street. Lily is just hopping onto a bus. *Wait, Lily...* he calls out.

Frame Two:

Adam reaches her. *Where you goin'?*

I'm moving. I...

Lauren threw down the pencil. "You're a jerk," she said to the cartoon. "A complete and utter jerk."

"Lauren?" She looked up to see Toby Hanson in the doorway. His curly hair was disheveled and he was scowling.

"Toby, what's wrong?"

"I quit the paper."

"What?"

He flopped wearily down onto a chair. "Perry and I had it out finally. He didn't budge, so I'm bookin'. I just gave two weeks' notice."

"What did you ask for?"

"A raise, and more challenging assignments. I want to do something with town politics. He says he has a political reporter."

"I'm sorry. I'd hate for you to leave."

He shrugged. "Well, you're not sticking around anyway, are you?"

She felt a chill. She hadn't discussed leaving town with anybody but Alex. And surely he wouldn't talk to Toby about it. "How would you know that?"

Her friend fidgeted. Then he glanced down. "*Dee and Me* stuff, I guess."

"Oh." She leaned over and squeezed his arm. "Is there anything I can do?"

"Have dinner with me tonight?"

She wanted to go home and bury her head in the sand. "Oh, Toby, I'm sorry. I can't. I've got something I have to do."

She was moving her stuff out of Alex's and she had to do it tonight, since he'd be home tomorrow and she didn't think she could face him again. "Tomorrow?"

"Sure." Toby stood. "Well, I'll go, I guess."

After Toby left, Lauren tried another tack with *Dee and Me*. She got nowhere so she finished up a few ad layouts for Perry and headed out to drop them off before she left at six. She reached the office just as George Yube was leaving it.

"Lauren, how are you?" At his fatherly, gentle tone, tears clouded her eyes. He drew her into Perry's office, which was empty. "What's wrong, dear?"

"Everything."

Gently he edged her to a couch and sat next to her. "Tell me."

She thought about Alex. "Some of it's private." She thought about the Ivies. "But a lot of it is this twin thing. Dana's my sister."

"Yes, I heard that from Vera." His tender look of understanding warmed her. She felt as if she could tell him anything. "Do they know what happened?"

She sniffled. "No, they're still checking hospital employment records to see if any of the staff of Courage Bay Hospital also worked at L.A. Hospital during the time of our births. Somebody did some kind of switch.''

"I'm sorry. This must be so hard.''

"It is. I'm not sleeping well.'' She thought about moving her things out of Alex's house. "I have something unpleasant to do tonight, too.''

"May I help?''

"No, I couldn't impose.''

"I'm free for the evening.''

In that moment, she realized she was sick of being alone. She wanted somebody with her to do this huge thing. She would have asked Hawk Longstreet if he was on duty later, but she didn't know the relief man well enough.

"You really don't mind?''

"No. What do we have to do?''

"Get my stuff from Alex's.''

"It's not going well with you two?''

"I don't want to talk about that right now if you don't mind.''

"No problem.'' He stood and held out his hand, just as her father might have. She took it and immediately felt better.

They drove to Alex's house in two cars, with the surveillance man behind them. They got her stuff, then headed home. Once they arrived, she cleared George with the new man, and they brought her things inside. On impulse, she asked George to stay for dinner.

His eyes had brightened. "I'd love to.''

When they went to the kitchen, she noticed the message light flashing on her phone. She ignored it, assuming it was Alex. She let the kittens out of the laundry room and shooed them to the backyard, then fixed a cold antipasto. All the while George chattered on about his family—Vera was wrong about his daughters—about his practice, about life in general. Once he excused himself to get his pager, which he'd accidentally left in the car.

Dinner was entertaining and distracting. Afterward, Lauren offered to make tea and, while he sat in the living room, she returned to the kitchen to heat the water.

She let the cats back in and filled their dishes, laughing when the ever-inquisitive Caramel bounded into the living room to see their company. She started after him but stopped when she saw the message light again. As the water heated, she pressed the button.

"Lauren, it's me Dana. I, um, jeez, I dunno. I've got a bad feeling about you. Are you all right? Things just don't feel...good. Call me back when you get this. I think...I should be there with you today. Stupid, huh? Call me and tell me how dumb I am."

There were two other similar messages from Dana.

Taking a deep breath, Lauren stared at the phone. She was suddenly overwhelmed by the need to talk to Dana. As soon as George left, she'd call her sister.

Gripping the tea tray, she headed for the living room. But she stopped in the doorway when she saw George Yube with his hands encircling Caramel's neck. The kitten dangled limply in the air.

Then, very quietly, he walked to the open window and dumped the cat outside.

Oh my God.

ALL RIGHT, George told himself. *Don't panic. The plan was already in motion.* It was time to end it all. If he could just get rid of the key players...first Lauren, then he'd go over to Dana's...and he might even take care of Shields. George laughed as he looked down at the body of the cat lying on the ground outside her window.

The cat moved. Hell, he thought he'd put it out of commission. He glanced back to the kitchen. Well, he wouldn't make the same mistake with the rest of them.

Then the doorbell rang. He fingered the cool steel in his pocket. Time to clean up the mess he had started thirty-two years ago...

HE'D KILLED HER KITTEN! Lauren was reeling from what she'd just seen. The doorbell pealed. Startled, she let go of the tea service and it clattered and clanged onto the floor. The brown liquid ran in rivulets over her tile, and the cups broke in pieces. In seconds, George Yube was beside her. Lauren knew she had to stay calm, and not give away what she'd seen him do.

Butterscotch mewed and sniffed around the mess on the floor.

The doorbell sounded again.

"Are you all right, dear?"

"Just clumsy." She looked down at the mess, unable to move.

"How about you clean this up and I'll get rid of whoever's at the door?"

Oh, no. "That's okay. I'll get it." She slipped past him and raced to the foyer. She whipped the door open. And there stood Dana. Looking big and strong and competent. But this was her sister. Lauren wouldn't, couldn't endanger her.

"Hi," Dana said, her face a little flushed. "Did you get my messages?"

"Um, yeah." She darted a quick look over her shoulder. "I don't want to see you right now, though. I'll call you." She started to close the door.

Dana put her foot in the opening. Her eyes narrowed as if she were reading Lauren's mind. "Something's wrong, isn't it?"

"No, of course not. I'm not feeling well and I want to be alone." She shook her head, her eyes pleading. "Just go, Dee."

Dana hesitated—then she stepped into the house. "Sorry, but I—"

"Well, we all meet once again."

Both Lauren and Dana turned. George Yube had come out of the kitchen. In his hand, he held a small revolver. Pointed at them.

Instinctively Lauren stepped in front of Dana. "Let her go, George."

His laugh was ugly. "Too bad you couldn't get rid of her. Now I'll have to do something about both of you, won't I? Again."

Moving out from behind Lauren, Dana put her hand on Lauren's arm. "What the hell's going on?"

"You know, don't you?" George asked Lauren.

"I saw you kill the cat."

Dana was staring at the gun. Then she said, "You're connected to all this twin stuff, aren't you?"

His face darkened. "Get into the living room."

Dana glanced at Lauren. *Do it,* their mutual looks said. Together they left the foyer and went into the living area.

"On the couch."

They dropped down, their shoulders touching.

Though she took comfort in Dana's presence, Lauren wished she'd been able to make her sister leave. She felt Dana's arm snake through hers.

"Isn't that touching?" Yube quipped.

Dana glared at him. "You bastard. What did you do to us?"

"Nothing intentional to you, missy." His eyes glazed over. "I switched around some babies, is all. But I figure I must have put you back in the wrong isolette." He focused on Lauren. "Now, *you,* I gave to the Conways."

"Why?"

"Because their baby died. They could have blamed me."

"You were on staff at Los Angeles Hospital?"

"Yes. I was an overworked surgical resident in Los Angeles, moonlighting in Courage Bay. The Conways were visiting L.A. and Sara went into premature labor. Her baby died under my care. I was afraid I'd be accused of something."

"Why?" Dana asked. "Preemies die. Doctors aren't always suspected of wrongdoing."

"Well, I'd been drinking that night. After the delivery, with the baby back in the nursery, I took her out of the isolette. Something happened...I'm not sure what. She just stopped breathing...and died."

"You *killed* the Conways' baby because you were drunk?" Dana's tone was horrified.

"Shut up." He pointed the gun right at her.

Lauren put her hand on Dana's arm and squeezed. "So what did you do?"

"I brought their dead child here, to Courage Bay, where I knew three little girls had been born. Twins, and another child. I weighed each of you, and you were the lucky match, Lauren. I made a slight error, though, when I put you—'' he waved the gun at Dana ''—back in the wrong place. You should have gone to the Barclays.''

Lauren swallowed hard. ''The Barclays? They were our natural parents?''

''Yes. Instead, Dana, you went to the Ivies. Later, the Ivies' real baby died, though it was reported that the second twin died.''

Lauren felt Dana stiffen. ''You let those poor people believe their children died when we were both alive?''

''Well, the Ivies and the Conways would have suffered, if I hadn't. Somebody was going to feel bad. I just decided who.''

''Oh, my God.''

His face darkened; he gripped the gun. ''God had nothing to do with it. He has nothing to do with anything. Doctors control life and death, as they should.''

Dana shook her head. ''You changed so many people's lives.''

Lauren asked, ''What happened to the Barclays?''

''They live in Woodville, about two hours from here. They were visiting Courage Bay for a festival of some sort. Far as I know, they're still there. I kept tabs on them for a while. Don't fret dear, they had another kid and have a very happy life.''

Oh, my God, they had another sibling.

''Your father's a policeman. Your mother's an interior designer.''

This was too much. Lauren felt her eyes sting. Dana had obviously taken after her biological father, Lauren after her mother. When she looked over at Dana, she saw that her sister's eyes were moist, too.

"Now, we have to get going." Yube gestured with the gun to the door.

"Going?"

"Yes, I have to finish what I started thirty-two years ago."

"What do you mean?"

"I have to get rid of you two. You've made it easy with your public animosity. Newly discovered sisters go for a ride to talk, have a fight while driving, crash their car."

Dana stood. "You can't be serious. There's surveillance outside."

"Not any longer. The poor man fell asleep—" he glanced at his watch "—oh, about a half hour ago. When he wakes up we'll be gone."

Lauren felt her heartbeat accelerate. "How'd you do that?"

"Remember when I went to my car for my pager?"

"Oh, God."

"I came up behind him. The window was down. I stuck him with a needle."

"He'll know he was drugged."

"He didn't see who it was. And after all, my dear, you've reported several stalker incidents. I've set the stage well."

"That was you?"

"Of course."

Yube waved the gun at them. "Let's get going."

Dana and Lauren exchanged looks.

"I assure you this is loaded. And I'll use it if you don't do as I say."

Lauren tried to stall. "What do you hope to accomplish, George? Killing us won't help."

"Of course it will. Everybody will be so saddened, they'll forget all about the investigation."

"That's crazy." And suddenly, Lauren realized the truth. Yube *was* crazy. And desperate. So none of this had to make sense.

"Stand up." Both of them did. He nosed the gun into Lauren's side. "Move."

They headed for the door. Dana shot her a look. One that she could read. *Don't let him get us out of here, or it's over.*

They reached the door. Yube growled, "Dana, you first." When Dana hesitated, he barked, "Open it."

She did.

"Mee...oow..." Caramel was on the stoop and tried to scamper around Yube. From inside came another meow, a screech really.

But it was enough to distract Yube for a second; he looked over his shoulder at the cat. Simultaneously Lauren and Dana reacted. Dana spun around and Lauren lunged. Together, they knocked Yube backward to the floor; Lauren landing on top of him.

A horrible noise rent the air.

Lauren felt a lightning streak of pain in her shoulder and the world dimmed.

"I'M ALL RIGHT." Lauren lay in her bed, her arm in a sling, and stared at Dana who stood over her like a worried mother. "My arm was just grazed."

"By a freakin' bullet." She picked up Lauren's hand and sat on the side of the bed. "You should have gone to the hospital."

"Do you know how many times I've been to Courage Bay Emergency in the few weeks I've been here? I'm not going again."

Brushing back Lauren's bangs, Dana smiled. "At least let me call Alex."

"He's on duty."

"Then his parents, and mine."

Lauren glanced sleepily at the clock. "It's three in the morning. They don't need to hear all this now, Dana." She felt the tears threaten. "It's so awful."

Dana bit her lip. "I know. Those poor people. The Barclays. Our...parents. I can't fathom..." She gave Lauren a half smile. "A police officer and a designer. Funny, isn't it?"

"Just like us." Lauren shuddered. "Yube was crazy. Years of guilt and stress."

"Yeah. He had to be crazy to do such an awful thing."

"I guess. His career was at stake. But he changed so many lives..." Struggling to keep her eyes open, Lauren peered up at her sister. "Did you have a good life, Dana?"

"Yes, the best. My family, Alex, the Shields. I loved—love—my life."

"Me, too. Though I always felt like an outsider. Mom and Dad were wonderful people." Again she experienced the sting of tears. "I guess it's a blessing that they didn't live to see this. It's why you fought this, right? Because you didn't want to accept that the Ivies weren't your biological parents."

"Uh-huh." She saw Dana swallow hard. "Poor Mom and Dad."

"They seem pretty strong." She squeezed Dana's hand. "Like you."

"Me? I was a pussycat. You were the strong one through all this. And you tried to take Yube on all by yourself."

Lauren yawned.

"You're tired."

"Yeah. I took that pain pill."

"Close your eyes."

"Okay."

"I'm staying here."

"Of course you are." She smiled sleepily at Dana. And nodded to the other side of the bed.

Without a word, Dana climbed into bed, next to Lauren's uninjured side, and switched off the light. Resting her head on Lauren's pillow, she sighed. "Lauren?"

"Hmm?"

"I had a good life. But I didn't have you. That sucks."

"I know."

"This is what it would have been like, had we grown up together."

Lauren chuckled. "We have a lot to catch up on."

Then she felt Dana slide a hand in hers. In the darkness, Lauren heard, "'Night, sis."

"'Night, sis."

FEAR WARRED with fury as Alex drove his Blazer through the streets, which were practically empty at six in the morning. He'd gotten back to the station house from a run at five when Vince strode in. Alex was having coffee with the guys, debriefing the call.

Vince had looked harried. "Alex, good you're back."

He felt a chill go through him. "Something's happened to Lauren."

"She's all right. But yes. The mystery's solved."

Alex had listened to the bizarre tale with increasing

anger. George Yube. The man his mother had loved. The man who had changed the direction of so many lives. He wanted to beat the crap out of the guy for what he'd done to Lauren, and to his father and mother.

"Dana called nine-one-one and since you guys were out on the run, truck two went along with the police."

"We missed the call." He pushed away from the counter. "Is she at the hospital?"

"No, the bullet just a grazed her arm. She refused to go to the hospital. The EMTs took care of it."

"What?"

"She said she'd spent enough time there and she dug her heels in."

"Tell me she's not alone."

"No, her sister stayed with her."

Her sister, Alex had thought. She'd wanted to stay with her sister.

"Why didn't she call me?"

Vince shot a quick glance at Begay, who stood by him. "She said she didn't want anybody notified. By the time we arrested Yube and took care of them, it was late. Besides you were on a run."

"Yeah, sure." Feeling bereft, he'd let the anger come. Kept it boiling inside him all the way over to her house.

Pulling into her driveway, he knew somewhere in his befuddled mind he was choosing anger over the terror he was squelching, but damn, she should have called him. He got out of the car and walked to the porch. Using the key she'd given him—it felt like a million years ago—he let himself into her house. Everything had been cleaned up, apparently. He could smell the potpourri and faint scent of tea. Immediately the kittens scampered over to him. Scooping them up, he held them close to his heart and whispered, "You guys get gourmet kitty chow for the rest of your natural lives." Vince had told him how the cats had distracted Yube and the girls jumped him. Damn it. He'd had a gun and Lauren and Dana had taken him down.

He headed through the house. Passing the spare room, he noticed that it was empty. Where the hell was Dana? In the doorway to Lauren's room, he stopped. And stared at the scene.

Dim light crept through the slatted blinds; the birds sang outside. Inside, Lauren, her arm in a sling, lay on her back, dressed in a white satiny nightshirt that begged to be touched. Her face was turned to the left, her injured arm secured against her chest. She was clutching Dana's hand. Dana lay on her left side facing Lauren. On the same pillow.

The scene stunned him. Twin girls separated at birth finally finding each other. The connection had been reestablished. They were going to be okay.

She said not to call you...

Are you saying you don't love me...

I should move out...

Already he felt cut out of her life. His anger resurfaced. Looked like Lily had Dee to help her through this. And she didn't want the muscle-bound boy involved.

Alex turned and let himself out of the house.

CHAPTER SEVENTEEN

DANA DROVE down the streets of Woodville, a small suburb of Los Angeles, with Lauren by her side. They were on their way to see their biological parents. Both were lost in their own thoughts, and conversation had been sporadic on the two-hour drive east out of Courage Bay.

Finally Dana broke the silence. "I hope we did this right."

"We did. A phone call would have been worse. They'd just worry till we got there. And it had to be done soon, before the story breaks in the *Courier*."

The events of two days ago had been kept out of the news until the Barclays could be notified. Lauren had told Perry she'd give the newspaper the scoop if he'd do two things: wait a day to publish it and let Toby write the story. He'd agreed to both. This was the biggest thing to hit Courage Bay in years. Toby was only too happy to pitch in and help, and Lauren knew they were negotiating his staying on permanently.

"At least we know they'll be there," Dana commented.

Vince Wojohowitz had called Cleveland Barclay, as a fellow police officer, and asked if he was going to be around this afternoon. Vince said he'd be in town and wanted to talk to him. He gave some vague excuse, but the Barclays said they'd be home.

From the driver's seat, Dana touched Lauren's hand. "Arm okay?"

"You looked at it yourself. It's already started to heal. I don't even need the sling."

"How about your heart?"

"Excuse me?"

"You haven't seen Alex since it happened."

"I know." She swallowed hard. "It's too much to handle right now. I can't deal with this—" she nodded to the quaint town they drove through "—and our relationship." She cocked her head. "You said he's angry."

"Pissed as hell, sis. And I don't blame him. You should have gone to see him after the thing with Yube. Before we left to see the Barclays."

Dana was right, but Lauren couldn't sort out her feelings for Alex right now. She was too overwhelmed to make big decisions that would affect the rest of her life.

Oh, you're just being lily-livered.

"Shut up," Lauren told Dee.

"What?"

Lauren giggled. There had been a lot of giggling and sharing between her and Dana since they found out the truth about being related. It felt great. "You'll think I'm crazy."

"Probably. And I'll tease you."

"I talk to Dee. She pushes me to do things."

"You called me Dee two nights ago, when you were trying to get rid of me." She smiled over at Lauren. "Did I tell you how much I appreciate your protecting me?"

"Hey, what are sisters for?"

The closer they got to the house on the hill the quieter they became. When they reached it, they sat parked at the curb, staring at the gray shingled structure with a huge front porch and flower boxes. "Come on," Lauren said. "Let's do it."

"I'm scared."

Reaching over, Lauren took Dana's hand. "I'll be with you, Dana. Through this and everything."

Together they exited the car. They'd dressed similarly today in cropped pants and blouses. It was funny, really, how much they had in common—same preferences in clothes, food, movies. It had been fun discovering that. On the porch, Lauren noticed a small tricycle. Gloria and Cleveland Barclay were in their fifties.

"Grandchildren?" Dana asked, reading her thoughts. "Jeez, I'm not even used to having two sisters. We've got nieces and nephews?"

"Let's see." Sucking in a huge breath, Lauren pushed the bell.

No one answered. Dana shifted on her feet. Lauren felt her pulse speed up.

Dana said, "Come on, let's get this over—"

The door swung open. They stared down into the face of a boy about six years old. His hair was bright red, his cheeks smattered with freckles. He looked like Lauren and Dana had as kids.

"Hi. Who're you?"

Oh, God. "We're...friends," Lauren said.

"What's the matter with her?" The kid pointed to Dana, who'd gone white.

"She's just anxious to meet Gloria and Cleveland."

"Nana and Papa?"

"Uh, yeah."

"Na-na!" the boy screeched from the door.

Lauren and Dana exchanged weak smiles.

"Coming," Lauren heard from the house. It was their mother's voice.

"Jeremy, how many times have I told—" Gloria stopped behind her grandson. She was the same height as Lauren and Dana, about five-seven, and had soft auburn hair just beginning to gray. Her eyes were deep, deep brown—not blue, like the Conways. And she had freckles. Dressed in jeans and T-shirt, she looked youthful for fifty-something.

The woman—their biological mother—simply stared at Lauren and Dana. The air crackled with electricity, just like it had when Lauren had met Dana. Finally Gloria touched the boy's shoulder. "Honey, go get Papa from the garden."

"I'm right here, Glo. What's going on—" Cleveland stopped in the doorway. He was a big man, over six feet, with completely white hair and dark brown eyes. His shoulders were wide, and he was very fit.

The frozen tableau was broken when Jeremy said, "You two look like my mom."

Lauren stared down at her nephew. "For good reason." Then she looked back at the adults. "There's no easy way to do this. We have something to tell you. May we come in?"

Gloria wavered on her feet and Cleveland grasped her around the waist. "I—something—you two—" She gripped her husband's arm. "I must have been outside in the sun too long. For a minute, I thought you two were…it's impossible…but you're twins and you do look like Jenny…"

Lauren and Dana simultaneously reached out and grasped Gloria's hands. Their mother's hands. "I'm sorry," Lauren said. "This will be a shock, but there was no better way to do it. We are who you think we are. We didn't die at birth, Gloria. We're your daughters."

LAUREN SAT on the couch, holding one of her mother's hands. Dana sat on her other side doing the same. A steady stream of tears tracked down Gloria's cheeks. Cleveland, their father, paced the floor. Jeremy and his brother, Mark, stood off to the side, wide-eyed.

"He really had a gun?" Jeremy asked.

Dana nodded. "Yeah."

"Cool." He looked at Lauren's arm where the bandage was visible under her sleeve. "You got shot?"

"Just grazed."

"Way cool."

Lauren smiled.

"Why don't you guys go out and play for a while?" Cleveland suggested.

Jeremy headed for the door. But little Mark came up to Lauren. He touched her face gently. "Are you my aunt?" he asked.

Lauren's throat closed up. "I guess."

"I'm glad." He leaned over, kissed her cheek, then Dana's, and took off. Lauren saw tears in Dana's eyes. She battled back her own.

"I can't believe it." Cleveland dropped into the chair opposite them and rested his hands on his knees. "It was horrible, what happened all those years ago. I blamed myself for making Glo take that trip to Courage Bay for the police convention."

"It wasn't your fault, Cleve."

He smiled, but kept stealing glances at the girls. *His* girls. He swallowed hard. "I don't know what to say."

"We had a nice life," Dana put in. Lauren knew she was trying to be brave, but this was *hard*.

"Tell us," he said.

Dana talked glowingly about the Ivies. "I'm a firefighter. I have EMT certification."

"I'm a cop and a paramedic." Cleve's voice was gruff. He smiled sadly. "What about you, Lauren?"

She told them about the Conways and her job. "And I'm an artist."

Gloria's head snapped up. "I'm an interior designer. I paint."

"I paint, too."

Gloria ran her hand through her hair, a gesture Lauren often affected. "I don't know whether to be happy or sad."

Cleveland did. "I'm goddamned pissed."

He sounded like Alex.

"I think we should all be happy," Lauren suggested. "We've found each other again. We should get to know each other now."

She felt Gloria squeeze her arm. "Are either of you married?" she asked.

"No." Dana winked at Lauren. "But Lauren has a beau. If she doesn't blow it."

Lauren loved having a sister to tease her, but she wished Dana would keep her mouth shut about Alex. "'Course, first he was Dana's beau."

"What?"

"It's a long story."

"Can you stay?" Cleveland asked. "For a while."

"I can," Lauren told them.

Dana smiled nervously. "I have to be on shift in two days. But I can stay till then."

"We have a lot to catch up on." Gloria threw back her shoulders. "I want to know everything about you." She frowned. "Your poor parents must be devastated, Dana." Lauren had told them about the Conways' accident.

"They're strong, wonderful people. They'll be okay." Still, Lauren could tell Dana was torn and uncomfortable. She leaned over and squeezed her sister's arm.

Cleveland rose and crossed to the three women. He crouched in front of them, encompassing them all in a big bear hug. "We'll be okay, too, ladies. I promise."

Quietly, still holding onto their mother's hands, Lauren and Dana, for the very first time, laid their heads on their father's shoulder.

ALEX HAD GOTTEN to the firehouse at five before the beginning of his shift and was in his office doing paperwork when Dana walked in. He swiveled in his seat. "Hey, girl." He studied her. "How'd it go?"

"It was the best of times and the worst of times," she said, quoting Dickens.

He leaned back in his chair, refusing to ask about Lauren, who had effectively cut him out of her life. Damn her. "How did the Barclays take it?"

"Gloria cried like Lauren would have. Cleveland got pissed as hell, like I handle things." Dana sat on the desk. "They're great people. We would have had a nice life with them, too." She shook her head. "It's gonna take a while to digest all this."

"I told you you could have had some time off."

"No, I didn't want to stay there. I wanted to get back to Mom and Dad."

"They're doing okay. My parents have been over a lot, and I spent some time with them."

"Yeah, I stayed overnight there after I got back."

"Oh." He wouldn't ask. He turned around to the computer.

"She didn't come back with me, Alex."

"Now there's a surprise." He sighed, then turned again. "Is she coming back at all?"

"What do you mean?"

"She told me she was moving back to Benicia."

"She doesn't know what she's going to do. She's rattled by this whole thing, like I am."

He could have helped her with it. He *wanted* to help her with it. But she'd shut him out.

Apparently Dana felt compelled to defend her new-found sister. "She hadn't figured out the whole thing with you two yet, and then this happened to her. Cut her some slack."

Throwing back his chair, he stood and kicked the wastebasket. It hit the wall with a thud. "I shouldn't have to do that. If she really loved me, she'd let me help her work this out."

Dana stood, too. "You're being an ass getting mad about this. It's so male."

"I don't need you on me, Dana."

"Yeah, well, you aren't gonna get what you need unless you find some perspective."

"When did you start taking her side?"

"*Listen* to yourself." She walked over to him. "Get a grip, buddy, before she comes home." After hugging him, she walked out. He kicked the wastebasket again, then dropped down into his chair. Hell, he didn't know why he was yelling at Dana. He *knew* he was behaving irrationally.

It's because you're hurt.

Damn, now he was hearing voices. Like her. He sank back and took the paper out of his drawer, the one that broke the story. The headlines read Local Surgeon Switches Babies At Birth. There was a picture of Yube to the right of the article. And ones of Lauren and Dana on the left. Slowly he lifted his hand and traced the curve of her mouth, which he'd once kissed with furious passion. The underside of her jaw, which he'd held with exquisite tenderness. She was soft all over, but tough, too. Apparently tough enough to go without him.

He sighed. "Well, sweetheart, it's over. I give up. You were right from the beginning. This was not meant to be."

LAUREN COULDN'T SLEEP. So much had happened... finding their parents, meeting yet another sister, nephews, it was all so disturbing. She stood by the window in the Barclays' kitchen and stared out at the backyard, wondering if she'd be a different person if she lived here all her life.

"Can't sleep?" It was Gloria's voice behind her— a little husky like Lauren's own.

Lauren turned.

Dressed in boxers and a UCLA T-shirt, her mother smiled at her.

"No. I'm sorry if I woke you."

"I haven't slept well since I found out what happened." She crossed to the stove. "Want some hot chocolate?"

Lauren smiled at the motherly suggestion. "I'd love some."

While Gloria fixed the cocoa, they made small talk. Lauren was surprised at how comfortable she felt with this family. Dana hadn't been as at ease, and she seemed troubled when she left. At the table, Gloria set a mug in front of her and smoothed a hand down her hair. The maternal gesture felt good. Then Gloria took a seat. "Something else is bothering you besides all this, isn't it, dear?"

"I don't know what's bothering me."

"Maybe that beau Dana teased you about?"

"His name is Alex."

Her mother sipped her cocoa. "Ah."

"He's a firefighter."

"America's bravest. I've always admired them. And cops, like Cleveland. But since nine-eleven, they have a special place in my heart."

"I know." She thought about Alex laying the foam blanket, rescuing a baby from a car accident, falling through the floor and almost dying as he tried to help others. "They're real heroes."

"You said Dana dated him. Is that the problem?"

"Partly. They were together before I came to Courage Bay. He lied to me about it."

"Oh, dear."

"But there's more. Right from the start we were mismatched. I never thought I'd be enough for him, right for him. We're so different."

"And were you, in the time you were together?"

"Was I what?"

"Enough for him? Right for him?"

She remembered how she'd come to him at the house that afternoon with sneakers and medicine and plans to take swimming lessons. How she'd taken care of him when he was burned. How they'd joked and laughed and made love.

"I thought so for a while. Now, I'm not so sure."

"Why?"

"All my life I felt like I never really belonged. I wasn't accepted for myself, even though my parents—the Conways—loved me dearly. Then I found Alex and felt different about it…like I belonged with him, like he loved me for who I was. But he lied about Dana and I began to think…"

"You were a surrogate."

She nodded.

"Do you love him, Lauren? Really love him? Do you want to be with him all the time? Worry about him, can't picture your life without him?"

"Yes. But so much has come between us."

Gloria sighed. "You know what I think about all this? Losing you two? Finding you?"

Lauren shook her head.

"That life is precious. Precarious, at the same time. You've got to grab for your happiness. Wherever you can." She cleared her throat. "Because you never know if fate's going to step in and snatch it away."

"Maybe," Lauren said. "Maybe you're right."

"THANKS FOR PICKING ME UP," Lauren said as she and Dana made their way back to Courage Bay. Since Dana had originally driven them up, she'd come back to get Lauren, and to see the Barclays again.

"You're welcome. Though you should have asked Alex to come and get you."

"Don't start, Dana."

Her sister shook her head. "You two are a pair, you know that?"

"What do you mean?"

"He bites my head off every time I mention your name, too."

The thought pierced Lauren's heart. He was angry at her with good reason. She'd played this whole thing wrong. She kept hearing Gloria's advice, Dana's chiding. They were both right.

"He's in bad shape," Dana told her as they maneuvered their way over the freeway.

Lauren's foot connected with a newspaper on the floor. She bent over to pick it up. "I'm sorry he's hurting." Actually she was despondent over the notion that Alex suffered. She kept picturing him...in the hut, in the bath, in the garden giving her his key...

His key. She still had it. "Maybe I should go over to see him." She was searching for a way to relieve the tearing ache she felt over missing him. It had been days since she'd looked into his face.

"Won't do any good." Dana switched lanes to pass an RV. "He's not there. He's at a party at the lake tonight. And he's got a date."

A date? "Oh, well then." He hadn't waited long.

"Me, I'd fight for him. But you're just gonna sit there, aren't you, and let him go." Under her breath, Dana whispered, "Lily-livered."

Sighing, Lauren shook open the paper to avoid reacting to Dana's comments and to escape her own thoughts of Alex on a date...how he would be kissing someone else now, maybe making love to her, maybe in their hut.

But she couldn't escape him. On the cover of the

Courage Bay *Courier* was his picture. He was holding a baby. "What's this?"

"Read it."

As Lauren did, she remembered the morning when Alex had come home and told her he'd delivered a child. "Oh. He told me about this, but I didn't know everything."

"What?"

"This is the baby's christening. They named him after Alex."

"Uh-huh. Alexos Alonzo Argulies. Poor kid."

Lauren lost herself in the picture of the big man holding the tiny infant. She wanted to paint it, only she'd make them both bare chested, the child cuddling against Alex's naked skin. She'd name it "Fatherhood."

Her throat closed up.

"I lied earlier. He doesn't have a date."

"What?"

"I just wanted you to see how bad you'd feel if he did."

"That's an awful thing to do."

"Hey, Dee would do it." She shook her head. "Besides, that's what sisters are for. To kick each other in the butt."

They got to the Courage Bay sign on the freeway and exited. "So," Dana said when she stopped at the light at the end of the ramp, "which way, Lauren?"

"What do you mean?"

"Left, I take you home, where you can wallow in your stupid insecurities. Which I don't understand at all. You're beautiful and talented and fun to be with." She nodded in the other direction. "Or right? To the beach where Alex is this very minute."

Lauren glanced at the picture. At Alex smiling down at the infant. Her heart somersaulted in her chest. "Right."

You dumb ass son of a bitch. This is so *stupid. It's only going to make you feel bad.* Still he kept walking down the beach. Toward the hut. He'd come to the party at his buddies' insistence and because he was sick of his own morbid moods. He'd played volleyball, eaten clams and even flirted with a new nurse from the hospital. But when she came on to him, he backed off and said he was going for a walk.

The June night was warm and the breeze soft. Lauren loved the weather here. Lauren. He missed her with an intensity that mocked him. He was letting his stupid pride get in the way of going after her. But he'd gone after her so many times…he just couldn't make himself do it again.

When he reached the hut, he stood on the shore for a minute. The water lapped at his bare feet and the moon kissed the ocean. It was beautiful, but it didn't move him. Finally he went inside. He remembered the first time he brought Lauren here…ripping at her clothes, backing her up against the wall, groans and grunts their only words. And the last time… *Wait, I want to tell you something…I've fallen in love with you, Lauren…*

And she'd cried, told him she loved him, and they'd gone home and made love that had transcended anything he'd ever experienced. He let himself get mad again. "Son of a bitch," he said, hitting one of the two-by-fours that held up the structure.

He heard a noise, a rustle really. Before he could turn around, someone came up behind him…encircled her arms around him. And he wanted to weep because he knew, by the smell and feel and touch of her, that it was Lauren.

Say something, he told himself. But he couldn't.

Neither, apparently, could she. Instead, he felt her hands on his belt buckle. His zipper. And suddenly it was all too much. He turned fast. In the moonlight he could see her…she was wearing a peach sundress and she looked so lovely. He wanted to kiss her.

And kill her at the same time.

He grasped her arms hard. "I'm mad as hell at you, Lauren."

"I know." Holding his gaze unflinchingly, she worked the belt on his jeans.

His hands went to her hips. He yanked her close. "How could you do this to me? Just leave me? End it?"

She backed him against the wall, while she reached into his pants and grasped him. "I'm sorry."

He leaned into her touch. "Oh, Lord."

Holding her tightly, he swung around so her back braced the pole. He buried his face in her neck, kissed her there. "You shouldn't have… I want you… How could you…"

"Alex… Alex…"

His hands dragged up the hem of her dress, ripped off her panties. Immediately she wound her legs around him. He thrust mindlessly into her.

They came in seconds, both of them, like hot lava bubbling out a mountain, too long contained, ready to burst.

He sagged against her. She buried her face in the open collar of his shirt. Inhaled him.

He drew in a heavy breath. After long minutes he said, "I'm still mad."

"You'd better get over it."

"What do you mean?" He didn't look at her, but kept her clasped to him, his face in her neck.

"We didn't use a condom."

"Oh, shit."

"And it's a dangerous time in my cycle. Right in the middle."

Holy hell, would she ever stop surprising him? He inched back. She clasped her hands around his neck. He was still buried inside her. "Lauren, what's going on?"

"I'm sorry. I shouldn't have cut you out. I was so afraid of my feelings for you, afraid you really didn't return them."

"I do. I love you."

"I believe that, Alex. I promise."

He sighed and clutched her close. "I'm sorry I lied about me and Dana. I was afraid, too."

Again she buried her face into his shirt. "I want to put all that behind us. I want a life with you."

"Me, too."

"Still mad?" she whispered.

He thrust forward. "Well, this took the edge off."

"I'll remember that."

"Did you mean it, about your cycle?"

"Yes."

"Did you realize we didn't use anything? I didn't. I wasn't thinking straight."

She hugged him tighter. "Uh-huh. I knew."

His chest rumbled. "So, what are we gonna do about it?"

She looked up at him. "What do you think?"

"I think you gotta marry me."

"Hmm. I probably don't have any choice." She rocked forward. "But see if you can convince me."

As he lowered his head, he whispered, "My pleasure, pretty lady."

EPILOGUE

FRAME ONE:

Lily and the muscle-bound boy sit on a two-seater swing in a garden filled with a variety of flowers. *They're beautiful, Lily. Thanks for doing a garden for me.*

Lily cuddles in close. *You're welcome.*

Frame Two:

Adam holds her hand. *We're gonna have a great time, pretty lady. I'm so glad you came back.*

Lily smiles and swings her pink-footed sneaker. *I know.*

Frame Three:

Adam stands and heads for the French doors, smiling. *I'll get some lemonade for us.*

Lily stares after him. A sappy look on her face. Bubbles indicate a huge sigh.

Frame Four:

Dee appears in the yard, grinning broadly. *I knew you could do it, Lil.*

Lily smiles over at Dee. *I couldn't have done it without you.*

Frame Five:

Dee grins. *Sure you could have.* She looks in the direction where Adam went. *But you don't have to. You got us both now, Lil, to keep you in line.*

It's gonna be a great life, Dee. Me and Adam. Me and you. Lily stares out at the reader. *What more could a girl ask for?*

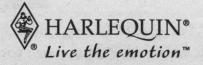

If you enjoyed what you just read,
then we've got an offer you can't resist!

Take 2 bestselling
love stories FREE!
Plus get a FREE surprise gift!

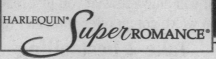

HARLEQUIN Super ROMANCE

Single FATHER

He's a man on his own, trying to raise his children.
Sometimes he gets things right. Sometimes he needs a little help....

Unfinished Business
by Inglath Cooper
(Superromance #1214) On-sale July 2004

Culley Rutherford is doing the best he can raising his young
daughter on his own. One night while on a medical conference in
New York City, Culley runs into his old friend Addy Taylor. After a
passionate night together, they go their separate ways, so Culley
is surprised to see Addy back in Harper's Mill. Now that she's
there, though, he's determined to show Addy that the three of
them can be a family.

Daddy's Little Matchmaker
by Roz Denny Fox
(Superromance #1220) On-sale August 2004

Alan Ridge is a widower and the father of nine-year-old Louemma,
who suffers from paralysis caused by the accident that killed her
mother. Laurel Ashline is a weaver who's come to the town of
Ridge City, Kentucky, to explore her family's history—a history
that includes a long-ago feud with the wealthy Ridges. Louemma
brings Alan and Laurel together, despite everything that keeps
them apart....

Available wherever Harlequin books are sold.

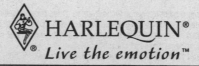

HARLEQUIN®
Live the emotion™